TO DIE FOR

PHILLIP HUNTER

HEAD
ZEUS

First published in the UK in 2013 by Head of Zeus Ltd. This paperback edition first published in the UK in 2014 by Head of Zeus Ltd.

9 7 5 3 1 2 4 6 8

A catalogue record for this book is available from the British Library.

ISBN (eBook) 9781781852064
ISBN (PB) 9781781852057

Typeset by Ben Cracknell Studios

Printed and bound by Clays Ltd, St Ives Plc

Head of Zeus Ltd
Clerkenwell House
45-47 Clerkenwell Green
London EC1R 0HT

WWW.HEADOFZEUS.COM

TO
DIE
FOR

PHILLIP HUNTER has a degree in English
Literature from Middlesex University
and an MA in Screenwriting from the
London Institute. He was also part of the
team that sequenced the human genome.
This is his first novel.

By Phillip Hunter

To Die For
To Kill For

Phillip Hunter has a degree in English literature from Middlesex University and an MA in Screenwriting from the London Institute. He was also part of the team that sequenced the human genome. This is his first novel.

*For my mum, Betsy, and
my sister, Louise*

I grabbed him and threw him into the wall. He crashed to the floor, tried to stand, tried to speak. His face was white, his eyes wide and wet. I hoisted him up and slapped him a couple of times. He focused on me and his head jerked back in horror. He tried to pull free, tried stupidly to bat away my arms. His breathing was wheezy and beneath that there was a squeaky whine. He landed a couple of punches on my face, but they bounced off and I had to slap him again, harder this time, to shut him up. The slap knocked his head sideways.

Beckett stepped forward, out of the dark part of the living room. He said, 'That'll do.'

I dropped the man. I remembered his name then. He was called Paul Warren. He was thirty-three, but looked older. He was short and pale-faced, freckles on his nose and puffy hands. He was slumping into middle age. He coughed for a while and gulped air and shook with shock. Then he did the smart thing and collapsed backwards against the wall, where he stayed, trying to work out what was happening. His grey suit jacket was twisted about him, and his shirt front was ripped. The fear had gone and left him limp, and now he looked scared and alone. That was good.

'Calm down,' Beckett told him. 'You'll be all right.'

Beckett seemed cool enough, but I saw the sweat on the back of his neck, and I heard the tightness in his voice. He

1

nodded to me and I moved aside. Warren looked up at us. We wore dark suits, white shirts, thin leather gloves. We wore stockings over our heads. That was deliberate. We could've worn balaclavas. Warren doubled over and retched. Nothing came out but spittle. He retched again. After that, he breathed more deeply.

'My wife,' he said.

Beckett turned and nodded to the darkness behind him. A shadow moved and a table lamp flared.

She was younger than her husband, and pregnant. We'd taped her to a wooden kitchen chair. She'd spent an hour fighting the tapes, and now her eyes were red and swollen from crying, and her dark-blond hair was stuck to her forehead with sweat. More tape kept a cloth gag in place. A line of spit ran from the corner of her mouth.

The thing standing beside her was called Simpson. He was a squat man, with small eyes, dressed the same as me and Beckett. He touched the woman on her cheek and his hand drifted down to the neck of her sweater. He stretched the cloth back and looked down. She tried to pull away, but there was no give in the bindings. Beneath the stocking, Simpson's face leered. He looked like a gargoyle. He looked like that without the stocking. I suppose I looked worse. He put a hand inside her sweater, groped and squeezed.

Warren leaped to his feet, a kind of wild fear on his fat, flushed face.

'Fuck's sake,' Beckett muttered.

I moved an arm out and wrenched Warren back and flung him to the floor. Beckett shot a look at Simpson. Simpson's greasy smile faded. He took his hand off the woman.

I'd never met Beckett or his men before this job. I'd heard of them, of course. From what I'd seen, they seemed okay. Walsh and Jenson and Beckett went back, but Simpson was new to the firm. I had the feeling he was trying to prove himself to me, show how hard he was. He acted like he was trying to prove something, anyway. That act with Warren's wife was all show.

I didn't know why I was there. Simpson was stupid, but he was good muscle and it should've been an easy four-man job. I didn't think they needed me, but Kendall had told me Beckett asked for me specially.

'He wants someone frightening, Joe,' Kendall had said.

Warren made another half-arsed attempt to scramble to his wife and I had to push him over with my foot.

'I told you to fucking calm down,' Beckett said.

The smoothness had gone from his voice. He was snarling now, his lips drawn back.

Warren put a shaking hand to his face. I moved back a step, gave him some room. He stood slowly. His face was grim and waxy, but he'd finally got the message.

'All right,' Beckett said.

We had to be careful with Warren. We couldn't hurt him because we needed him later. Even signs of a struggle would be bad. But we also needed to scare the shit out of him. A pregnant wife was good leverage, but we couldn't touch her. In her state, anything heavy might have bad results and then Warren would be useless, too angry or too scared or whatever.

We could've used guns – Beckett and Simpson were tooled up – but guns sometimes scared people too much, turned them into wrecks. Besides, few things shocked a man as much as a quick, effective beating. So, Beckett had needed someone violent, someone massive, someone cold. Anyway, that's how Kendall had explained it to me, and I'd believed him.

'What do you want?' Warren said.

'The casino,' Beckett said.

Warren shook his head.

'But . . . don't you know – ?'

'I know. Is the schedule for tonight the same?'

'My wife – '

'Shut the fuck up and listen.'

Warren seemed dazed again, shocked. That was one of the dangers; he was in an impossible situation. He sagged and staggered, backing up until he hit the wall. He kept staring at his wife, and every now and then he shook his head. I'd seen this before. I reached out and grabbed him. He flinched, lifted his hands to protect his face. I hauled him upright and Beckett walked forwards, blocking his view of his wife. Beckett leaned in close to Warren. He talked quietly, but his voice rumbled.

'Listen to me. Your wife's fine. But I'm leaving this man here. Look at him. Look at him.'

Warren looked up at me. I looked back. It was all I had to do; he could see what I was. Beckett touched Warren on the shoulder.

'If he doesn't get a call from me before seven, he'll hurt your wife. He'll fuck her up and then he'll leave. You understand?' Warren nodded. 'Good. Now, is the schedule for tonight the same?'

Warren nodded again. It was like someone had hit a switch and put him on automatic.

'Yes,' he said.

'I want you to tell me the procedure and times for moving the money to the armoured car,' Beckett said, the smoothness back.

Warren told him. Beckett made notes and read back what he'd written.

'The casino closes at five. The money is collected by two security guards inside the casino and taken to the counting room.'

'The auditing room.'

'Right. Where you and the manager supervise the count and log it. The armoured van arrives at the back door at six forty-five. There are cameras over the back door and a keypad. When the correct number is entered by the guards from the van, they open the door and are given the money by the casino's own security. Is that right?'

'Yes.'

'That's good. You're doing okay. Now, here's what you're going to do: you drive back to the casino – we'll be following you all the way – and you tell them the reason you went home was because your wife thought she was going into labour, but she's all right now. Got that?'

'Yes.'

'You're going to call up the security firm and tell them there's a half-hour delay. That's built into their contingency, so there won't be a problem. Make the call from your mobile and make sure no one's hanging around when you do it. Then go straight into the office.'

'They'll phone the casino to confirm.'

'Make sure you answer it. Nobody else at the casino must know you've contacted the security firm. Do it when the office is clear, if you can. There's only one person there most of the time, right? You should get a chance.'

'If I can't be alone?'

'Just make sure your manager isn't there. You and your manager are the only two who can confirm the change of times, so even if someone else is in the office, you answer the phone. The security company won't need to speak to anyone else. If you're overheard, keep your talk to a minimum.'

'Yes.'

Beckett handed Warren a pad and pen.

'Write down the security code for the back door.'

Warren's hands shook too much to write. He took a breath and got a grip and then wrote a number on the pad. Beckett took the pad and pen from him, looked at the number and made him repeat it back.

'That's good. Now get yourself tidied up, put on a clean shirt. Then you, me and Mr Smith over there are going to leave, get in our cars and go back to the casino. Got it?'

'Can I talk to my wife?'

'Sure.'

Simpson pulled the tape off the woman's mouth. She spat the cloth out.

Beckett took a phone from his jacket and called Walsh, who was in the car with Jenson, cruising the area, avoiding main roads and CCTVs. Their route had been checked, but in a suburban neighbourhood like this it was easy.

'Five minutes,' Beckett told Walsh.

Warren walked stiffly towards his wife. He stopped a few feet from her, straightened his clothing. She looked up at him.

'Just do what they want,' she said.

'I will. Are you okay?'

'Yeah.'

'It's going to be okay,' he said.

He looked at her a bit, but he'd run out of things to say.

'Do it, Paul,' his wife said.

Beckett tugged his arm.

'Let's go.'

Simpson stuffed the gag back in the woman's mouth and reapplied the tape. He was all professionalism now. Warren moved forward and kissed his wife on the forehead, then turned and walked back to us. He wouldn't look at me.

'Make sure he doesn't hurt her,' he said to Beckett.

'You make sure.'

I heard them go up the stairs. The woman was quiet, watching. The room was still. The only sound came from the movement above. Floors creaked; a cupboard door opened. The three of us waited. Simpson glanced at me and then looked away. He flexed his hands, stretching the thin leather, and began to walk back and forth. The woman watched him with large eyes, but he ignored her now and paced, jaw tight, neck stiff. Water flowed into a sink somewhere upstairs. Simpson looked at the ceiling.

This was the easy part. I didn't know how much grief they were expecting when they hit the casino. One thing was for sure, though, Simpson was close to bottling it.

I didn't know Simpson, didn't know what jobs he'd done, how he'd done them. I wondered.

Truth was, I didn't know much about any of the others either. Jenson was a tall gangly man with white-blond hair and a constantly joking manner that quickly became annoying.

Walsh was the smallest of the outfit, wiry, covered in tattoos. I hadn't spoken to them much; there hadn't been time. I'd only been told a few days before what I was supposed to do. Beckett and Walsh and Jenson worked as a crew and had done some decent jobs. They'd been together a few years. Kendall had told me they were tight. But they didn't trust me, the outsider. That was fine. I was doing the job because Kendall had always been careful not to mix it with cowboys.

Simpson stopped his pacing and looked over at me.

'Hey, what do you make of this?' he said.

I was about to ask him what he was talking about when Beckett came back, with Warren in tow. Warren looked neat now, and calm. Simpson turned off the table lamp. The room filled with shadow. The three of them left the room. I heard the front door open and close. It was 1.45 a.m. Less than an hour had passed since the woman had phoned her husband.

I moved a seat over to the back wall and sat down. And waited. I had about five hours left.

At first, she stared at me, her eyes on mine, unflinching and fierce. She had bottle, this one. More than her husband. I sat there and looked back at her. She hated me with everything in her. I didn't take it personally. I didn't take it any way at all. After an hour or so, she grew tired of hating me and started fidgeting, shifting in her seat as far as the tape would let her. When she realized she wasn't going to get free, she bent her head forwards and closed her eyes. I didn't think she was asleep. At about 4 a.m., I took a bottle of water from my jacket pocket and drank deeply. I took the bottle over to the woman and removed her gag. Her head snapped back.

'Untie me,' she said. 'Please. I won't try to run or anything.'

I lifted the bottle to her mouth and tilted it. She spluttered, trying to talk while the water sloshed around her mouth. She swallowed enough and I lowered the bottle. I waited until she'd finished coughing.

'I need to go to the bathroom. Please. Please.' I wiped her mouth. 'Please.'

I put the cloth back in and reattached the tape. She fought me, twisting her head back and forth savagely. I took my seat again and watched her fight her restraints for forty minutes, the words of pleading muffled, sweat on her forehead. Finally, she urinated and her body jerked with sobs. After that she was quiet, sagging in her seat. There was a sour smell in the room now, mixing with the sweet-smelling flowers and the warmth of a house well lived-in. It was cloying.

It was 6.52 a.m. when my phone rang.

'We're done,' Beckett said.

When I stood, she looked at me with fury. I went into the hallway, removed the stocking, unlatched the front door and pulled off my gloves, letting the door close behind me.

The air outside was cold. I walked for a half-hour towards the bus stop I'd scouted earlier. There I'd catch a bus to Walthamstow Central and then change. I didn't think anything more about the job or Warren or Warren's wife or Beckett.

It was starting to get light. The sky was the colour of concrete. I walked past a playing field, churned up and guarded by a row of lime trees that looked scratched in charcoal on grey paper. Rooks' cries cut through the early stillness. I walked past an old man bent over a walking frame, dragging himself somewhere for some reason that he probably didn't know or care about, dragging himself onwards for the sake of it. I walked past rows of the same semi-detached houses, drenched in the same shades of grey, coated by grime from the traffic, from the acid rain, from the wash of sameness, as if the life of them had become washed out from contact with their surroundings. I walked on, past these things, hardly aware of them, not caring.

TWO

When I woke, it was early afternoon, and still dull. Something like daylight crept through the small windows and gave up halfway across the room, leaving the far ends dark. Below, the traffic on the High Road whirred, the odd lorry or bus humming with a deeper sound. I lay there and listened to it and gazed up at the cracked ceiling, a long way from it all. It was another day to face, another one to cross off.

I thought about Brenda again. I turned my head to one side and looked at the picture of the ship, old and worn out and being dragged to its death by some ugly brute. It was a good painting. It made me feel something, anyway, though I don't know what. It made me think of her, I suppose. I looked at it, as I often did, and tried to call the picture of her to my mind, to fill the empty moment. But it was getting harder to remember her, and the empty moments were getting emptier, and every second that passed took me further from her, further from the image of her. I looked at that picture more and more, and the picture itself became her, or she became the ship. Or something.

So I looked at that picture and counted the cracks on the ceiling and stared at the wall and looked at the picture some more, and all the time I was getting further from her, inch by inch, second by second, day by lousy fucking day until those small things added up and became one big blur. And all the time that blur became duller, darker, emptier. And the jobs I did meant less and less until I was doing them for the sake of it, just to keep on doing something, just to keep from being swallowed up by the emptiness.

'That poor old ship, Joe,' she'd say.

And while the blur became bigger, and my memory of her became blurrier, and I became older and more worn out, the jobs became smaller. I was dying by inches.

And then this job came along. A big job. And all I had to do now was sit and stare at the picture and try to think of her and wait for my cut and wonder why the fuck I was getting so much for doing so little.

I'd decided to stash some of my cut, though I wasn't saving for anything especially. I had nothing much to spend it on. I was saving for the sake of saving. I was like that old man, clinging on to his walking frame. I told myself it was emergency cash, it was a retirement fund. It was some fucking thing.

I hauled myself out of bed, feeling the ache in my muscles. I washed and shaved, trying to clear away the muzziness that seemed to stick to me more these days. I did a set of push-ups and a set of sit-ups, did stretching exercises for my back. When I finished dressing, I went into the kitchen and made tea, and cooked a cheese and onion omelette. Omelettes were about the only thing I could cook well. Still, I liked omelettes.

I sat at my small table and turned on the radio and ate as I listened to stories of lies and murder and mass murder. The world turned. Then the local news came on and the casino job was the second item after a stabbing in Kilburn. One million quid, that was the haul. I worked for a flat fee plus two and a half per cent of the take. I could've got a better cut if I'd joined up full-time with some firm, but I didn't want to do that. I switched the radio off. I felt okay.

My cut came to twenty-five grand. Say, fifteen, if the money had to be cleaned. I didn't know about that. Less twenty per cent. Plus the flat fee of four thousand. Sixteen thousand total. At least. That was the most I'd ever earned. For sixteen grand, I could lay off work for a while. I didn't know what I'd do, but I could find something. Go somewhere, maybe. I couldn't think of anywhere to go. I'd always had half an idea that I might go live in the country, but I knew that was bollocks. I belonged in the country like a traffic jam.

I finished the omelette and tea and sat for a while, not thinking of anything. All I had to do was wait for Kendall to tell me where and when to collect the money.

I'd met Kendall eight years back. I'd been fighting a bloke called Hadley. He was nothing special, and I should've had him on the canvas inside of three. He moved well, though, and I realized too late that he was after a TKO. He was quicker than me, and younger, and I couldn't keep up with his punches. By the fifth, my left eye had closed up and I spent so much time covering it I forgot about the right, and Hadley, who was orthodox, was making a good show of being a southpaw. He connected with my right eye a few times and opened it up. I had to get in close and jam him up, but with the left closing and blood in my right, I was swinging blind. If I could've connected, I'd have flattened him, but I couldn't find the fucker and finally I got counted out.

I climbed from the ring and was led into the changing rooms where Browne did a quick patch-up job, gave me a handful of pills and told me I'd probably have headaches for

13

a week or so; told me I'd have to quit soon or risk permanent brain damage.

'I'm serious, Joe,' he said.

I nodded. I'd heard it all before.

I had a quick shower, switching the water from hot to ice-cold, trying to soothe the aches and wash some of the dullness out of my head, and when I came out, a small fidgety man in a camel-hair coat and tailor-made suit was pacing up and down, smoking a cheroot. He had dark hair, greased back and greying at the temples, and olive skin. He moved like a young man, full of pent-up energy, but his face was without flesh and the hollow, shadowed cheeks and deep-set dark eyes made him look old and sick, and his constant movements made me think that if he stopped for a moment he'd realize he couldn't go on.

When he saw me, he crushed the cheroot underfoot. He looked me up and down, nodding to himself.

'I seen you fight a coupla times.'

I grabbed a towel and started drying myself. My head hurt. My head always hurt. It was just one of those things. I didn't need someone to make it worse.

'You got a great left,' he said. 'I never seen a jab with so much behind it. And you can take punishment, I'll give you that.' He hesitated, looked down at his crushed cheroot like it was an old friend he'd lost. 'But you're old.'

Everyone was telling me that. The doctors, the other fighters, the crowds.

'You're too slow for these kids,' he said. 'They're running all over you.' He held out his hand. I looked at it. It was small and sweaty. 'My name's Kendall. Dave Kendall. Ever heard of me?'

I hadn't heard of him, but didn't say so. When he got tired of holding his hand in the air he pulled it in and used it to scratch his ear.

'I used to fight. Crystal Kendall. Crystal on account of my glass jaw.'

I still hadn't heard of him.

He glanced at his watch. It was an expensive watch. Or maybe it was a good fake. He looked like the kind of person who'd try and con someone with a dodgy watch. Maybe he'd got confused and sold it to himself.

'Look, I gotta get over to Deptford in a coupla hours, but I'm free till then. Fancy a pint?'

I was waiting for the pitch. I was bored of him. He smelled of hair oil and cheroots. He moved too much.

'Don't talk much, do you?' he said. 'That's all right. I don't need a talker. Look, I'm not trying to con you or nothing.'

I started dressing. Kendall backed away from the lockers, giving me room. He scratched his ear again.

'Look, you're getting seven shades of shit knocked out of you, what, once, twice a week? How long you gonna be able to do that? How would you like another job?'

He pulled a cheroot from a pack in his coat pocket. He lit it, blew out some smoke and said, 'A decent fucking job.'

I sat down. My head throbbed. My eyes stung. My ribs were trying to unhinge themselves and run away. Even my hair hurt.

Eight years later and he seemed to have kept his promise. A decent job, decent money. Easy. All I had to do was wait for him to call.

I didn't own a phone. There was a newsagent a couple of doors along and the owner there, bloke called Akram, would take the call for me. He'd come up with a message, then I'd go see Kendall or phone him back from a public phone. Akram was also my landlord. He owned three buildings along the road. I had an arrangement with him: he paid all the bills and I gave him the cash. Nothing was in my name. Recently, I'd moved flats to a smaller, single-bedroom place. I'd done this because some of Akram's old relatives had come over from Pakistan, and Akram, who was paying their living costs, wanted them to live as cheaply as possible and because his old grandmother couldn't manage stairs so well.

The attic flat needed updating, as estate agents would say. The putty around the edges of the single-pane windows was cracked and falling away, and cold air leaked in. In summer, the flat would probably be hot. In February it was fucking cold. The previous owner – an old man who smoked roll-ups and wheezed more each day climbing the four flights of stairs – had never had money to spend on things like a new cooker or a coat of paint. It didn't matter. The flat was far away from other people, which was fine by me. I didn't plan on holding many dinner parties.

I sat in all day Monday. Nobody called.

On Tuesday, I went to my local gym, an old-fashioned boxing place called Murray's which smelled of sweat and menthol and rubbing oil. I was on nodding terms with the punters there, but I hardly ever talked to them. Sometimes one of the old-timers would have a word about boxing, but that was about it. I stood by myself, pounding the heavy bag, trying to ignore the glances I got from the others, the change in mood. There was less banter when I was there, less joking, as if the air had changed, become thicker, heavier.

On my way back from the gym, I stopped at Akram's to see if there was a message for me. The shop was long and narrow, with discoloured yellow and white vinyl floor tiles, and a layer of dust and filth in the unused corners. One wall had racks of magazines from floor to ceiling, and newspapers bundled along the floor. Along the other wall were shelves of groceries, sweets, crisps, drinks. Stuff like that.

Akram always wore the same beige-striped shirt and brown trousers, and never seemed to realize they were too small for him. He was always behind his counter, always sweating behind his thick black beard, always worried about something and apologetic, always surrounded by women, or so it seemed. The shop was always open and always staffed by Akram or his sisters or his mother. His wife spent her life at the back, behind the bead curtain, where she cooked spicy food and listened to a London-Asian radio station. She never came out, as far as I could tell, but she would call out to Akram in her sharp voice, getting him to do some task or other.

When I walked in, an old Asian woman in a purple sari was ranting at Akram. She jabbered away and he, palms towards her, shook his head and tried to answer. Akram's wife called out something and Akram sighed. The old woman saw me and flinched. Akram said something, pointing at me. The old woman muttered a reply and shuffled off, keeping her eyes to the ground. Akram smiled and lowered his arms.

'My grandmother,' he said. 'She thinks everyone here is trying to rob her or rape her. She wants to go back to Pakistan.'

'She should go back,' Akram's wife's voice said.

There were no messages for me. I left them to it.

17

On Wednesday, I went to my local library. The young assistant was at the front desk, busy cataloguing or whatever they do there. I'd said hello to her once and since then she'd avoided my eye, busying herself, like now, with some job that needed her to look down or up or anywhere else. I walked past her. Maybe I'd said hello too aggressively.

Mostly, I read history. I wanted to see how the great figures had risen, how the great crimes had been carried out. You got to see what people were up to, what their angle was, how they disguised their self-interest, how they fooled and bullied others into following. You got to see where the con was, how the winners had got it right, how the losers had got it wrong. Wars, especially, interested me. Like boxing, they were the end of things, human nature at its most basic.

I spent the rest of Wednesday reading about how people in history had fucked up, and in that time I'd heard nothing, and that was strange. Usually, Kendall would at least call and tell me when to expect the money or the reason for the delay. I didn't mind waiting, but three days after a job with no word wasn't right.

And there was something else. I was waiting to hear about another job that was supposed to go off in a week or so. I didn't need the money so much now, but I'd still agreed to do the job. I had a reputation for being reliable and I had to keep that. It was the most valuable thing I had. The job was a jeweller's over in Brent Cross. The outfit was local, from Tottenham – Nathan King and his crew. King, I knew. We'd worked together a couple of times. He was a neat operator. He'd found me in Murray's gym and had asked me to do the job.

18

'Quick in and out,' he'd said. 'But we need to go mid-afternoon, and it's a big place. We could use some crowd control.'

That had been a couple of weeks ago and by now King should have fixed it up with Kendall who would've waited until the casino job had been done before confirming.

On Thursday, I decided to give Kendall a call.

I went down from my top-floor flat and along to Akram's. He was handing change to an old woman who muttered complaints about her missing free scratch card. After she'd shuffled off, I bought a phonecard and went out to use the phone box on the corner. I called Kendall's number. I got his answerphone and hung up and went over to a greasy spoon called Sam's. I tried Kendall an hour later. There was still no answer. I left a message this time, telling him to call me at Sam's.

I sat in the greasy spoon as the day slid into muddy dusk. I stirred my tea and looked out of the plate-glass window, through the pockmarks of dust and dirt, and watched the people trudge past, watched the world trudge past. My head wasn't hurting, my thoughts were clear, and a question snagged in my mind:

Why me?

I'd done the job because it was just a job, and I was just a lump who wasn't in on the planning, who only did the heavy stuff and took a small cut. But all I'd had to do was frighten Warren, knock him around a bit, and then sit with the woman for a few hours. Beckett had had his usual crew, and the job, from what I could see, had been easy enough. Simpson could have leaned on Warren. Why did they need me for that? And why did they need anyone to sit with the woman? If she was tied up and Warren was sure that she was in danger, they could have left her by herself. The house was detached: nobody would hear. Better still, they could have taken her to some isolated place and left her there.

It was dark now and the drizzle hovered and drifted on the cold air. The traffic, the sky, the buildings seemed sluggish and the few people who tramped along the road held their heads down, their coats huddled about them.

I walked a couple of blocks to the multi-storey car park where I kept my old Vauxhall Carlton on a long-term parking permit. I checked I had enough petrol in the tank and drove off on a trawl of places across north London.

The third place I tried was a pub called the Earl of Roxburghe in Enfield. Everyone called it the Roxie. Kendall was in a booth when I got there, seated by himself with a glass of vodka-tonic. He sipped the drink, stirred the ice cubes with a finger and sipped it again, putting it down carefully on the table. When he looked up and saw me standing above him he smiled broadly. He pulled a cheroot from a pack on the table, lit it and took a deep drag. He blew the smoke out and said, 'I was gonna call. Been busy. You all right?' I nodded. 'Good. Good.'

He made to draw on his cheroot again, and noticed the no-smoking sign fastened to the window beside him.

'Shit.' He dropped the cheroot to the floor and stamped it out. 'I hate this fucking no-smoking bollocks. Sit down.'

He wore a nice suit, but he made it look cheap. I took the seat opposite and waited. He looked at the vodka-tonic in front of him and pushed it with his finger, like he'd forgotten what the drink was for.

'Heard you were looking for me,' he said. 'What is it?'

I waited. He went to light another cheroot, remembered the sign and cursed, flinging the pack away.

I knew that I should try and be subtle. People responded better to that kind of thing, I'd learned. The trouble was, I'd never really known what that meant. Being what they called subtle seemed to me like a waste of time. All it meant was you spent too long talking around a subject. I tried to think how I should be subtle and then gave up and said, 'Where's my money?'

Kendall took a gulp of his drink, then, while still swallowing, shook his head. After that performance, he said, 'What's wrong with you? Haven't I always got you your money?'

'Yes.'

'Course I have. So what's the fucking problem? There's a bit of a delay. Nothing to worry about.'

He was taking the long way around saying that he didn't have my money. Maybe he was being subtle.

'Where is it?'

'I dunno. Beckett's gone. I can't find the cunt.'

'What about the others? Walsh, Jenson.'

'I've been trying to reach them. Look, I know Beckett. He's all right. If he's taking his time, it's for a reason. Maybe he's having trouble cleaning it or something.'

He tapped the tabletop with a stained index finger, just to make sure it was made of wood.

'Look,' he said, 'I'll pay you out of my own pocket. I mean, I fixed the job up, right? I'll get it off Beckett later. Okay?'

Right then I knew something was wrong. It was like Kendall to stall if there was a delay, sure, but handing over his own money? Forget about it.

'I'll bring it over later,' he was saying. 'You still at that Paki's place? Tottenham High Road, right?'

'I moved.'

'Yeah?'

He'd stopped tapping the tabletop.

'Where to?'

'Upstairs. Number fifteen.'

'Well, I'll bring it later. Hey, you ain't got a drink.'

He stood up.

'I'm not thirsty.'

He hesitated. He didn't seem to want to sit down again.

'I gotta have a slash,' he said. 'Wait here, okay?'

He swayed towards the back of the pub. He'd had a few more drinks than I'd realized. While I waited, I thought.

It was possible Kendall was worried Beckett had been caught, or had got into trouble and would grass him up. Possible, but not likely. Kendall wasn't important enough to worry about and he sure as shit didn't give a damn if I got caught. Could he think that Beckett had done a bunk with the cash? Again, possible but unlikely. He would lose the cut from my end, but it wasn't so much that he would care about it.

I turned and scanned the pub. It was almost eight o'clock, still too early for the main custom. There were a few men in the place, no women. Mostly the men were in groups of two or three, but one man was alone at the far end of the bar, as far from me as possible. It occurred to me then that Kendall had taken the very end booth and was seated with his back to the wall so that everyone in the pub was in his sight. He'd also sat on the bench at the end nearest the aisle, preventing

22

me from sitting next to him. The man at the bar was big, with a thick upper body and developed arms. He had a tall, slim glass of clear liquid in front of him. There was ice in the glass. It might have been lemonade or gin and tonic or vodka. It might have been water. Whatever it was, he wasn't drinking it. He had his elbows rested on the counter and, with one hand, he held the glass and tilted it every now and then so that he could look down into it.

Kendall came back to the booth. He was sweating more now. Trying to be subtle, I said, 'Haven't heard from Nathan King.'

He didn't say anything to that.

I said, 'You got any work for me?'

'No, Joe. Nothing. There's nothing much happening at the moment.'

He was back to looking at the table.

I stood up and almost felt the relief slide off him.

'You don't want a drink?' he said.

'No.'

Kendall was scared. More than that, he was scared of me. Someone had called him up and told him I was out looking for him, or he'd heard it on his answering machine. Then he'd found a nice safe public place to sit and wait, and a nice friendly bodyguard to watch his back.

'Don't worry about it,' Kendall was saying. 'The money.'

I left the pub, got into my car and drove a hundred yards up the road. Then I waited, watching the pub entrance in the rear-view mirror. Kendall and the other bloke came out after a couple of minutes. They stood in the light of the pub's windows and exchanged a few words, and then they parted.

Kendall went to his car and drove off. I followed him. After a minute or so, I knew he was going home. I eased back and let him leave me behind.

THREE

He lived in a detached mock-Tudor place in Palmer's Green. It was bland enough to give him businessman-like cred, big enough to let him see his money. He'd never invited me over, had never, in fact, told me where he lived. I'd decided one day to find out. Just in case.

When he opened the door, he said, 'Urgh.'

I barged through, shoving him backwards. I kicked the door shut and guided him through the house. He tried to pull his arm free.

'What the fuck you doing?' he said.

The living room was large and full of old-looking furniture, hunting prints, those Staffordshire figures, stuff like that. There was a white shag rug, two thickly padded leather sofas, a dining-table set. Kendall's wife must have thought her husband was a stockbroker or something. I let go of his arm.

'What's this all about?' he said, rubbing his biceps. 'I told you I'd bring the money.'

'Sit down.'

He sat at the small dining table.

'I'm sitting. Happy?'

I grabbed him and shoved him across the room. He fell on to a low sofa. He was starting to look worried.

'Look – '

'Where's your wife?'

'Out. Bingo. Look, I don't know what this – '

'Who was that bloke?'

'What bloke?'

'The bloke in the Roxburghe.'

His body sank into the sofa.

'One of my boys. Name's Robson.'

'Why the protection?'

He fidgeted in his seat, trying to make himself more comfortable, trying, I thought, to buy time. He leaned forward with his elbows on his knees. I went over to the drinks cabinet and pulled out a bottle of vodka, filled a glass and handed it to him. He drank it down quickly and held his glass out for more. I poured him another.

'Look, just take it easy, okay?' he said.

I waited and watched his small dark eyes flicker from me to the doorway.

'It's nothing personal, Joe,' he said finally, wetting his lips. 'We've done enough jobs together, haven't we?'

'Why the protection?' I said again.

'Haven't you heard?'

'What?'

'That bloke,' he said. 'The one on the job with you.'

'There were five of us on the job.'

'The new one, the muscle.'

'Simpson?'

'Yeah, Simpson.'

He knew damn well who was on that job. Now he was playing forgetful. I had to wonder.

'What about him?' I said.

'He's dead.'

'How? When?'

'Three days ago. Day after the job.'

'Where?'

'In his house. Beaten to death.'

The job was a fuck-up now, whatever way you looked at it.

'Who did it?'

'How the fuck am I supposed to know that?'

'What do the law know?'

He poured the rest of the vodka down his throat. I tossed him the bottle. He flinched.

'Joe, look – '

'The police, Kendall.'

'They don't know nothing.'

'Have they made Simpson for the job?'

'No. Not as far as I know.'

'What about Beckett and Walsh and Jenson?'

He pulled a cheroot from the pack on the coffee table. He patted his pockets for a light. I saw some matches on the table and tossed them to him.

'Beckett, Walsh, Jenson,' I said, after he'd fired up the cheroot.

'I dunno about them. They're gone.'

He blew smoke out.

'Where?'

'I dunno. Haven't heard from them.'

'The money?'

'Well, if you haven't got it, Beckett's got it. Or he ain't. I dunno.'

'What do you mean, if I haven't got it? Is that what you think? That I ripped Beckett off, killed Simpson?'

27

'I don't think anything. Christ, we've worked together long enough, right?'

'But you still wanted protection to meet me.'

'Look – '

'Forget it. If Beckett's gone, why doesn't anyone think he's legged it with the money? He could've killed Simpson.'

'Well, he's prime suspect, sure. But . . .'

'But what?'

'It's not just that.'

He hesitated and sucked on his cheroot. Ash fell into his lap.

'Go on.'

'That other mob. What's his name? Them black blokes. Ellis.'

'What about them?'

'They got turned over.'

For a moment I didn't understand him, and then I got it.

'That Brighton job? That was four weeks ago. I wasn't on that.'

'You worked with them on the job they did before,' he said.

Something cold moved over my skin.

'That was the job before.'

'They never use an outsider, Joe. Then, the one time they do, they get done on the next job.'

They'd used me that one time because Caine was a wreck after his wife left him, back on the smack. After the Brighton job, they'd had a haul of cash, but they got hit by some unknown firm. Someone had told someone about the cash. I thought that Caine had said something, perhaps in exchange for heroin, but since he and two others were blown apart by twelve-gauge shot I supposed it would never be known. There was no point me saying all this to Kendall. He wasn't the one that needed convincing. I looked at him and he half shrugged and made it look like it hurt him to do so.

'You think I did the one job with them, learnt a bit about their next one and then passed the information on?'

'No, Joe. I don't. Course I don't.'

'But others think I did? Nathan King, for instance? That why I haven't heard from him about the jewellery job?'

Kendall held his hands up.

'Like I'm saying, I know you're okay. It's just people are careful. Mud sticks. You're covered in fucking mud, Joe.'

'Why would Beckett use me if my name's bad?'

'It wasn't. Not then. Now that Simpson's dead . . . well, now it ain't so good.'

He was right, it looked bad. And if people thought I was bent, London was dead for me. The only people I'd ever get work with would be the type I'd never want to work with. It was nothing personal. I would've been just as nervy if I'd known someone with my kind of luck.

When I turned to go, Kendall struggled from his seat. He grabbed my hand and shook it. His handshake was limp, his hand warm and clammy. He held on a few seconds too long. When he finally let go, he patted me on the arm and told me again that he'd never doubted me. I wanted to throw him through the window.

So, that was that. I was fucked. My money wouldn't last long without any other income. My name was dirt. I was getting old.

Back in my car, I thought things through. There were two problems, as I saw it.

The first was this Beckett thing. Where was he? Where was the money? What had happened to Simpson? It might still be possible for me to survive if I could find out these things.

The other was more immediate. Nathan King. I was supposed to be doing that job with him. If he thought I was bent, I could be in trouble.

I decided to go to King's house. He wouldn't like me doing that, but I didn't think he'd try anything on his own property. I had an old Russian Makarov PM pistol taped to the underside of the passenger seat. I'd take the gun with me but stash it outside King's place. That way I could walk in without causing friction but still have some protection when I left. If I left.

The Makarov was a small piece, and heavy, but the blow-back action gave it accuracy, and it was more reliable than most other automatics. I cleaned the gun and checked its action.

I drove the car to Oakwood tube station and left it in the car park. I walked a couple of blocks to a semi-detached house in a quiet road. I walked up the driveway and stopped next to King's black BMW. I slipped the Makarov beneath the car, just next to the nearside rear wheel.

The woman who answered the door was short, young and dumpy. She had bleached blond hair and make-up you could bang a nail into. She looked up at me and sighed, held the door open with one hand, put the other on her hip and called over her shoulder:

'Nat, it's one of yours.'

She walked away, leaving the door open. I stepped in, but left the door ajar. I could hear a TV playing, kids arguing.

There was a thick smell of fried meat and perfume. King came through from the lounge. He was a big black man, with greying temples and a hard, creased face. He was carrying a can of lager. He stopped when he saw me and the good humour slid away, its place filled with a deadened look. His eyelids closed slightly.

'Joe. What are you doing here?'

'I need to talk.'

'About?'

'Business.'

He took a swig from his can and, as he did so, his eyes moved quickly over my body. I stood still with my arms by my side. A man's voice called to King from the back of the house.

'Come see who's here,' King called back.

Tony Daley was a stocky white man with a thing for chunky gold jewellery. He'd partnered King for the last twenty years. They'd grown up together in Wood Green, within sight of the Ally Pally. They owned a second-hand car lot in Muswell Hill that gave them their legitimacy. They never did anything half-cocked, never took chances, never tried to take down too big a score. I'd worked with them a couple of times and we'd got along well enough. King and Daley knew what their job was; they did it without fuss. They were smart and careful. If my name was dodgy, these two would tell me. They were also the two who might have most to lose if I was a grass.

Daley smiled when he saw me. It was an easy smile, and I thought that he at least didn't think me a threat. I relaxed a little and felt the tension in my shoulders ease.

'Joe. What you doing here?'

31

'Business, he says,' King said.

They exchanged quick glances. I didn't know them well enough to know what was in that look. If they suggested we leave the house, I'd agree, then grab the gun.

'Must be important business,' Daley said. 'You don't ever leave Tottenham, far as I remember. 'Cept for a job.'

'It's important.'

They exchanged glances again, weighing things up.

King said, 'Come alone?'

'Yes.'

'Where's your car?'

'Oakwood tube. I walked from there.'

He looked at Daley, nodding his head towards the street. Daley moved past me and out through the front door. We waited, not speaking. After a few minutes, Daley came back in.

'Fine,' he said.

'Come with me,' King said.

He led the way back through the house. I passed a few kids sitting in front of a TV. They were playing games on some computer console thing, arguing about whose turn it was. Two women, King's wife and another woman – Daley's wife, I guessed – were sitting on a sofa, drinks in hands. King's wife glared at her husband as we passed. He sighed and looked away from her. She was going to give him a bollocking later. Daley's wife glanced at me. She looked like she'd seen it all before. She turned back to her drink.

King led us into the bright kitchen, cluttered with dirty dinner plates and stacked pans, and hot from steam and cooked food. We went through the back door into another room that had once been the garage. A pool table had been set up in here, and a bar had been built along one side. Daley slumped into a black leather chair and reached to the ground for his glass of Scotch. I'd interrupted their game of pool. King leaned against the table. Nobody offered me a drink. I hadn't expected them to. I took a position between the two men, but away from them, near the bar. I had them both in sight. I could grab a bottle if I had to.

'So,' King said. 'Tell us.'

'I hear you two don't want to work with me any more. That right?'

King took a deep breath.

'No. That's not right. Not exactly.'

'We were told you might not be safe,' Daley said.

'And the job? You cutting me out?'

'No, Joe,' Daley said. 'You ain't in or out. We're not doing the job.'

'Because of me?'

'What does it matter?' King said.

'It matters.'

'We're not doing it,' Daley said, 'because something smells fishy. No offence, Joe. We gotta take precautions.'

'Uh-huh.'

'But that doesn't mean we think you're a scalper. Nat said that was bollocks soon as he heard it.'

'Right,' King said.

'Besides, we didn't think you'd want to surface for a while. Certainly not to do a job.'

'What do you mean?'

King picked up the cue ball and put it down again. Daley shook his head and said, 'Fuck's sake, Joe. You can't hit a man like Cole and not expect any shit to come down on you.'

'Cole? Bobby Cole?'

'Of course Bobby Cole. The casino job.'

'That was Cole's casino?'

'Didn't you know?' King said.

'No.'

Robbing Cole was madness. He wouldn't rest until he had us all strung up. Maybe he'd killed Simpson. And Beckett. If he had, why didn't Kendall realize it? But then, maybe he did. Maybe he was distancing himself from the whole thing.

'Who told you I wasn't safe?' I said. 'Was it to do with the Ellis thing?'

'We didn't hear it from Ellis,' Daley said. 'That was just bad luck, even Ellis says so. He blames Caine for that.'

'It was Dave Kendall told us,' King said. 'Last week. Said he was worried about you, wouldn't be putting any more work your way.'

Kendall. That explained his behaviour earlier, why he'd felt he needed a bodyguard. He must've thought that I'd heard he was throwing shit on my name.

'I never liked Kendall,' King was saying. 'Never trusted him. He talks too fucking much.'

One of Daley's kids, a small blonde thing, ran into the room and stopped dead when it saw me. It stared at me with huge eyes and mouth agape. Then it remembered it had legs and turned and ran from the room.

Daley said something to me about the kid's name meaning something or other in Dutch.

'My mum was Dutch, see,' he said.

34

Something King had said was getting caught somewhere. It didn't fit. When Daley finished giving me his family history, I said to King, 'Last week?'

'Huh?'

'You said he told you this last week.'

'Yeah. After I saw you that time in the gym I called him up and told him we wanted you for the jeweller's.'

'This was before the casino job?'

'Yeah, of course.'

I felt a weight in the back of my head.

'Did you tell Kendall that you'd seen me about the jeweller's?'

'No.'

Kendall.

FOUR

Things didn't make sense. Kendall had told King I was no good before we'd done the casino job. So why hadn't he warned Beckett? Kendall wasn't stupid. He wouldn't risk fucking Beckett up. Another thing, Kendall had told me that it was the raid on Ellis *and* Simpson's death that made me look suspicious: two jobs, four deaths, two missing cash hauls. I couldn't argue that the combination made me look guilty of something, or unlucky as shit, but to sling mud at me before the casino job . . . that didn't make sense.

I was thinking these things as I trudged up the stairs to my flat. When I opened the door, I held my arms up high in a blocking motion. I didn't know why I'd done it – the old instinct, maybe. The first blow landed on my right shoulder. Pain shot through my back, my ribs. I gritted my teeth and fought the wave of nausea. The second blow came from the left. I moved quickly, leaning into it, killing its power, but it caught me on the side of the head and sent an electric shock into my neck. Everything spun around and blurred, but I was used to that sort of thing. I hunched over and barged into the direction the blow had come from. I glanced off someone. I threw a left jab, felt it connect with gristle and flesh, felt the smash of bone, heard a grunt and a heavy crash. There was another flash on my right. I stepped back through the doorway. Something whooshed through the air in front of me. It was a baseball bat, I could see now. My right arm was deadened and I'd be unbalanced if I used my left. I charged the man with my shoulder. The two of us fell through into the kitchen, smashing into the sink at the far end, shattering the chipboard cabinets like matchwood. I grabbed shirt, skin, whatever I could. I heard a yelp. I used my body as a pivot and threw the man over my shoulder. I saw a grey mass land heavily on the floor, heard the air rush out of him in a cry of panic and hurt. I raised my foot and stomped on a head. I slammed my foot down, again and again, putting all my weight into each blow. After a while, the grey mass stopped moving. There was a slimy mess on the floor. My shoe was slippery with blood. I was shaking; my heart was in my throat; I felt dizzy. I fell to my knees and tried to breathe. It took a moment for the adrenalin to sink. My arm was throbbing and warm now, but the numbness was going. I stepped over the mess and walked back to the hallway, to where the other man was lying on the floor. He wasn't moving. I flicked on the light and closed the front door.

The bloke on the floor was young, in his twenties, with shaved blond hair. He was big, like a body-builder, too fresh-faced to have been in many fights. He'd crashed backwards into a low table. There was a hole in the plasterboard where his head had hit. His neck was twisted around, blood trickled from a gash above his eye. His breathing was shallow, his face a grey, washed-out colour. I thought maybe his neck was broken. I didn't need to worry about him, so I went back to the kitchen. The man there was older and smaller. There wasn't much else I could make out. He lay face down in a thick and deep crimson pool of blood and gore. I pushed my boot into his face enough to move it around. His eyes were open. He wasn't breathing at all.

I went into the bathroom, shucked out of my jacket and ripped off my shirt. My gun clattered to the floor. I'd forgotten about that. I looked at my right shoulder in the mirror, flexing it, rubbing it, moving my arm above my head and around. The skin was already discoloured where a bruise was breaking out, but nothing was broken. A pain moved through my head and, for a second, the world went dizzy. I splashed cold water on my face then went into the bedroom and grabbed a leather travelling bag. I went from room to room, packing essentials, some clothing, some dried food.

I left the flat to get some stuff I'd stashed under the landing floorboards. Below me, Akram's grandmother stared up, eyes wide, hands clasped before her. She was terrified. She said something I couldn't understand, then turned and scuttered back down the stairs. I ripped back the carpet and pulled up a floorboard. Beneath it lay a black plastic bin bag, taped up to form a package the size of a hardback book. I grabbed the bundle, replaced the floorboard and carpet, and went back into the flat. I opened the package and poured its contents into the leather bag: a Smith and Wesson M10 .38 Special, two boxes of cartridges, one for each of my guns, a silencer for the Makarov, and £5,000 in twenty- and ten-pound notes.

I put the travelling bag by the front door and looked around the flat. It was no bother to dump my old life. There was no point wiping the place down. I could spend hours trying to clear all traces that I'd lived there and still miss something. Besides, they'd still get my DNA. No, I had to go, leave it all behind. The flat was under a false name, anyway. I hadn't used my real name since I'd left the Paras. So long as I didn't get caught, I'd be okay. I'd have to lie low, though, go to ground for a while. I needed a new car. If, as I thought, these were Cole's men, my car would soon be known.

Back in the kitchen, I checked through the dead man's pockets. I pulled out £500 in new fifty-pound notes and £100 in used twenties, a key ring with various keys, including one for a car, and a bank card in the name of Brian Dirkin. I took the money and the keys. I considered taking whatever vehicle this Dirkin had used, but that would be as hot as mine once his body was discovered, and from the look on Akram's grandmother's face, that wouldn't be long.

The boy out in the hallway hadn't moved. I stood and looked at him for a moment. He had a black tribal tattoo on his upper right arm. Something tweaked at the back of my mind and I felt as though a far-off part of me was crying out a warning. It was like a horror lurking.

I crouched down and searched his pockets. There was a condom, a penknife and, as with Dirkin, £500 in fifty-pound notes and £100 in twenties. There was something strange about that. I looked at both bundles of fifties and checked the serial numbers. They were sequential. It looked like someone had paid these men a grand to do this job on me.

I wondered how far they were supposed to take it. Had they been paid to kill me? A thousand didn't seem much for that kind of thing. And baseball bats weren't the best choice of weapon. No, they'd been paid to beat me badly. But then, Simpson had been beaten to death. And maybe the £500 each was a down payment. It was strange, though, for Cole to do it like this. He had men on his payroll, he wouldn't need to employ a couple of outsiders, and amateurs at that.

I heard a rasping sound and froze. The boy was trying to breathe. I watched him for a while, then went into the living room, where I pulled the skirting board away from the wall and reached into the recess behind. I had a driving licence and a British passport made out in a new name. The passport was okay as long as I didn't try to leave the country, but the driving licence was one of those old paper ones. I wasn't sure if they were still valid. I grabbed my large overcoat and a balaclava from a hook in the hall.

It was then that I saw the canvas bag. It was the kind that athletes carry with them. I opened it up. It was empty. Two men wouldn't bring an empty bag to my flat. Either they were going to take something or they'd left something. I went back to the boy in the hallway. His eyes were open now. They rolled around and looked up. He jerked back and that made him cry out.

'Who sent you?' I said.

'Can't move my leg.' He started crying. His lips quivered; snot dripped from his nose. 'Help me.'

'Who sent you?'

'I don't know. Brian knows him.'

His eyelids flickered and fell. I checked his neck for a pulse. It was there, but weak. I slapped him a couple of times to bring him round. After a while, his eyes opened. When he saw me, he panicked and a spasm jolted him. But he couldn't move.

'Don't . . .' he said, his voice breaking.

'What was in the bag?'

The boy mouthed the word before finding a voice.

40

'Money.'

'What money? Why?'

'Don't know.'

'Where is it?'

'Bath – '

'Bathroom?'

He tried to nod and grimaced in pain.

I went into the bathroom. I looked in the cabinet and around the sink. I opened up the cistern and there it was: a clear plastic bag with tape around it. I pulled the bag out and ripped it open. Water poured over the floor and bundles of rolled fifty- and twenty-pound notes fell out. Each roll was £1,000 thick. All the notes looked new. I counted the rolls. There were twenty-four of them. I thought about that and realized that the £1,000 I'd taken from the two men had come from this pile. Likely, they'd been paid £100 each and had then decided to steal £1,000 and split it. So, they weren't paid to do me any kind of harm, they had been paid to plant the money. The baseball bats could have been for protection. They'd probably thought of that themselves. When I'd come back, they'd panicked. There was no way out of the flat except through the front door. They must've thought they'd beat me and leg it. It was guesswork, but it did fit. I decided to keep the notes for the time being. They were evidence that I'd been in on the casino job, but then, if I was caught, they'd hang me for more than robbery.

I stopped short. How had they got in? The lock hadn't been forced and they couldn't have entered through the window without a ladder and ropes, and even then they would've had to break the window, which they hadn't. And I hadn't found any picking tools. I took Dirkin's keys from his pocket and compared them with my own. One of the keys matched: same cut, same dull khaki colour, same company.

I glanced at the boy as I went out. His eyes were open, but not focused. His breathing was short and rapid.

Akram was alone in his shop. He stood behind the counter with a ledger book and calculator in front of him, a look of concentration on his face. There was a faint smell of spicy food, but the smell was stale. There was no sound of music. Akram looked up at the sound of the door opening.

'Hello, my friend,' he called out. He held a hand up briefly and smiled. 'What can I do for you? You need a phonecard?'

I stood for a moment, scanned the place. Pain pulsed from the base of my skull through to my forehead. I tried to push it away. I needed to think.

In the far corner of the shop, near the bead curtain, the lower magazine shelf was missing. The magazines had been stacked in a pile, but the top few had fallen off. Akram's smile faded as he watched me approach. He looked back at his ledger book, ran a dirty finger down a column and punched some numbers into the calculator.

'What happened to the shelf?'

He shrugged, keeping his eyes on the book.

'Kids,' he said. 'They play around.'

'Where's your wife?'

'My wife? She's ill.'

'What's wrong with her?'

He looked up then, his finger on the ledger still.

'Ill.'

'Uh-huh,' I said. 'Tell me about your grandmother.'

42

'My grandmother?'

'Yes.'

'What about her?'

'She was in here Tuesday. She was upset.'

'She's always upset.'

'She was telling you about some men who tried to break in, wasn't she?'

'Did she tell you that? She's old, a bit crazy. She thinks everyone here is trying to rape her.'

'Your wife's ill, your grandmother's crazy and your shop is vandalized by kids. Bad week, huh?'

He tried to smile. He couldn't quite make it.

'Is there anything you want, please?' he said. 'I'm busy.'

'Did they have a key?'

'What?'

'When they went into my old flat, where your grandmother now lives. Did they have a key?'

'She gets confused. I told her: no one has a key. You gave yours back.'

'So she said they had a key, then?'

Akram looked flustered now. He ran a hand over his thick beard and glanced at the bead curtain.

'How many keys are there for my new place?' I said.

'I have one. You have one.'

My head throbbed heavily and my right arm ached and felt like a dead weight. I didn't want Akram to see that my arm was almost paralysed. I didn't want Akram to see the pain I was in. I held my left hand out.

'Let me see yours,' I said.

'What?'

I had to stay patient. I needed Akram to keep calm. Another time and I'd have torn his fucking, sweating head off.

'The key you have to my place,' I said. 'Show it to me.'

'What do you want it for?'

'Give it to me, or I'll come over there and take it.'

He hesitated, looking at me. His mouth hung open and he started to say something and stopped. He patted his pockets and looked inside a drawer.

'I don't have it on me,' he said. 'Why don't you come back, huh?'

'They came in here,' I said. 'Two of them.'

'What?'

'They threatened you? Beat you?'

'I don't – '

'I haven't got time for this bollocks. They came in here, right? Two men. One young, big, shaved head. The other older, smaller.'

He took a step back and slumped on to his stool. He was no hard man. His shoulders sagged. He looked at the missing shelf. He reached behind him and took a packet of cigarettes from the display, unwrapped it, pulled one out and lit it.

'They beat my wife. With bats.'

'Baseball bats?'

'They smashed up my shop.' He took a drag on his cigarette. 'They're bastards,' he said. 'I should have tried to stop them.'

'Then they would have hurt you badly.'

'But they wouldn't have hurt my wife. She has got two broken ribs.' He held up two fingers, a rush of anger forcing him from his stool. The anger shrivelled and he slumped back

44

again. 'Broken ribs. They said if I told you or the police they'd come back and beat my grandmother.'

'They won't come back.'

'How do you know that? You can't know.'

'They won't come back.'

He looked at me steadily.

'Yes,' he said at last. 'I believe you.'

'Your grandmother?' I said.

'She didn't want to come here,' Akram was saying. 'She said London was dangerous, gangs shooting each other. I told her it was safe.'

'They used a key to get into her place, my old flat.'

'Yes. She screamed at them and they ran. She kept telling me strange men had come into her flat. She's old. I thought she must be crazy.'

'And when they came in here, they wanted the key to my new place?'

'Yes.'

'What time?'

'This evening.'

'What time?'

'What does it matter?'

'What fucking time?'

Kendall's wife was unconscious. Her jawbone jutted out, pushing into her cheek. I thought she might have a fractured skull too. There was a mess underneath her head. Kendall didn't care about his wife just then – he had problems of his own. He was on his hands and knees spitting blood and teeth and trying to speak, trying to push words through a broken mouth, trying to tell me not to hurt him any more.

'Please,' he managed to say.

I lifted him up off the floor and threw him into the drinks cabinet. Glass and wood erupted.

I was sweating, snarling, my teeth bared. I hardly noticed the aching in my arm now, with the adrenalin pumping through me. I couldn't understand it. I was shaking. I did this sort of thing all the time. I never lost it, like some. That was why people used me. I didn't go manic. Now I was standing in the middle of Kendall's living room and the place looked like Armageddon. Kendall's wife still hadn't moved, but that didn't matter. What mattered was that I needed Kendall conscious and talking, and if I wasn't careful, I might kill the fucker.

There were suitcases lined up by the door. If I'd got there a few minutes later, Kendall and his wife would've gone.

I couldn't think straight. Christ, the pain in my head was endless. It thrummed. It was like someone pumping molten lead into my skull. Lights danced before my eyes.

He moved, crawled from the wreckage of the cabinet. I stood above him, put my foot on his back and pushed him down.

'You set me up.'

'No,' he said into the shag carpet.

'You waited until I was out of the flat – at the Roxie, with you – and you called your boys and told them to go plant the money on me.'

'Joe, please.'

'They were too slow, and greedy.'

'I don't know what you're talking about.'

'Dirkin. I found him. I killed him. He'd gone to Akram and beaten his wife, taken the key to my flat.'

'Please, Joe.'

I was soaked in sweat and each time the pain, in spasms, reached through me, more cold sweat broke out.

'But you fucked up, Kendall. They tried before but you didn't know I'd moved, did you? You sent them to the wrong flat.'

I put more weight on him, pressing him down into the carpet.

'I can't . . . breathe.'

'You and Beckett were going to feed me to Cole. That it? That's why I was on the job, wasn't it? Wasn't it? Get me on the job, keep me out of the way so I wouldn't be with the others when they legged it with the cash.'

His feet pushed against the floor. His arms flapped around. He looked like a dying fish.

'I . . . can't . . .'

'Talk, Kendall. Talk, you fuck. Simpson was beaten to

death. Everyone knows I'm handy with my fists. Did Beckett do that?'

I pressed him further into the floor. He wasn't breathing now. His face was red; his hands groped for something to help, but there was nothing there.

'Joe,' he said, his throat gargling.

'That's why you've been smearing my name with King and Daley, blaming me for that Ellis botch. You've been laying the ground, right?'

He'd stopped moving now. I lifted him up and threw him across the room. He crashed to the floor and didn't move.

My head throbbed. I needed Kendall capable of talking. I went into the kitchen and put my head under the cold water tap. I filled a glass with water, took it back to the living room and threw the water over Kendall. He stirred and moaned.

I had to think. It didn't all fit. Giving me up to Cole as one of the robbers wouldn't make Beckett safe. Cole would still be looking for the man behind the job. He'd still be looking for his million.

I knelt down and flipped Kendall on to his back.

'Don't. No more. It was Beckett.'

'Go on.'

I lifted him up and rested him against the wall. I found some vodka and poured it down his throat. He sputtered and coughed and pushed the vodka away. He spewed up blood and alcohol, and doubled up coughing. I forced myself to wait, to watch, to ignore the itch to destroy him, to rip him apart. After a few minutes, he straightened himself up. There were tears in his eyes.

'Look, Joe – '

'Talk about Beckett. He knew it was Cole's place. Why did he hit it?'

'Set-up. All of it. Cole offered Beckett a split if he robbed the casino.'

'Cole?'

'Cole.'

'Beckett had inside knowledge.'

'Yeah.'

'So why use Warren?'

'That was for show. Had to look like an outside job.'

And to keep me out of the way for a few hours.

'Beckett was in it for a cut? Hands the rest back to Cole?'

'Yeah.'

'But it was a big haul. Too big for him to give up, right? So he decided to keep the money and he wanted some dumb bastard like me who was supposed to have fucked Beckett over and taken the money for himself. So he came to you.'

'He wanted – '

'He wanted what? Someone stupid?'

'Joe, please.'

I slapped him.

'Is that right? He came to you, said he needed some mug to fuck over.'

'Yeah.'

'But I've got a good reputation, always have had. Too good. Cole might have been suspicious. Beckett needed to smear it a bit so he'd fixed it with you to put the rumour about that I'd had something to do with Tony Ellis's gang getting knocked off. That muddied the waters, made me look iffy.'

'What could I do?'

49

'Why was Simpson killed?' I said.

He was crying now. He passed a shaking hand under his nose to wipe up the snot.

'Beckett,' he said.

'What does that mean?'

'It must've been Beckett. That's all I know.'

He looked towards the doorway.

'You won't make it,' I said.

He coughed back a sob.

'Money,' he said. 'How much?'

I kept my gaze level, fixing Kendall with my eyes, pinning him. He held up his hands, like he was trying to fend off an attack.

'Oh, God,' he said.

I slapped his hands aside.

'How much did he pay you?'

'Ten grand down, five per cent of the take. It's yours.'

He lifted his hands again. I don't think he knew what he was doing, only pushed on by some urge to defend himself. I smacked his hands away again.

'When do you collect the rest? Where?'

'Beckett was going to give it me after . . .'

'After what?'

'He just said he'd give it me later.'

'After I was dead?'

He held his arms out, touching my hands, holding them.

'Look, Joe, I made a mistake. I know that. I'm sorry.'

I pulled my hands away from his wet grasp. He tried again to touch me, his hands flailing around, trying to cling to life. Tears rolled down his cheeks.

'We've known each other a long time, haven't we? Eight years, more. I remember when we met. Remember? It was after that fight in Leyton. You got counted out 'cos you was blind. You'd still be doing that shit if it weren't for me. You'd be blind by now, or dead, if it weren't for me. So I made a mistake. You never made a fucking mistake? I'll make it up to you. Just tell me what you want. What do you want, Joe? For Christ's sake.'

His eyes were wide, his chest heaving.

'Finished?' I said.

He dropped his arms. He dropped his head.

'Why was Simpson killed?'

'I don't know. Scared, maybe, lost his bottle. I didn't have anything to do with it.'

'Why did Cole want his own place knocked off? Insurance job?'

'I dunno. Yeah, probably. My guess.'

He reached a hand out for the bottle of vodka, pulled it to him and took a swig, coughing. I took the bottle and tossed it away. He watched the bottle smash into the wall.

'Why hasn't Cole come for me already?'

'Huh?'

'We did the job four days ago.'

'Maybe . . . maybe he hasn't made the connection.'

Was it possible that Cole hadn't joined the dots as Beckett had planned? Maybe Cole realized Beckett was behind the double-cross. Maybe Cole had men out looking for me at that moment.

Kendall sat up.

'I'll clear it with Cole,' he said. 'I'll tell him you weren't part of it. I'll tell him it was Beckett.'

'Where is Beckett?'

'How the fuck should I know? He's done a bunk, stitched me up. Walsh and Jenson too. Cunts have disappeared.'

It would've surprised me if Kendall had known. He'd served his purpose, why would Beckett let him in on his hiding place?

'I been trying to find them,' he said. 'Give me some time. I'll get them; you'll get clear; we'll sort it with Cole.'

'How?'

'Huh?'

'How have you been trying to find them?'

'I've got a phone number,' he said. He pointed to a desk in the bay of the living-room window. 'In the top drawer.'

I stood and turned to the desk. It was a mistake. Kendall leaped to his feet. He was quick, moved by desperation. I thrust my arm out and grabbed a handful of his hair, ripping it from its roots, wrenching him back, spinning him around. He screamed, his face contorted by fear and shock and pain. I slammed my fist into his face. I heard the crunch of cartilage as his nose shattered. His head snapped back with a crack. He fell to the floor, spasming, gurgling blood from his ruined face. His body jolted; his hands grasped at his face, clawed at the carpet. He rolled and tried to get to his knees but collapsed. His breathing became strained; his movements stopped.

When I knew he was dead, I walked over to the desk. I opened the drawer, riffled through the papers and photographs. There was nothing. I wiped the desk clean. I searched the rest of the house. I found stashes of cash, about a thousand total. I found Kendall's mobile phone in one of the suitcases. I waited for Kendall's wife to come round so that I could question her. After a while, when she still hadn't moved, I checked on her and found that she'd stopped breathing and was going cold. She'd probably been dead a half-hour or so.

Somewhere, maybe, Kendall would have documents, a diary, an address book, that would help me find Beckett. I ripped the place apart. There were bills, photographs, letters, but no part of his business life was here, no sign that he had men on his payroll who robbed banks and extorted money with menaces and collected debts with sledgehammers. Maybe his wife had made him separate his lives, or maybe here Kendall could pretend to himself that he was just an ordinary upstanding citizen. I searched the garage, and through the cars. Nothing. I remembered that Kendall had once mentioned an office, but I didn't know where it was.

I flicked Kendall's mobile phone on and fiddled about with it until I found the address book. I scrolled through until I found 'Beckett, J.' There were two numbers, one of them for a mobile. I tried the number, there was no service. I made a note of the other number, then scrolled through the rest of Kendall's address book, looking for a Walsh, a Simpson, a Jenson. I couldn't find anything. I hadn't expected to; Beckett was in charge. I found a telephone directory, flipped through to the Becketts and ran my finger down the list looking for a match with the phone number I had. There was none. I called directory enquiries and asked for the address of a J. Beckett. There were lots of J. Becketts, the operator said. I gave her the phone number I had. She couldn't help me. I used Kendall's landline, hitting 141 first to hide my number, and dialled Beckett's home phone.

'Yeah?' said a man's voice. The voice was not Beckett's.

'Is John there?' I said.

'Who's this?'

'A friend of his.'

There was a pause.

'He's not here right now. I'm trying to find him myself, you wouldn't –'

I dropped the receiver. One of Cole's men, probably. I looked around the room trying to find something solid. I was used to action, quick sometimes, slow at others. Now I didn't know what to do. Uncertainty was like an itch I couldn't reach.

Kendall and his wife were on the floor in front of me, crumpled like rubbish. I looked at them for a moment before I realized the obvious: I hadn't searched their bodies. I tried the woman first, turning her over with my foot. Her arm flapped out across the floor as her body rolled. The fat on her neck wobbled. She wore a cotton dress, too thin to hide anything except the wrinkles of her skin, too thin even to hide the outline of her underwear, which pushed through the fabric and made her seem stupid, even in death. I'd met her once when Kendall had stopped off at the gym to hand me some money. That had been a long time ago, but I remembered she was snooty, deliberately turning away from me when Kendall had introduced her.

I hadn't meant to kill her. She'd panicked and tried to run from the house and I'd had no choice but to slap her. She'd hit the ground heavily, but I didn't think my blow had killed her. Maybe she'd had a weak heart or something. Now, in death, all that thick make-up, all those gold bangles made her life look like a waste of fucking time.

It was in Kendall's rear trouser pocket that I found the scrap of paper. On it, scrawled in Kendall's hand, was a list of names. None I recognized. All the names had been crossed out except the last: 'R. Martin'. It didn't mean anything to me. Martin was a common name. I found nothing else on him.

I searched the house again, trying to guess where Kendall would hide his important information. If I hadn't been in the front bedroom, I would've missed the headlights as they pulled into the driveway. I dumped the drawer I was holding and went to the window. Below me, a black Mercedes had pulled to a stop behind Kendall's car, blocking it. Three men slipped out of the car. One of the men looked up and I saw a long, thin, white face stare at me. The small dark eyes and small mouth and sharp cheekbones gave it a mask-like appearance. It was a delicate-looking face, pretty in a way. It belonged to a man I knew, and there was nothing pretty about him. I knew him from years back. His name was Kenny Paget. Back then he'd worked for a man called Frank Marriot, a pimp and pornographer, one of the biggest in London. Paget had been his hatchet man. Our paths had crossed a couple of times. What the fuck was he doing here? I didn't move. He kept looking and then turned his face away. He hadn't seen me in the darkened room. He said something to the other men. The three of them fanned out, two going to the front door, one around the left side. The doorbell rang.

By the time I'd got into the kitchen, the third man was at the door, trying the handle. I'd left my car up the road, and I'd left my guns in the car. That was stupid of me. I'd been reckless, impatient to smash Kendall.

Keeping in the shadows at the rear of the house, I moved through to the dining room. Here, French windows led to the patio. When I heard the smash of glass in the kitchen, I slipped the catch on the French windows and eased them open enough to slide through. I closed them, moved around to the side of the house and vaulted over the fence into Kendall's neighbour's garden. Crouching, I moved along the fence, over the soft earth, until I came to the street. Behind me, I heard Kendall's front door open.

'He's dead,' a man said. 'The place has been searched.'

When I heard the door close, I stood up slowly. Paget and his men had gone inside the house. I walked to my car.

I drove aimlessly, sliding around the streets, not aware of where I was going. Things were closing in on me. If I wasn't wanted by Cole and the law yet, I soon would be. My name was shit. I'd just killed the man who was my link with the only kind of work I could do these days. Most of all, my reputation was being shot to hell. That mattered.

I'd never trusted Kendall, but I should've been more careful. I'd let my guard down. Kendall was stupid enough to fuck with me. And I was stupid enough to let him.

I pulled the car over, fished Kendall's mobile phone from my pocket and punched in King's number.

'The fuck is this?' he said, his voice still croaky from sleep.

'Joe.'

'Shit. Hold on.'

I heard the sound of King's wife asking who it was, and King telling her to go back to sleep. I heard the sound of King getting out of bed, a door closing. I kept my eyes on the road, and a hand on my gun. The street was deserted. The sound of any vehicle approaching would give me clear warning. I was jittery. I didn't like being jittery – it made me jittery.

'What is it?' King said.

'I need to find someone.'

'What am I, the police?'

'Beckett's gone. I need to find him.'

He let out a laugh.

'Yeah? Well, good luck.'

'You won't help me?'

'What's this about, Joe?'

'He's taken Cole's money.'

'Leaving you to take the blame?'

'Will you help me or not?'

'If Beckett's gone to ground, I won't find him. If anyone knows, they won't tell me.'

'They'll tell me.'

'Okay, sure, you can make them. But then you'd have to kill them, otherwise they'll just call Beckett and he'll move.'

'I don't mind killing them.'

'No, I'm sure you don't. But you'll have a shit load of heat on you.'

I had enough heat on me. What was a little more?

'Who might know?'

'I don't know. I don't know Beckett, never liked the cunt.'

'You know some people. They know people. Call them up, ask them.'

There was a pause. When King spoke again his voice was quieter. 'I could do that, but I'm not going to. If I start asking questions, it's going to get back to Cole. He's going to want to know what my involvement is. Sorry, Joe, that shit's too heavy for me. Don't you think Cole is going to know who to ask? If he hasn't found Beckett, I won't be able to.'

He was right, of course.

'Give me a name,' I said. 'They won't know it was from you. If I don't find Beckett, I'm finished.'

There was silence down the line. He was thinking it through. His loyalty was split. He knew me, and I was known as a good man to work with, reliable. And he hated Beckett. I was pushing him. I had no choice. After a few seconds, he said, 'Go to ground, Joe. Quit while you're still alive.'

It was no good. King wasn't sentimental about these things. I wouldn't have been. I was about to hang up when I thought of something.

'Do you know someone called Martin?' I said. 'Initial R.'

'Martin,' King said. 'Name rings a bell. Ray Martin. An old face, I think.'

'Why would Kendall want to find him?'

'Fuck should I know? Ask Kendall.'

'I can't.'

'Why?'

'You don't want to know.'

There was another pause.

'Fuck. You're really in it, know that?'

'Just tell me where I can find this Martin.'

'I don't know.'

'Tell me someone who might. Your name'll be out of it.'

He sighed and muttered something. Finally he said, 'Know Jim Bowker?'

Bowker. I knew him. 'Remember Paget?' I said.

'Yes,' King said slowly.

'I saw him tonight. At Kendall's.'

'So?'

'He work for Marriot still?'

'Not any more. Got a better offer. Works for Cole. Didn't you know?'

'No. Since when?'

'Since Marriot got banged up. Paget switched then. Go to ground, Joe. If Paget's after you, you're in trouble.'

Bowker was one of the old sort who'd worked in London in the seventies when the law was as bent as the thieves and you only had to fall out of your car with a sawn-off to net fifty grand. He'd done a couple of long stretches in Wandsworth and the Scrubs, and when they'd finally kicked him out he found that his time had gone, his profession had changed and nobody gave a fuck what he'd done twenty years ago. I hadn't seen him for years, but I remembered him.

I found him in the Connaught Arms club, a snooker place on the Holloway Road. It was an old haunt of mine. I'd last been there about six years before, when I'd worked nearby.

It was members only and I had a bit of trouble getting in, until I fed the bloke on the counter a fifty. He was happy then. Giving him money meant I wasn't law. That was all he cared about. That and the fifty notes.

Upstairs was a large open room, dim and dusty, with a long bar down one side, a handful of tables with mixed chairs and stools, and a dozen or so shabby snooker tables filling the middle of the floor. It was late, but this place had never shut as far as I knew. They served alcohol until the early hours and, because of the bloke downstairs in reception, they had a heads-up on any law, so they let their punters smoke if they wanted to. Smoking wasn't all that went on there. At one of the tables a group of young black men were smoking spliffs, chatting and texting on their mobiles. Yardie-connected, probably. Small-time, though. During the days, the club ran a book. They had a few TVs behind the bar and punters would sit and drink and blow their money on long shots at Goodwood or Haydock Park or wherever, and always it was the gambling, not the winning or the chance to win, but the gambling itself that they sucked up and fed on, because that told them they were still alive.

Bowker was a gambler, which was how I happened to know him. It was his gambling that got him in stir. He'd become desperate a few times too many. He was one of those people who always won small and lost big. That's why King had suggested him, I suppose. He'd spill anything for anyone if you dangled a score in front of his face. Everyone knew he was a grass but for some reason nobody cared, though they made damned sure they didn't talk business around him.

I saw him in the far corner, leaning over a table, cue in one hand, fag in the other. I walked towards him. He was a small man and his three-piece suit was a couple of sizes too big. He seemed to have shrunk since I'd last seen him. Something was killing him: the fags, the booze, the constant losing. He still tried to keep the Teddy-boy quiff he'd had as a young man, but his hair was too thin, and the black sheen it had was too black and just made his face look older and paler.

He lined up the blue with a corner pocket. He put the fag in his mouth, leaned over, cued up and smacked the cue ball. The blue missed the pocket by half a foot and bounced into the reds, scattering them everywhere. He dragged on the fag, coughed a lung up and walked around to line up another shot. He didn't seem to mind that he'd missed.

He didn't see me until I was at the table. When he did see me he didn't react, and I thought that was strange. I should've realized.

'Joe,' he said. 'Been a while.'

'Yeah.'

'Game?'

'No.'

He bent over as far as he could and hit the cue ball into a pack of reds. One of the reds went in the centre pocket.

'You shouldn't be here,' he said, moving around the table and aiming along the cue at a long black. 'People are looking for you.'

'Don't worry about it.'

I watched the cue. It was shaking. I remembered when I'd played poker with him. He would have been good, if it hadn't been for the shakes he got. He missed the black and stood up. He drew on his cigarette and let the smoke out in a sigh. He took a gulp from a glass of Guinness he had on the small table. Sweat stuck to his upper lip and he was taking a while doing things and I knew he was terrified.

'Really, I'm serious, people could be here pronto.'

'Nobody knows me here, not any more. Except you.'

'Sure about that?'

'I'll assume it.'

He looked at me fully for the first time. His face had a yellowish colour that I hadn't noticed in the dimness. His eyes were watery, and the skin around them sagged so that you could see the blood vessels below the eyeballs. His skin was like his suit, two sizes too big.

He said, 'Don't worry about me, if that's what you're

thinking. I'm too old to make enemies. What can I do? You know I can't hardly leave the flat now. My wife, her legs are all swelled up so she don't go out. So I stay in, keep her company. Don't even get to the bookies any more. Can't afford it.' He bent over the table again, lining up another failed shot. 'Coming here is all I can do to get away,' he said. 'It's cheap.'

When he'd finished his sob story, I took a couple of hundred from my pocket and laid the notes on the green baize, right in front of his nose. He gathered the money without straightening up.

'Ray Martin,' I said.

'Martin? What for?'

'I need to speak to him.'

He jerked the cue forward and the white went bouncing around. I didn't know which ball Bowker was aiming at. I don't think he knew. Anyway, he missed. He stood up and slid the cue on to the table surface.

'You mean speak to? Or question?'

'Speak to.'

'Because he's an old mate and I couldn't land him in it.'

'You haven't got any old mates.'

'Nevertheless.'

'I'm not looking for aggro with him.'

He nodded and looked at his feet for a moment, pretending to weigh up whether to say anything, like he was caught in a moral dilemma. I let him pretend. We both knew he was going to tell me.

'Okay. You say he won't get in no trouble over this. I'll take your word for it. I know him. Well, I knew him. Haven't seen him for years. Fifteen at least. He did a stretch, then went straight.'

'Tell me about him.'

'He was a tough old bird. Long time ago, though. Like I say, he's straight as these days.'

'What was his work?'

'Banks, armoured cars.'

'You know Dave Kendall?'

'Kendall? Yeah, sure.'

'Know of any connection between the two?'

'What, Kendall and Martin?' He thought about that while he had another gulp of Guinness. The Guinness left a creamy line on his top lip. 'Can't think of anything,' he said, wiping his mouth with his sleeve.

'Where's he live?'

'I can find out.'

'Do that.'

He picked up the cue and looked along it. I reached for some more notes, peeled off a hundred and fed them to him.

'Might take a while.'

He shuffled off towards the bar. I watched him take a seat next to a wall-mounted telephone. One of the young black men was sitting on a stool next to him watching football replays. I watched Bowker for ten minutes or so. The smoke in the place was starting to make my eyes sting. It was grimy and hot in the club, and it made my hands sticky. I felt tired. My neck ached; my back ached.

I went into what the club had for a bathroom and splashed water on my face. I picked up the soap, washed my hands and dried them on a roll-cloth towel that didn't roll and probably made my hands as dirty as they'd been before I'd washed them. One of the young black lads came in to use the bog. His clothes smelled of the sickly-sweet ganja he'd been smoking. He gave me a narrow look. I walked past him.

'You know him?' he said.

I stopped and turned.

'What?'

'Geezer on the phone. Bowker.'

'What about him?'

'Fucker's dirty, you know. I see you talk to him. Just telling you upright, case you might want to get out of here.'

'Go on.'

'All I know is he's a grass and he sounded like he was grassing someone up, you know. Telling someone that someone was here. You might be one of the someones, and the police might be another. All I know.'

When I went back into the snooker hall, Bowker had disappeared. I didn't think he'd have the bottle. It had been about ten minutes since he'd first used the phone. I made for the exit, taking the stairs two at a time. When I hit the cold air, I scanned the street and couldn't see him. I was a dozen yards from my car when I heard the high-low pitch of a powerful car changing gear and gunning towards me. I looked up. The black Merc screeched around the Highbury Corner and fishtailed as it straightened. I wasn't armed.

My car was parked facing the oncoming car. I got in and keyed the ignition. The Merc came abreast of me and slewed across the middle of the road as it braked. I saw Paget in the front passenger seat. His eyes were on the pavement. He hadn't seen me. The two rear doors opened. I waited while the two men in the back of the Merc were halfway out, then I locked the wheel over left and slammed the accelerator down. The road was slick and my car made a 180-degree spin, tyres squealing and smoking with the burning rubber. They'd noticed me now. Paget swung round to see what the fuss was about. When he saw me his eyes became slits, like thumbnail marks. He yelled something to the men at the back, but I'd timed it right and they were caught. I touched the brakes, straightened up and stamped on the pedal again. The man on the far side jumped back into the car and the one on the nearside dithered, started back for the car and changed his mind, diving into the middle of the road. I missed him by inches and smashed my car into the side of the Merc, mangling the open door and sending the car ten feet down the road. I backed up a few yards. I could see the driver frantically trying to get the car going. I took the Makarov out of the glove compartment, got out of the car and walked towards the Merc and put a few rounds in the front tyre. It blew with a puff and the car sank, lopsided. Paget was getting out of his car as I was getting back into mine. He had a gun in his hand. I didn't think he'd use it; Cole would want me alive and singing.

The windscreen shattered as his rounds hit. I ducked and put the car in reverse, locked the wheel over and spun the car round. I heard a couple more rounds hammer into the body-work. I got out of there, leaving them a crumpled mess.

I threw the car round a few turnings, bypassing Paget, and came back on to the Holloway Road, further up. I cruised for a while, scanning the scene. I had an idea where Bowker would go. I saw him in the distance, scurrying away, his shoulders hunched, his hands in his trouser pockets, smoke billowing from the fag in his mouth. I pulled up beside him. He looked over at me, looked at the mashed front of my car. He didn't try to run. I got out. He pulled the fag from his lips.

'I had to do it,' he said. 'You know I did. Paget would've torn my face off if I'd seen you and not told him.'

He was probably right. I didn't care. He backed up against the front of a kebab place. A couple of teenagers in there were seated at a table, looking at us over their kebabs, vacant expressions on their faces. Bowker reached into his jacket pocket and pulled out a piece of paper.

'Ray Martin,' he said.

On the paper was an address.

'Let me go, eh?'

'So you can grass me up again? Did you tell Paget what I wanted?'

'No. Straight up. I knew he wanted you. He told me to keep me eyes open. Last thing I expected was you to come to me. Christ, I shit myself. I mean, what was I supposed to do? I grass you up and you kill me. I don't and Paget kills me.'

'What do you know about the casino job?'

'Only that you ripped Cole off. You and Beckett, I hear. Beckett's disappeared. That's all.'

I shoved him towards the car. He turned.

'Don't do it. Please. For old times, Joe. Remember?'

'No.'

'That bird of yours.' He lifted his chin. 'There. The Sportsman.'

I turned. Across the road from us was a tall and wide Edwardian building, the brick orange-brown, the gabled windows spilling their yellow light on to the pavement. The name had changed. It called itself a club now.

'I always liked her,' Bowker was saying. 'She liked me.'

From the outside, it looked solid, respectable. Perhaps it was now. I hadn't realized we were so close to the place, though I'd known it was probably where Bowker was going. He was a rat who scampered home whenever he was threatened. The Sportsman was his home, or used to be. Bowker said something else, but I missed it.

It was the first time I'd been back. I didn't know if there was anything in that, or if it was just because I'd never had a reason to go there. The door bounced open and a young couple came out of the place, their breath smoking the moment they hit the coldness. They strolled down the stairs. He said something and she laughed and put her arm through his and snuggled into him to keep warm. They wandered off up the road, leaning into each other. I watched them go.

When I looked round, Bowker had gone. I hadn't known that he'd known Brenda. I felt like I was falling back into it all, into that mess. Paget, Bowker, and now here.

SEVEN

The first time I saw her was in the Sportsman. I'd been working there as security for a few weeks, adding to the stuff that Kendall was feeding me. They let me play whatever I wanted on my own time. I played poker. I was okay at it. People couldn't read me. I had no expression.

My shift was over and I was at a table with £175 in front of me. I'd been there maybe four hours and all I had to show for that was a loss of £68 and an empty stomach. We were playing Texas Hold 'Em and I was in a three-way with a fat Indian bloke and an old woman who had orange hair and orange skin and red fingernails. The Indian had a stack of chips up to his chin and he would've wiped me out if he'd gone all in, but he didn't, so I thought he probably had nothing. The woman kept fiddling with her thick gold bracelets and I hadn't worked out if this was a tell or not. There were two others who'd both folded early on, a man called Roger from Manchester and a bald bloke. The reason I knew Roger was from Manchester was because he'd told me so when I sat down. Nobody said much of anything except Roger, who said way too much for his own good. When he stopped talking everyone folded. He was losing a lot, but he had a lot to lose and seemed happy to see it go. He was on some free business trip, I guessed, probably the only time he ever got to slip the leash.

I was holding a couple of jacks and the flop threw up a third one and nothing bigger, so I decided I'd string it out a bit and then go in heavyish and hope someone had a high pair. The turn card was a four of clubs and that made three clubs showing, so then I thought I'd better not give anyone a chance to get a flush on the river and I went all in and, sure enough, I won. That pot was worth a hundred and fifty odd, which gave me a profit of about twenty quid per hour. I could've earned more on the door.

A voice behind me said, 'Can I join in?'

'Always room for more,' Roger said. 'Where you from?'

When she sat next to me, I had her down straightaway as a pro. Her perfume was too strong, the make-up around her eyes too thick, trying to cover the crow's feet. She was pushing forty and all that make-up just made her look older. I hadn't seen her before, but I knew that some of the pros were pimped by Frank Marriot. He had a scam going with the Sportsman's management. The idea was the pros would pick out mugs from the floor, chat them up, ply them with comped drinks, egg them on at the tables, getting them to lose that little bit more. If they lost, the women would take them to their pad and charge them a fair rate. If they happened to win, the women would try and rob them and split the money with the management. The marks weren't going to complain too much. What were they going to say? It helped if the bloke had a wedding ring, as Roger did.

I wondered if I should hang around a while and see if Roger had any more money to lose. If this woman flirted with him, he might get cocky and start laying it down in piles. But I was tired and my head was pounding and I couldn't give a fuck about Roger's money, so I gathered my chips and left the table.

The Sportsman had a lounge. The lounge had thick red carpets and easy-listening music that was just plain annoying. I assumed the idea was to force the punters back on to the tables as quickly as possible. As staff, I was allowed free drinks after work. I usually didn't bother, but tonight I needed something to loosen me up.

Matheson was leaning against the wall, reading a tabloid, or looking at the pictures anyway. I took a seat at the bar. He looked up and saw me and brought over a beer.

'Win?'

'Some.'

'Good,' he said, and went back to his wall.

I nursed my drink for a few minutes, trying to relax and hope that the headache didn't get a grip like they sometimes did.

'Was it something I said?'

I glanced round. The black pro was sitting next to me. I hadn't heard her arrive.

'What?'

'I take a seat and you leave.' I shook my head. 'Does that mean it wasn't something I said?'

She had a northern accent. Yorkshire, I thought.

'It means I'm tired.'

'Yeah,' she said, rubbing her neck. 'Me too.'

She lit a cigarette and looked at me. She seemed to be waiting for something. I tried to ignore her. Finally, she sighed and said, 'Bloody hell. A girl could die of thirst around you.'

I signalled to Matheson. He strolled over.

'Get her a drink, will you?' I said.

He hesitated for a bit, like he'd forgotten who he was and what he did and how to pour a drink. I just wanted to get rid of the woman. I flicked a glance at him.

'What does she want?' Matheson said to me.

I shrugged.

'I'm over here,' she said. She was smiling.

He pulled his eyes in her direction.

'Double Bacardi and Coke,' she said. 'No. A treble. Make it two.'

She laughed and Matheson snatched a glass and dragged himself to the optics. He poured a double rum and added a splash of Coke and dropped the glass in front of her.

'Thanks,' she said, sarcasm in there.

Matheson had wandered off.

After she'd taken a long gulp of her drink, she turned to me and said, 'I'm Brenda.'

I finished my beer and signalled to Matheson. He grabbed another for me and walked by, sliding the beer on the counter as he did so.

'You're Joe,' Brenda said. I turned to look at her. 'I asked the croupier,' she said.

I nodded, wondering why she would be asking about me. For a moment, I thought she might be the law, but I threw that idea straight out. She was too worn out to be law, too deflated.

'You don't say much, do you?' she said. 'What's wrong? You punchy or something?'

'No.'

'You done some fighting, though. Right? You look like you did.'

72

'Yeah.'

'Professional?'

'For a while.'

'Heavyweight? You must've been or else you put on a lot of weight.'

My head hurt. I wanted to ease it with alcohol, not make it worse with talk. I wanted her to go.

'So, you ever been in any fights I would've seen?'

'How'm I supposed to know that?'

Her smile faded.

'Yeah, right. Stupid question. What I mean is, have you ever been on TV?'

'Only *Crimewatch*.'

She laughed out loud, throwing her head back. I hadn't been joking. I looked at her then, looked properly for the first time. When she'd finished laughing, she sat smiling. The smile transformed her face. Her eyes, heavy-lidded, sparkled and her wide mouth gleamed with white teeth. She looked okay. I downed my drink and got another from Matheson. I wanted some alcohol now, just to take the edge off, just to escape for a while from the dullness.

I saw her turn and look around the casino. She froze for an instant and turned back round. The glint had gone from her eyes.

'So why don't you talk?' she was saying. She sounded a little drunk and I wondered how many other rum and Cokes she'd earned that night.

'I got nothing to say, so I don't say it.'

'I just thought maybe you were kinda punchy or something.'

Another one who thought I was dumb. I'd been getting

73

that all my life, and now I was getting it from some over-the-hill drunk prostitute. The thing was, this time it bothered me. I didn't know why.

'I'm not punchy,' I said.

'I didn't say you were, I just said I thought maybe you were.'

We sat there in silence for a while. Brenda had become tense, awkward. And yet when she'd sat down and started talking to me, she'd seemed relaxed. Cheerful even. I wasn't used to that from people.

'Well, maybe it's because you don't like me. Huh?' she said quietly.

'I hadn't thought about it.'

'It's just you don't talk so much. I thought maybe you didn't like me.'

'I don't care about you one way or the other. I'm just not in the market.'

I heard her swallow hard. It sounded like a sob. She got up from the seat and walked quickly away. Matheson came over.

'Know her, Joe?'

I shook my head.

'Tart,' Matheson said. 'We get lots of them. Me, I don't like 'em. Lower the tone.'

Everyone wanted to talk tonight.

A man took a seat at the bar, two stools up. I glanced over and saw that the man was Kenny Paget. Back then, Paget was the rising star. He'd started out as a bouncer in one of the Soho clubs. He was small for a bouncer, but he'd had a run-in one night with a couple of drunken loudmouths and he'd put them both in hospital. One had a knife wound from one side of his gut to the other. Paget was nicked for that, faced an attempted murder charge, but other bouncers testified that the knife had belonged to the drunk and Paget got off on self-defence. The bloke who owned the club was Frank Marriot. He recognized talent when he saw it and pushed Paget up until he was pretty much running the whole outfit, acting as Marriot's enforcer. It was a hard, dirty business and Paget fitted right in.

When Matheson saw him, he unglued himself from the wall sharpish and tried to look like a barman. He smiled and walked over and said, 'Usual, Mr Paget?'

Matheson selected a clean glass, polished it up some more and measured out vodka and tomato juice. He threw in a few other things to make it look fancy and put it on the bar counter, on top of a paper coaster thing, and slid it an inch towards Paget. Paget looked at it. Matheson waited just long enough to see he wasn't going to get thanked, then floated off.

'It's Joe, right?' I turned back to my beer. 'I've heard about you.'

'Uh-huh.'

'Heard you're one of Dave Kendall's boys.'

I downed some more beer. He didn't say anything for a while, but I knew he was looking at me. I was too tired to play that game. He finished his drink and slid the glass along towards Matheson.

'Get me another,' he said.

Matheson did as ordered, not bothering with the chit-chat this time. Paget slid off his stool and slid on to the one next to me. He was like that. He slid.

'You don't want to talk to me?'

'No.'

'You know who I am, though. Am I right?'

'Yeah.'

'And yet you don't want to talk to me. I consider that rude. Or stupid.'

He leaned forward. Matheson was edging away down the bar.

'They say you're a bit stupid. That right? A bit lacking in brain matter? Maybe I'd better explain something to you. Drinks are free. The whores aren't. Got it?'

I downed some more beer. The man was beginning to annoy me. His voice was buzzing in my head.

'That bird you were talking to, for example. She's what we call a whore. She fucks for money. The money she gets goes to Mr Marriot. I make sure of that. Got it?'

He leaned closer still. I could smell his breath. I could hear the click in his throat as he spoke.

'That nigger is of especial interest to me. So leave her alone.'

It was an effort not to shove his nose back into his head. Instead, I got up and walked away, leaving half my drink.

I decided to walk home and try to clear my head with fresh air, if that's what you could call it in London. If I walked down St Paul's Road, I could cut across to Green Lanes and follow that up to the Seven Sisters Road. It was only a couple of miles. I left the warm fuggy air of the Sportsman and hit a crisp, cold January night. It helped to clear my head, freshen me up a bit.

I'd gone a few dozen yards when I saw her, standing in a doorway, trying to light her cigarette. She was wearing a short black jacket. The collar was up. Her shoulders were hunched against the cold. I walked past.

'Hey,' she called after me.

I slowed and stopped. I didn't turn around. I heard her trotting on high heels. When she reached me, she stood a moment. Her unlit cigarette was between her fingers. She moved from one foot to the other to keep warm. A jacket like that was useless in this weather, plain daft.

I thought that if I just gave her a few quid she'd leave me alone. I was waiting for the pitch, thinking she'd charge fifty quid tops for a quick one, figuring I'd give her a score and be off. Instead, she said, 'That hurt, you know.'

'Huh?'

'What you said in there.'

I didn't know what she was talking about. I waited for her to say something else. She managed to light her cigarette, took a deep drag and blew out a cloud of smoke and breath.

'I wasn't trying to solicit you, you know.'

'Weren't you?'

'I'm off duty.'

She smiled then. I wondered why. She looked nice when she smiled. She didn't look all washed-up and wasted. She looked as if she could still think life was fun, like a kid.

She had a slim body and she was tall, lanky really. In her heels she came up to my chin and not many women can do that. Her skirt rode high up on her thighs, and her blouse was thin. She stood shivering and her knees were together and she looked about as awkward as a woman can look. Her face became serious again. She frowned and there was something in there, something she couldn't hide.

'He a friend of yours?'

'Who?'

'That man, Paget.'

'No.'

Her frown lifted. 'Didn't think so.'

'What do you want?' I said.

She looked down at the ground and pulled her jacket tighter about her. When she looked up, her eyes were wide, her eyebrows raised.

'I wouldn't mind a cup of tea,' she said.

I looked at my watch.

'Nothing open round here.'

That was a lie. We both knew it.

'We could go to my place,' she said softly.

I was about to give up on her and go when she said quickly, 'Just for tea.'

I sighed. 'Yeah. Sure.'

We walked off, me striding like a walking wall, she tottering to keep up, smoking as she went.

It took us a while to walk to her place and all that time I was wondering what the hell I was doing. She'd say something now and then, making small talk, telling me about what a bloody awful day she'd had and how she just wanted to sit down with a cup of tea and all that kind of thing. I might have muttered something or other, but it was an effort.

She lived in a high-rise off the Caledonian Road. We passed a group of kids as we went in. They stared at us. I stopped at the lift and one of the kids laughed.

'It's not working,' Brenda said. 'Hasn't ever worked as far as I know. I think they put it there for show.'

So we climbed the stairs. The building was a sixties thing, falling apart at the seams, cracked cement, damp in the stairwell. They should've pulled it down ten minutes after they'd put it up. Some of these buildings are getting tarted up these days, sold to City types for a bomb. This one hadn't had that treatment, and if it ever did Brenda and all the others would have to go find some other piece of shit to live in.

'Fancy a cuppa?' she said, as she disappeared into the kitchen.

It was a one-bedroom flat, basic, but she'd done what she could with it. There were a few ornaments around and an Indian-style cotton throw on the settee. There was flowery wallpaper, but it was discoloured and peeling in the corner where the damp was coming through. It was warm, though. She used a blanket as a draught excluder for the front door.

In the lounge, there were pot plants all over by the window and a large plant in one corner. She was trying to bring life into the place.

I was looking at a print on the wall when she came in with the teas.

'Sorry I took so long.' She handed a mug to me. 'Bloody kettle packed up. I have to boil water on the stove.'

She waited for me to drink some of my tea before drinking her own.

'I saw that in a shop in Camden,' she said, pointing to the picture I'd been looking at. 'It's called *The Fighting Temeraire*, by J. M. W. Turner.'

'I've heard of it.'

'The *Temeraire* was a famous ship, can't remember why. But, thing is, here it's being taken in to be broken up.' She held her tea. When she spoke again, her eyes glistened.

'It's one of the saddest pictures I ever saw. That beautiful ship and it's being dragged in to be pulled apart. Its time is up.'

We both looked at the picture for a while. The once-glorious fighter, now ghostly, was being pulled to its end by a squat black tug while Turner lit a funeral pyre in his sky. I'd never bothered with art, but as I looked at the picture, I saw she was right, it was sad. And yet, glorious also. I didn't know why, I just felt it.

'She fought at the Battle of Trafalgar,' I told her. 'She helped save Victory. At one point, she was locked between two French battleships and managed to outfight them both.'

Brenda looked at me for a moment.

'You really know a lot.'

'I know bits and pieces,' I said.

'And them holes, they're for the guns?'

'Yeah. She was a ninety-eight gun ship of the line.'

'That's a lot of guns.'

'Yeah.'

'Frightening.'

'They were killing machines, those ships.'

'Killing machines?' she said. 'Killing machines.'

She looked at the picture again, tilting her head to one side.

'Why did they have to break it up, Joe? Why kill it?'

'Like you said, its time was up.'

'Yeah,' she said, looking back at me. 'I suppose so.'

She took her tea over to the settee. I took mine to a small table on the far side of the room. I sat on a wooden chair at the table, turning it slightly to face her. She moved across the settee so that she was closer to me. She smiled and I clenched my jaw. I was still waiting for the pitch. The silence stretched. Brenda fidgeted. I drank my tea. It was good tea.

'Where are you from, Joe?' she said, finally.

'Tottenham.'

'Yeah?'

She looked like she was trying to say something about Tottenham, but she didn't seem able to come up with anything. Most people know it for the football club and the riots. She said, 'I'm from Leeds. You ever been there?'

'No.'

'You ever been to Yorkshire?'

'One time.'

'Where'd you go?'

'Sheffield.'

'Yeah, well, Sheffield's nice, but Leeds is, like, nicer.'

'Maybe I'll retire there.'

She laughed nervously. She was trying and I suppose I wasn't making it easy for her.

There was another lull in the conversation. It was more lull than conversation.

'I remember the riots in Tottenham,' she said, having finally thought of something to say about the place. 'I remember, I was going to go to a club there with my friend and I told her at the last minute that I didn't really feel like it and then on the news they had about all them riots.'

'The riots were in '85.'

'Oh. Must've been some other riots then.'

I was still waiting for the pitch. She waited for me to say something. She might as well have waited to be young again.

'It's funny, you know?' she said. 'The way things happen sometimes. You believe in God?'

'No.'

81

'No. Neither do I. You believe in fate?'

'No.'

'You believe in anything?'

I looked at her.

'What for?'

Maybe I spoke harder than I'd meant to. There was a slow throbbing in my head and I was still riled about that encounter with Paget. I could've taken him apart in two seconds flat, but that would've meant trouble for me. I could've at least told him to fuck off, but that would've soured me with the casino. Once, I wouldn't have given a fuck about that. What bothered me now, sitting in this damp flat, drinking tea, my head aching, was that I was losing my bottle, getting fearful of where I was, where I would be in five, ten years. I was getting old and my future was lousy and I damned well knew it, and someone like Paget could see it too and knew he could slap me down without any comebacks.

Brenda shifted in her seat, looked up, looked down. She put her mug on the ground, got up, went to a white, vinyl-covered cabinet and pulled out a bottle of gin and a glass. She filled the glass with gin and held the bottle up to me. I shook my head. She put the bottle down.

'Mind if I smoke?' she said.

'It's your place.'

'Actually, it's not. I rent it. Frank owns it. He owns lots of places and rents them out to his tarts. Sometimes he comes here to film stuff.'

She lit a cigarette and, while the smoke was still in her lungs, downed her drink. She poured another.

'What do you want from me?' I said.

'Nothing. I mean . . . Oh, Christ, I don't know.'

'Everyone wants something.'

'Do they?'

'Yes.'

She stood slowly and brought her drink over to the table and put it down. She stood and watched me for a moment before sitting next to her drink, pulling it towards her, looking at it like it was her child.

'I just wanted someone to talk to,' she said to the drink. 'That's all right, isn't it?'

'I'm not the talking type.'

'I know. We established that.'

'So, why me?'

'Bloody hell,' she said, looking up sharply. 'Are you always so suspicious?'

I was about to tell her that I wasn't being suspicious, but I stopped. There I was, looking for her angle. That was suspicion, wasn't it?

'Why?' I said.

'Why what?'

'Why do you want to talk to me?'

'I dunno.'

'You've got to have a reason.'

'Have I?'

'Yes.'

She thought about that for a moment.

'I think,' she said, 'I think because I thought you were like me. I thought that you wanted someone to talk to, you know? I thought you were, well, lonely.'

I didn't know what to say. I didn't feel lonely. I didn't feel

83

anything. I wondered if not feeling anything was what feeling lonely was like. I wasn't sure. I couldn't remember anyone ever just wanting to talk to me. Maybe that was loneliness.

'I think you are like me,' she said. 'A bit, anyway. I think you do want to talk.'

'Why would you think that?'

She smiled a small, sad, uncertain smile.

'Well, you're still here, aren't you?'

She was right. I was still there.

I went to see her a few days later. I gave her a new kettle and a book about the Battle of Trafalgar. She smiled then, one of her wide smiles.

EIGHT

There were lights on, but nobody answered, and I couldn't see any movement inside the house. I banged on the door again. After a while, I could see a small figure through the frosted glass. The figure hesitated and then moved quickly forwards and snatched the door open. I found myself looking down at a woman. Her face was pale; her eyeliner had streaked from crying. She was scared, but she looked straight into my eyes and held my gaze. She was a good-looking woman, slight in frame, with large brown eyes that had a cat-like slant to them. In her hand, pointed at me, was a kitchen knife.

'I've called the police,' she said.

I wondered if Bowker had called ahead and tipped them off. The woman didn't seem to know how to react to my calmness. She kept edging backwards and then forwards again. She was lost, caught between anger and fear and bewilderment and a bloody great kitchen knife.

'Go away,' she said at last.

She tried to slam the door, but I held out a hand and caught it. She fought me for a moment, trying to push the door shut. She gave in and the door flew back against the wall. She held the point of the knife a foot from my stomach.

'I'm looking for a Ray Martin,' I said.

I didn't force my way into the house, and that seemed to

confuse her more and for a few seconds she forgot how to talk. When she remembered, she said, 'Who are you?'

'Nobody he knows. I need to talk to him.'

'Haven't you people done enough?'

'What?'

'Bastards.'

She spat the word, then started sniffling. She reached her hand up to wipe her eyes, forgetting that the knife was in it. I could've slapped her down easily enough, but smacking sobbing women and smashing down doors leaves a trail. She remembered the knife and brought it back to aim it at me.

'Others were here?' I said.

There was doubt now in her eyes.

'You're with them.'

'I'm not with anyone. I don't know who the hell "they" are.'

I took the gun slowly from my jacket pocket. When she saw it, she gave no sign of fear except to grip the knife more firmly. I held the gun out to her.

'I only want to talk to him.'

I put the gun on the floor, took a step forwards into the hallway. She didn't stop me. She was scared, but she wasn't panicky, and she had the determination of a she-cat protecting its young. She moved backwards so that she was lit by the ceiling light. I pushed the door closed.

With the light of the hallway now on her face, I could see that she was older than I'd first thought. Lines had been scratched into her face. You could see a history of hardship. Martin had done a long stretch, King had told me. Had she waited years for him to come back? She was probably in her middle forties, but still attractive. I moved forwards slowly and she moved backwards, equally slowly, keeping the knife pointing up at me, keeping her fierce eyes on mine. It was a dance, of sorts – two-step with blade. I could have taken the knife from her anytime. I don't know why I didn't.

She crumbled then. The knife wavered in her hand and then fell and landed on the carpet. Her face creased.

'I can't lift him,' she said.

'Where is he?'

She pointed to a room at the back of the house.

'He won't let me call anyone.'

I eased past her. She caught her sobs and followed.

The room was small and dark, but it was comfortable. There were flowered curtains and quilted cushions and those small bowls of dead, dried petals that smelled. It was a woman's place, a cluttered refuge full of books and easy furniture and warmth. On a mantelpiece over the fireplace were framed photographs of a smiling couple. There was no money on show, but there was security. The room didn't fit with my profession. There couldn't be anything here that would link with Beckett and Cole and a missing pile of cash.

And then I saw the man.

He was on the floor with his back against the wall. He'd dragged himself over. There was blood spattered on the carpet in the middle of the room. He looked like he was in his fifties, but it could have been that he was a damaged forty-something. He'd done some fighting once. His nose had been broken long ago, and there was scar tissue around his eyes. His hands were broad and gnarly, but they'd gone soft. He'd been big once, but he'd thinned so that the skin around his face was loose.

He was a mess. His brown hair was matted with dried blood, his right eye swollen and livid, his lips split and bloody. I lifted him from the floor and put him in one of the two comfortable chairs. He looked up woozily and made a weak attempt to push me away and stand up. I eased him back and he gave up trying.

'Martin?'

He didn't try to answer and when he looked at me he had trouble focusing. I sent the woman off to get water, ice and a cloth. When she came back, I wiped the blood from the man's face, put ice in the cloth and pressed it to the swollen eye. I held the glass of water to his lips. He swallowed a little, then winced and pushed the glass away. He took the ice-press from me and held it to the left side of his face. He wasn't making a fuss about it. He shook his head and looked up, noticing me for the first time.

'Who are you?' he said.

'It doesn't matter.'

'Right.'

'You're Martin.'

'Yeah, sure.'

'Who did this to you?'

'Two men. Dunno who. Have an idea.'

'Describe them.'

'Both white. One thin, tall, blond, and a shorter one, heavy, with red hair, shaved short.'

'What did they want?'

'Same as you, I expect. Wanted to know where Beckett is. Told them I don't know.' He gestured to his face. 'They didn't believe me.'

'I'm calling an ambulance,' the woman said.

'No,' Martin said.

'Look at you. Look at your face,' she said.

'I've had worse. Don't get hysterical.'

'I'm not getting hysterical. I'm going to call an ambulance, that's all. What's so fucking hysterical about that?'

'Call them and they'll report it to the police,' I said. 'Get the law here and this'll be peanuts to what'll happen next.'

'He's right,' Martin said.

I held Martin's face in my hands and probed it. I knew what I was doing and he knew that I knew. I suppose we each took one look at the other and knew we'd both been there before. He jerked back once in pain, but said nothing. I lowered my hands.

'I can't feel any broken bones. You might need a brain scan.'

'Tell me if they find anything,' the woman said.

'What did you tell them?' I said.

'Who says I told them anything?'

I tilted my head towards the woman. She was staring at me, her face gaunt, her hands clutched before her.

'They didn't touch her,' I said.

'She wasn't here.'

'You must've known she'd be back sometime. You knew they'd use her as leverage.'

I was guessing. It made sense, though, and the grim look that ran across Martin's face told me I was right.

'Ray.' The woman had taken a half-step forward. 'Is he right?'

She'd started crying again. Martin waved her back.

'Is there a first-aid box in the house?' I said to the woman.

'I can find some things around,' she said, wiping her eyes. 'What do you need?'

'Antiseptic, gauze, bandages. Anything like that.'

She hurried off. When she'd gone, Martin said, 'Gauze ain't gonna do it.'

'I wanted to get rid of her.'

'Right. Thanks.'

'You know where Beckett is?'

'No.'

'What did you tell them?'

'Maybe they could find Walsh.'

'How?'

Martin let the towel drop. He took the glass from my hand and swished some water around his mouth and spat it out on to the carpet. The water was pink. All the while he did this, he kept his eyes on me.

'I know you,' he said.

'Do you?'

'Yeah. Joe something. You're a fighter, right?'

'I was.'

'Right. Long time ago. Got a fag?'

'No.'

'Over there,' he said, pointing to a packet on the shelf. I fetched the cigarettes, a lighter and ashtray. He fired up a cigarette and put it carefully between his lips. His face must have hurt, but he didn't show it.

'This has got something to do with that casino job,' he said.

'What do you know about it?'

'I know Cole owned that place. I know Beckett did it over.'

'How do you know?'

90

'I still have a few friends. They talk. That's all.'

Everyone in London knew we were raiding Cole except me.

'Those men worked for Cole, right?' he said.

'Probably.'

'But you don't.'

'No.'

'But you do want to find Beckett,' he said.

'Yes.'

He took another drag from his cigarette. He doubled up coughing and spat out some blood.

'Shit,' he said, wincing. 'I better get to a hospital.'

'I'll call you a cab.'

'You might run into the two who gave me this face,' he said.

'I might.'

'Will you kill them?'

'If they get in my way.'

'Good enough.'

He pulled at the cigarette again. It seemed to me that he was buying time, trying to think things through. I pulled over the other chair and sat facing him. I wasn't going to push him. For one, he might be better as an ally. He already had a grudge against Cole. For another, the woman might go and call in the law or stab me or something like that. She looked about ready to go crazy.

'Do you know a man called Kendall?' I said.

He watched me, looking me right in the eyes.

'What's this to you?' he said.

'I got stitched up.'

'By Kendall?'

'Yes.'

91

He nodded, as if it all made perfect sense.

'I know Kendall. Least, I knew him years ago. He called me a few hours ago. Said he had to find Beckett. I told him I didn't know where he was. He offered me a thousand quid. Told him I still didn't know.'

'Did he say anything else?'

'No. He trying to get a cut of this cash?'

'More likely he was going to sell Beckett out to Cole.'

'*Was* going to?'

I shrugged. Martin didn't push it, but the flicker in his eyes told me he'd understood.

'Cole must be fucking desperate,' Martin said, more to himself than to me. 'I've got to be way down the list. He must have men out all over London. That exposure's not like him. Liable to draw attention.'

'What?'

'He's looking for Beckett, right? So why the urgency? Surely he's got time enough to find Beckett quietly. What he's doing here is signalling weakness, exposing himself to attention. Cole's a hard man, but he's discreet.'

Martin was right. Sending his men around to Kendall's like that, looking for someone like Martin, having him beaten like this; Cole seemed desperate all right.

'Something else is going on,' I said.

Cole had a big set-up. He could afford to let some money slide off for a while, just as long as he got it back again. And so what if it took him a few months to find Beckett? And wouldn't Beckett have known that Cole could take his time? That he'd find him eventually?

Which led me back to the other question that had been

plaguing me: why would Beckett have risked stealing the money in the first place? He couldn't surely have expected Cole to believe I'd been solely responsible? Besides, at some point Beckett would've known that Cole would catch up with me and realize that I hadn't taken the money.

'What does Beckett know?' I said.

'How d'ya mean?'

'If Cole's desperate, Beckett knows it. So, what does he know?'

'I dunno. How would I? I work in a warehouse. I move fucking boxes for a living. Know why?'

I didn't know. I didn't particularly care.

'It's so I know I'll come home in the evening. Every evening. All that other shit's behind me.'

He looked up. I followed his gaze and saw the woman standing in the doorway. She came forward stiffly. She kneeled and from her arms poured a pile of bandages, creams and antiseptics. Her face was flushed; her eyes glistened. When she looked at Martin, he winked with his one good eye. He was letting her know that she was helping, and that he was okay. It was a lie, of course, and she knew it, but she smiled thinly.

'Go make us a cuppa, love,' Martin said.

'All right.'

She was quiet now, thoughtful, fearful. It seemed like an odd relationship. He, the hardened former pro, the battered shell of something that had once been dangerous; she, the quiet, domestic type, without guile, without malice. He'd always protect her; she'd always keep him warm and bring him a cup of tea.

93

'You want something?' Martin said.

'Huh?'

'Drink or something?'

'Some food.'

'Food?' the woman said. 'How about a pipe and slippers?'

Now that Martin seemed to have recovered, her suspicion was returning and with it the resentment that her home had been marred. I was here; I was a part of them. It didn't matter that I wasn't the one who'd beaten Martin.

'A fry-up'll do,' Martin said to her. 'Nothing for me.'

She dragged herself away. When we could hear her in the kitchen, Martin crushed his cigarette and said, 'Walsh has a habit. Was smack. Might be crack now, from what I hear. He buys from a bloke called Travis Moore. They call him T-bone for some fucking reason.'

Walsh had kept his habit well hidden. I cursed myself a thousandth time for getting involved in this shit.

'How do you know this?'

'I used to work with Walsh. Don't see him much any more, but he's had that fucking habit for fifteen years. One of the reasons I stopped working with him. Brain turned to mush long time ago. Beckett's a fool for working with him. Anyway, the last time I saw Walsh, he was buying his stuff from Moore.'

'Where do I find Moore?'

'Clapton.'

'And you told this to the others?'

'Yeah. Don't worry about it. Moore has his place done up like Fort Knox, and he's in with the Yardies, up in Hackney. He pays them off, and even if Cole had the bottle to go up against them, he hasn't got the clout. His name don't mean much to those wankers. His men won't get in unless Moore wants them in. Besides, I gave them his home address, but he doesn't deal from there. Owns three houses in a row, all in different names. The business is in the end one, and the door to that is on the other street. Those two wankers'll be watching the wrong place, waiting for Walsh to show up.'

'So I'm supposed to go and ask Moore to tell me where Walsh is?'

'He wouldn't tell you unless you put a gun to his head. And you won't get a gun to his head.' He lit another cigarette. He was still shaken by the beating and he was trying to get over it. 'Moore uses couriers. He's paranoid about being ripped off. Way it works is, someone makes a call, Moore makes a call, courier comes round, collects the shit and takes it away. Cole's two won't know which courier to follow.'

Martin smiled, and winced with the pain of smiling.

'But I know something I didn't tell them other two. Walsh is queer. One of Moore's couriers is a bloke called Waylon something. This Waylon has a habit, all them couriers do, and Walsh had a thing with him. He'd be the one to take Walsh's gear round. He'd stay a while and hope for a free hit. If Walsh has bought any shit since he disappeared, Waylon would've delivered it.'

'So, I find this Waylon, I may find Walsh.'

'That's about it.'

'How do I find Waylon?'

'Can't help you there. Have you got an in with the Yardies?'

'No.'

Martin shrugged.

95

'It's all I got, but if Walsh's flush, he might feel like partying.'

'Right. You got anything else for me? Anyone else who might know?'

'All I know is what I told you.'

'Why did you tell me? You're grassing out Walsh.'

'Better you get to him before Cole. Walsh ain't a bad man, he's just stupid. All that shit's gone to his head. Beckett . . . well, fuck him. You take him out, I won't cry. But Walsh is all right. Take it easy on him.'

'If I can, I will.'

'Good enough.'

After a while the woman appeared at the doorway with a mug of tea, which she gave to Martin.

'Your food's in the kitchen,' she said to me.

She stayed next to Martin, her arms crossed. I got up and followed the smell. She'd done a good job: fried eggs, bacon, beans, bread, even a couple of sausages. I set to the food. I was suddenly starving. I could hear Martin and the woman talking. They were keeping their voices low, but there was urgency in their tones. I heard the front door open and close. I wolfed the food down, wiping my plate with the bread. I might not get another chance to eat for a while.

When I went back to the lounge, she was waiting for me, sitting where Martin had sat. She leaned forward, her elbows resting on her knees. My gun was held loosely in her hands.

'Where's he gone?' I said.

'Don't worry, he's not going to the police. He's gone to the hospital. He wouldn't let me go.'

That made sense. If anyone at the hospital was suspicious, they'd question the woman.

'He told me you were okay,' she said. She glared at me. The defiance I'd seen earlier was there, but it couldn't quite mask the fear. I looked at the gun. 'I threw the bullets away.'

'I've got more.'

'I bet you have. He said you wouldn't do anything to me.'

'Why would I?'

'Are you going to come back?'

'No reason to.'

'Will the others come back?'

'They might do. I doubt it, though. Martin gave them good information, as far as it went.'

As I watched, her expression changed, became faraway.

'He's a fool,' she said. 'About these things, I mean. He still believes in things like honour and fairness. That's why he went inside. He thinks all you people live by a code. He trusts you. He thinks you're a decent man.'

'And you?'

'I know what you are. I can see it a mile off.' She stood and tossed the gun to the floor. When I bent to pick it up, she said, 'Don't ever come back.'

It was past midnight when I got to Clapton. I parked the car a few streets away from the road I needed and walked until I reached the T-junction. To my left and right, along both arms of the Chatsworth Road, everything was quiet enough. In the distance, a young couple came out of a burger place, huddled against the cold, holding their burgers in front of them. I watched them walk away. For some reason I thought of Brenda, and a hole opened up inside me for a moment. Then I turned away from them.

There was a pub across the road. Its lights were off. It was too late for pub traffic. I moved towards it and slid into the shadowed recess of the side door. From here, I had a clear view down Moore's road. I watched for a few minutes, trying to get a feel of the place. Edwardian terraced houses, their brickwork more grey than red, ran down both sides. Cars were packed tightly, end to end. Parking was a problem around here. Some of the houses had lights in one or two rooms, but mostly they were dark, quiet. Moore's house was number twenty-eight. I looked across the road at the first house and saw that it was number two, so Moore lived on that side of the road, another thirteen doors along. I counted down the row until I could make out Moore's place. It was the third from the end, as Martin had said. That last house was the one where the business was done. The door to that one was at the side and so in another street that went off at a right angle. All those houses were dark, no windows open, no sign of anyone.

I would call at Moore's place and talk to him, maybe offer him a cut of any recovered money. If he didn't know where Walsh was, he might point me towards this Waylon character. One thing was for sure, I couldn't go in heavy. I'd have my gun taken from me before I even got inside. Places like this, a dozen armed police with a battering ram had trouble getting in. And I didn't have the time to try and get Moore outside of his place.

I closed my eyes and listened. The odd car passed along the Chatsworth Road and I could hear vehicles far away, travelling down the Lea Bridge Road; otherwise all was quiet, everyone tucked up in bed, far away from the cold dank night, far away from blood and murder.

I pulled up the collar of my overcoat so that it buried the lower part of my face, pulled my woollen hat down low so that it covered my ears. I plunged my hands into the deep pockets, feeling the .38 in my grip. I pushed myself away from the shadows, crossed the road and started to walk towards Moore's place. I kept a steady pace, all the time listening, flicking my eyes left and right, all the time calculating how long it would take me to get back to my car, where I could find cover, how long it would take to fire off the six rounds and reload. I felt exposed, useless. I was used to the simplicity of the job: learn the plan, go in, execute, leave. Easy. Here I was alone, not knowing who my enemies were, not knowing what was going on.

I saw the car when I was about ten yards away, a black Ford with steamed-up windows. If I stopped and they saw me, they'd be instantly suspicious. I hunched my shoulders, lowered my head, making myself as small as possible, and ploughed on: just another man trying to get home on a cold night. I gripped the Smith and Wesson and slowly pulled back the hammer.

There were only a few parking spaces so the car had had to park on the same side as Moore's house, and halfway along the road. They wouldn't have a good view from there.

I drew even with the car. Through the cloudy window, I could just make out a pale head, the stubble of red hair. The man turned when I walked past. I flicked my gaze back to the pavement. I heard the car door open and the red-haired man step out. I braced myself, my hand gripping the .38. I heard the one inside the car complain about the cold. The red-haired one told him to quit moaning. I kept walking, expecting any moment to hear a shout, a gunshot, pounding feet. But there was nothing, and I guessed they'd been given specific orders: find Martin, question him, find out what he knows and follow it up. Cole would've had other men doing other things, men who might be looking for me, men who, at that moment, might be questioning Akram or searching my flat. It was likely these two had no idea who I was.

I passed number twenty-eight without looking at it and turned the corner. In the clear night the icy concrete gave a ring to my footsteps, as if I was walking on solid iron. They could hear me well enough and they'd pay attention if I stopped. I carried on walking for another fifty yards, and heard the slam of the car door. After another minute or so, I stopped and backtracked.

This street was much like the other: rows of terraced houses, cars parked solidly. The one difference was a small off-licence opposite Moore's business place. Graffiti-covered metal shutters hid the windows.

I looked at Moore's house, silent, dark and impenetrable. Asking Moore for information was no good. I knew that, I'd known it all along, but now I had to admit it was a fucking stupid idea. If Moore was suspicious, as he should be, he'd close up entirely. He might even call Cole, not wanting to tread on any toes.

I was making one mistake after another – doing the job with Beckett without checking it through, killing Kendall, blundering from place to place without stopping to work things out. It was time for me to start acting smart.

I walked over and scoped out the off-licence. There was a space along one side leading to a rear door where deliveries would be made. If I stood a few feet along this alley, I'd be in darkness, shielded from the street light by the bulk of the building. From here, too, I had a good view of this other entrance to Moore's place, and I was safely hidden from Cole's men. If those two had stood watch, as they should have done, they'd have had the whole of Moore's place covered: one opposite and along from the house; one here, where I was standing. But Martin hadn't told them about this other entrance and, besides, it was a cold night and Cole's men weren't in the mood for standing outside indefinitely. A person could come and go from Moore's place on this street without being seen by the two in the car.

I still had Kendall's mobile phone in my pocket and I used it to call King again. When he'd finished swearing at me, I told him what I wanted him to do. He called back a couple of minutes later.

'It's done,' he said. 'Can I get some fucking sleep now?'

I pulled my coat tighter around me and stepped back into the alley. I put my hands in the coat pockets, placed my feet evenly and fixed my eyes on Moore's place. I was perfectly balanced, ready to move quickly in either direction. I settled down for a long wait.

I'd done this many times over the years, one way or another – bodyguard duty, casing a place, sentry duty. I always liked it. I liked the darkness, the silence of the night. I could let my mind go blank, let the world slip away. I could live, for a while anyway, in nothingness. The darkness around me was like a blanket to me. It was comfortable.

But as I waited, the silence seemed to slide into my guts, the darkness sank in on me and closed around. I took a deep breath. In everyday life, there was so much clutter that you got used to it. Silence, stillness, these were foreign things. It seemed to me a long time since I'd felt the peace of nothingness. Had I ever? I fixed my eyes again on the building opposite and shook my head to clear it. I was tired, and I ached from the earlier beating I'd taken, and I couldn't keep my mind concentrated. Images flitted through my head. I gritted my teeth, clenched my fists and tried to block out the thoughts.

Still I stood immobile, my eyes unwavering, dead to see, if anyone could have seen them, not flickering, not moving, not blinking. The cold bit into me. I ignored it. The sound, far away, of traffic carried through the still, thin air, and droned. I smelled the woollen mustiness of my coat.

My mind began to wander again, slinking back like a dog to its own vomit. I saw Kendall's wife flop over, her white flesh wobbling. I saw my dad, too drunk to stand upright but still able to smash my mother's face with a right hook.

How much time now had passed? A few minutes? Half an hour?

I tried to blank my mind, shake out the thoughts, but they buzzed around and caught.

And then I was on a hill and the air was biting cold and the fog was all around me and I was alone. The boy stared at me, his eyes sunken, his cheeks hollowed so that it looked as if he'd been dead for many days, but he'd died just a few hours earlier. I knew this. I'd killed him. And he lay there, with eyelids lowered so that, if it weren't for his mouth, he would have had a sleepy mask. But it was that mouth, that rictus grin with the lips pulled back, the teeth bared in a mocking snarl, that I couldn't stop looking at. It drew me in and held me. It was just the two of us, me in the foxhole, wet and frozen stiff, gripping my SLR with hands that I could no longer bend, and the boy a dozen feet away, staring at me, laughing at me.

Maybe it was the blow to my head. Or maybe I'd fallen asleep for an instant and had dreamed. That happens. I don't know. I hadn't thought about that boy for a long time. There was a time when I'd thought of nothing else. I call him a boy, but I was probably younger than he was when I killed him. I got older. He didn't. That was all there was to it.

A light came on in Moore's place. Someone had made a phone call. The light was good. It gave me something to focus on. After another few minutes, I saw a figure, a man, far off to my left, coming towards me.

The man was tall and thin and, in the neon glow of the street lights, he had a sickly white face. He looked, from a distance, to be old, bony and bent, but as he came closer, I could see that he was young, early twenties at most. Despite the cold, he was wearing a thin canvas jacket in which he'd planted his hands. He walked with his head down, shuffling along with the look of someone going to do a job he hated. He looked dopey and might've had a hit of something already. I watched him turn into Moore's place. He knocked, waited, said something to the door. The door opened and he went in. Within the minute he was out, shuffling back the way he'd come. All of this was out of sight of Cole's men. My luck was in there. I waited for the light in Moore's place to go out, then I left the shadows.

I waited until he walked by a small park. He hadn't heard my footsteps. He didn't turn until I was upon him and by then it was too late. He let out a sort of gasp as I grabbed him and hurled him over the low wall and into the park. He tried to defend himself, but his arms were like twigs and, besides, he had no strength. He gave up quickly, curling into a ball.

'I ain't got nothing.'

I hoisted him up. He fumbled in his pockets and pulled out some notes and coins.

'Here. It's all I got.'

I smacked the money aside.

'What's your name?' I said.

'What?'

I raised my hand.

'No, wait. Derek, okay? Derek Lewis. Do I owe you money or something? I thought I was clear now.'

'You know a man called Waylon?'

He bent down to retrieve his money. He kept his eyes on me.

'Um, Waylon? That his last name?'

I took a step forward and kicked out with the flat of my foot. I caught him on the side. He landed heavily, sprawled on the floor with a face full of dirt. I took another step forward. He rolled over, holding up his hands.

'Okay. Yeah. I know him.'

'Where do you live?'

'Up the road. Half-mile.'

'You live alone?'

'Yeah.'

'Call Waylon, get him to meet you at your place.'

'Now?'

'Now.'

'What am I gonna tell him?'

'Tell him you've got a load of smack and you want to share it around.'

'He won't believe me.'

'He'll come.'

Lewis lived in a bedsit on the ground floor of a small grey block. The place was a mess of empty beer cans, used takeaway packaging, dirty laundry, magazines, newspapers. It smelled like he did – stale. I took his mobile phone, unplugged the landline from the wall, and threw them in the toilet bowl. He complained about that for a second or two, then gave up.

He was fidgety and kept walking around, glancing at me, worried, probably, that he was getting caught up in whatever I had going with Waylon. I told him to sit down. He found a clean spot on the sofa and sat and looked at me through sleepy eyes. I told him if he behaved there'd be a reward, so long as he didn't open his mouth afterwards. I hadn't made my mind up what to do with him yet.

We waited half an hour, me by the door, Lewis falling asleep on the sofa. When the bell rang, I slapped him a couple of times and took him to the door, keeping my gun in the small of his back. He looked through the spyhole and opened the door without a word. A young black man walked in and said, 'How much you got?'

Then he saw me and said, 'Shit.' Then he saw my gun and said, 'Shit,' again, only with more conviction.

I pushed him into the bedsit and closed the door.

'The fuck, Del?'

'What could I do, man? He wanted to see you. Look at him.'

I told Lewis to go and lock himself in the bathroom.

Waylon was a little older than Lewis, and a little shorter, but just as thin. He had his hair in an afro, and there was something like a goatee on his chin. He wore a baggy green T-shirt and baggy blue jeans. They didn't help his appearance.

'What do you want with me?'

I gave him a short punch to the diaphragm. He doubled over and hit the floor, gasping for breath. After a while, he was sick. He'd pissed himself. I waited until he could sit up and told him I wanted to find Walsh.

'If you tell me you don't know where he is, I'll hit you again, harder. Tell me where he is and you get a grand.'

'Dalston. House there.'

'How do you know?'

'Called me yesterday. Said he wanted some stuff, said for me to bring it over.'

'You took it over?'

'Yeah.'

'Anyone else there?'

'I dunno. He wouldn't let me get past the front door. I say how come you invite me over and then don't let me in? He say he's got friends in, they wouldn't like me hanging around. All a bit paranoiac, you ask me.'

Paranoiac. They had reason to be.

I made him describe the place. I was going to take him with me and if the place didn't pan out like he'd said, I'd get heavy.

'What you gonna do to Walsh?'

'It doesn't matter.'

'Walsh, he's a friend of mine.'

'Right.'

'You won't tell him, right? That I told you?'

'No.'

I let him clean himself up. He borrowed some clothes from Lewis. They fitted better than his own. Lewis didn't seem bothered by Waylon's trouble, which suggested he wouldn't go running to Moore. As we were leaving, he said, 'Um, hey, man. You said there was something in it for me?'

'You got some smack on you, right?'

'Huh?'

'You had a call from Moore, or one of Moore's people, to make a delivery tonight.'

'Uh . . .'

'Keep the smack for yourself.'

He hesitated. He wanted it, but he didn't want to cross Moore.

'Can't do that, man. There's someone waiting for this stuff.

If I don't get it there, I got Moore on my back, and I definitely don't need that right now.'

'The call came from a friend of mine. He doesn't want it.'

'Really? You sure?'

'I'm sure.'

'Who pays for it?'

I fished out a bundle of notes and tossed them to him.

'Give the money to Moore. If he asks, say you never saw the man before. Say he was in town one night and someone had given him Moore's number.'

'Right. Won't tell Moore.'

'Take some shit now.'

'I don't need any now. I had some.'

'Take it now.'

'Okay, all right.'

I waited long enough to see that he'd taken a hit, then I pushed Waylon out through the door and walked him back to my car. We headed for Dalston.

The roads were clear, only a few cars, taxis. I drove fast, watching the slick black road heading towards me.

Waylon sat beside me, sulking. He wouldn't speak and kept staring at his hands, which were folded in his lap. Every now and then he'd shift in his seat and look over at me. He probably wondered if he was going to walk away from this.

I was keyed up now and could feel the strain in my neck muscles, in the backs of my arms. It wasn't like the tension I felt before a job, or even before a fight. This was different. This was more like dread. Something was bad and I was in the middle of it and I kept seeing that white, mask-like face of Kenny Paget, and I kept thinking of Cole, out there, waiting.

I kept thinking of what I had, which wasn't much, and what I could lose, which was my reputation, which was everything. Most of all, I thought of Brenda, and I didn't know why. It was a feeling I had, a cold, dark, empty feeling. It was that hole opening up.

It was one of those three-storey Victorian terraced affairs, part of a row of twenty or so that stood like a cliff opposite a small square. They were firm buildings, deep and tall. Lights were on in the ground-floor front room of the house Waylon pointed out. The curtains were drawn and there were no gaps that I could see through.

I gave Waylon the money and told him if he said anything to anyone I'd cut his bollocks off. He believed me.

I walked around the block. The rows of houses were solid all the way around, except for several places where there were alleys or driveways. Even with these access points, I would have to cross a dozen gardens to get to the back of the house.

So, I could go in through the front door, or I could get access to the rear garden. The garden option meant first getting access to the garden that backed on to it, and that would mean going through the house of that garden.

I sat for a while in my car and thought things through. Then I reached over to my bag, pulled out the Smith and Wesson .38 and checked that the chamber was full. I attached the silencers to both the .38 and the Makarov. Fuck subtlety.

I was going in blind. Was Beckett alone? Was he there at all? Were Walsh and Jenson with him? Were they expecting me?

I took off my coat and hat and dumped them on the passenger seat. I got out of the car and crossed the road, keeping my eyes on the front door. I moved quickly. I kicked the iron gate to one side and raised the .38 and emptied it into the lock area. The gun coughed, the rounds hit the wood like fast hammer blows. I dropped the .38 into my pocket and charged the door, hitting it shoulder-first, smashing the lock apart. The door splintered with a crackling screech, flew open, crashed into the wall and rebounded back behind me. I had the automatic in my hand now, and I was steaming. I burst into the front room, gun raised, saw Beckett in one chair, the other two on a sofa. I let go with the gun, firing three rounds into Beckett, the gun kicking in my hand, feeling good, feeling like revenge, each round tearing into Beckett's body, taking with it my fury. I spun around to let the gun loose on the other two, to destroy them. But even as I was turning, I knew it was all wrong. My finger tightened on the trigger. And stopped.

They were dead. All of them. I was killing corpses. Beckett stared at me, his face slack, white, a black hole in his forehead. I lowered the gun. My heart banged in my chest and something crawled up my spine.

I stood and listened, every part of me ready to spring. I waited for a creak, a knock, anything that would tell me someone else was here. I gripped the Makarov, strangled it. Its heat travelled through my hand.

I heard nothing but the television, facing Beckett, which muttered away quietly.

I still waited, rigid, listening. My breathing was shallow, my neck, shoulders, arms tight. I was an animal in the night startled by some unknown sound, some dangerous smell. I waited, feeling the dread rise, feeling the horror.

Finally, I let my body relax.

There was no way into this room except from the door I'd just burst through. Maybe I should've gone over the rest of the house, but I wanted to check the bodies first, see what I could find out. I kept my gun up, and one eye on the door.

From the spread of the powder burns on Beckett's skin I reckoned he'd been shot from near point-blank range, probably a couple of feet away. Someone had stood above him and fired into his face. The blood and brain and shattered bone spread out behind him, over the back of the chair.

He'd been dead about twenty minutes, maybe half an hour, wiped out minutes before I'd arrived. The other two had been killed in the same way, both with wounds in the head and upper torso, both shot where they sat.

I stood in front of Beckett and lifted my gun level with his head. I aimed, then turned and aimed at Jenson and Walsh. I followed the trajectory that any rounds from my gun would take. I went over to Jenson and Walsh and examined the wounds and bullet holes. They were consistent with shots fired from four or so feet in front of them and not from where I'd stood, which was five feet to their right side.

I had a look around their corpses. Walsh's jacket, on the floor next to him, carried a small automatic in the jacket pocket, easily within reach. Jenson's left hand held a can of beer that had half toppled over. They hadn't been bound. They hadn't been otherwise injured.

All three of them had been killed within a second or so of each other. There had been no reaction from any of them, which there would've been had one been killed before the others. The trajectories the bullets took and the speed of execution meant that there had been more than one killer. Probably two. I guessed that at least one of the three dead men had known the killers, and maybe trusted them. They'd been sitting watching television when they were killed. They hadn't been on their guard. They hadn't expected to die.

The killers must have used silencers. The bullet that had killed Beckett looked like a .32, and fired at point-blank range, but it was still embedded in the back of the chair, which meant that its velocity had been reduced. A silencer would do that. The fact that there weren't coppers all over the place meant that nobody had reported hearing gunshots.

If the killers had used silencers, then they must have had them already attached. That all meant one thing: they'd come here to kill. This hadn't been the result of an argument. This hadn't been impulsive. This had been a hit.

I went through to the back and looked at the kitchen door. It was locked: no sign of forced entry there, or through the kitchen window. The same went for the rear lounge windows.

I went back to the front door, which was still partly open. I pushed it to and studied the lock. It was a mess, smashed to pieces. But the chain and the dead bolts were untouched. They hadn't been used when the door had been closed. That meant Beckett hadn't been expecting trouble. Probably, too, he'd let his killers in.

Beckett should've been on his guard. He would've known that Cole would be after him.

I didn't have much time to search the place thoroughly. Maybe nobody along the road had taken any notice of my entrance. It had been loud, but not so loud that anyone would think murder was taking place. Still, I didn't want be found around three dead bodies.

But I wanted that money. It could have been that Beckett had put the money somewhere off-site. More likely, it had been here and was now gone, taken by whoever had killed Beckett. I had to check anyway. I sectioned the rooms into quadrants and searched rapidly, looking through drawers, cupboards, anywhere that a million in cash could be stored. There was nothing downstairs. I went up.

There were two bedrooms and a bathroom on the first floor. I tried the bathroom first, opening the cistern, the cabinet. I ripped off the side of the plastic bath and tried the floorboards. Nothing. I tried the smaller bedroom. Someone had slept there and left clothes and things around. I pulled the place apart, tearing at the clothes, looking for a key, an address, anything. I was sweating when I finished, and I'd still found fuck all.

The larger bedroom, at the end of the hallway, had probably been Beckett's. From the state of the double bed, I guessed he'd had a girl there. I saw a canvas bag by the side of the bed and made a grab for it. It was empty. I found another empty bag underneath the bed. The money, probably, had been in these bags. I threw them away. Then I made a mistake – I decided to be thorough. I went over to the large wardrobe and threw open the door.

At first, I didn't know what I was looking at. It came to me in pieces. Eyes, large, scared. A smooth dark face. A young face. A girl's face. A small body crouched in the corner of the cupboard.

She was twelve or so. She was thin. She had hair braided in what they call cornrows. She didn't move. She stared out with such a look of fear, with such terror in her eyes that it paralysed me. She lifted a hand upwards. And then she shot me.

ELEVEN

I was sitting at her table one morning, drinking coffee, eating an omelette, reading some book about John Hawkwood, the fourteenth-century English merc, who was smart enough to make himself rich in a plague-infested, war-ridden, fearful, religiously insane Europe. I'd been up an hour and had had a long cold shower and my head had only just about cleared. It was a day off for me and I was going to spend it doing nothing except reading, if I could keep my eyes focused that long.

Brenda was out, had been out all night. Every now and then Marriot had her do some kind of hostessing gig, usually for Middle Eastern types. She'd given me a kiss on the cheek late the night before and told me she'd be back in the morning, told me not to wait up, told me she'd miss me. I didn't sleep too well that night. Already I was getting used to her body next to mine, and when I woke and found myself alone in the bed I'd wonder if I'd been dreaming or remembering something from long ago. It got like that, sometimes, my mind, wandering back and forth so that I didn't know when I was, or where, or who.

So I was sitting at her table, reading the book, my torso bare and still damp from the shower, my head clearing. I had the window open and a cool breeze brushed over me, soothed my aching muscles. I didn't hear the door, but I heard her steps. She came up behind me and I felt her hand stroke my neck.

'Miss me?' she said.

'Sure. You want coffee?'

I could smell stale cigarette smoke on her clothes, and alcohol on her breath.

'Why, Joe,' she said, 'you old romantic.'

I could tell, now, by the tone of her voice, when she was taking the piss out of me.

I made to stand up but she pushed me back down. I waited for her to say something, but instead she traced a line down my back with the tip of her finger. She did it softly, so that it felt like a teardrop slipping slowly away. I felt her finger move left, then right, zig-zagging. I knew what she was doing. I knew what was coming.

'Where did you get these?' she said.

'An old job.'

'An old job? An old job. Just that? That simple? An old job.'

'Yeah. That simple.'

Her hand dropped away and she put her handbag on the table and walked to the kitchen.

'Shall I do you a coffee?' I said.

'Forget it.'

She spent a few minutes bashing things about and then I heard the kettle boil. After that, she was quieter and I figured she wasn't so pissed off with me. When she came back, she carried her mug and a plate of biscuits, which she put down on the table. She took a seat opposite me and sipped her coffee and watched me.

'For someone so smart, you're bloody stupid at times,' she said.

'I know.'

'Tell me, Joe,' she said. 'Tell me your story. How did you end up with those scars?'

I finished eating the omelette, mopped up the juice with a piece of bread, and pushed the plate away.

'What does it matter?'

'It matters to me. Surely that's all you need to know. Tell me, from the beginning. Tell me a story. Tell me about the first scar you got. It was that one on your thigh, wasn't it? The one I touch at night. Start with that. Start from the beginning.'

She reached behind her for an ashtray, then leaned back in her seat and lit a cigarette and sipped her coffee and waited. I shifted a bit in my seat, not knowing what to say or how to say it. And then I thought, fuck it.

'When I was seventeen,' I said, 'I worked in Wembley, on a large building site next to the North Circular.'

It was a lousy job, I told her, hod-carrying, cement-mixing, all that shit. I'd wanted to be a carpenter but the site boss wouldn't let me give it a go. He'd taken over from some other bloke who'd been sacked for taking backhanders to employ illegals. That other bloke was all right. When he'd been site manager, he'd let me watch the chippies, let me try it out. He'd given me a chance, at least. The new geezer didn't like me, wouldn't let me near the wood.

'That's a shame,' she said.

'Yeah. So I'd just about had it with the building trade. I sure as fuck wasn't going to carry bricks for the rest of my life.'

Anyway, I told her, one night, as I walked back to my rented bedsit, I passed an Army Recruitment Office. It might have been a Navy Recruitment Office in Portsmouth, or an unemployment office in Romford. I might have been a fireman or a gardener.

'You might have been a carpenter,' she said.

'Yeah,' I said. I hadn't thought of it before. 'I might've been. Who knows? That's the way things happen. As it was, I walked in and that was that. I joined the fucking army.'

She looked angry, her eyebrows angling in.

'That's not how to tell it,' she said, flicking ash into the ashtray.

'What?'

'Don't just say, "I walked in and joined the army." Tell me what happened.'

'Fine.'

The sergeant behind the desk asked me some questions, I told her, and then he looked at me carefully. At that age, I was big, but still fresh-looking, still clear-eyed. The sergeant hesitated. He listened to the answers I gave him, weighed me up, my size, my ability to fight and take hardship. 'I won't lie to you,' he said, 'we could do with men like you. Have you thought it through?'

'He asked me what my girlfriend thought,' I said to Brenda. 'I told him I didn't have one.'

'You didn't?'

'No.'

'Never?'

'No.'

The sergeant asked about my parents. I shrugged. He

struggled on, asked me what I saw myself doing in five years' time, if I thought I'd stay in the army. I didn't know the answer to that. It seemed a stupid question. How did I know what I'd be doing in five years? I might be dead. But I played along and said I'd like to have a career in the army. 'It's a good life,' he told me, 'if you're prepared to work. I'm a Para, myself,' he said. I told him I'd always wanted to be a Para, not caring one way or the other. He brightened up. 'Smart man,' he said. 'The Paras can give a lot to someone like you.'

'I didn't know what he meant by "someone like you",' I said to Brenda, 'and I didn't give a shit what the army could give me. I just wanted something else. The army was something else.'

Just to make it look good, this sergeant asked me what I thought I could do for the army, what I could offer. I looked at him, bright and smart, ribbons and stripes and all. I looked at the posters of neat uniformed soldiers. What could I do for the army? What could I offer?

'What did you say?' Brenda said.

'I told him I could kill people.'

The sergeant's face lost its smiliness and I saw him for what he was. 'Perfect,' he said.

Brenda took a biscuit from the plate and looked at it and put it back. She took a drag of her cigarette and watched the smoke coil.

'Did you mean it?' she said. 'About killing people?'

'I told him what he wanted to hear. That's all.'

She nodded, but I don't know if she believed me.

Anyway, I told Brenda, I was a good recruit. I did what they told me and I was tough. Obedient and hard, that's what they wanted. They bumped me up to lance corporal in my first year. Then corporal. It was extra money.

Eighteen months later, my company was spread out on a place called Mount Longdon. I was with a couple of men from my platoon and we were taking cover in a ditch while dug-in Argentinian conscripts and regulars sprayed the area with Browning M2s. It was dark and icy cold, and the damp grass and mud had made my clothes wet and heavy, and the smell of stale sweat was mixed with a musty earthy smell. My body ached with fatigue, but there were too many threats of death, too much adrenalin, too much fear to feel anything but a kind of edgy, tingling aliveness.

The bloke next to me stuck his head up and a round pinged off his helmet. The man said, 'Fuck was that?'

And I felt a burning in my hip, as if someone had pushed the tip of a cigarette into it. I knew I'd been hit. It was unmistakable. I couldn't do much about it.

'And that's the scar,' Brenda said.

'That's it.'

'Okay, so what happened next?'

'I left.' Brenda sighed. 'Okay. If you want to know – '

'You were a good soldier, I bet,' Brenda said, taking a biscuit from the plate and pushing it into her mouth.

'I was okay. I even liked it. But then people were trying hard to kill me and I didn't like it any more.'

'Don't blame you,' she said around her biscuit.

Of course, I'd never been fooled by the reasons they gave me for fighting: for Queen and country, or for honour, or for your regimental colours, or for your comrades or your family or your way of life or whatever. I knew that was all bollocks.

I knew the reason I was there: I was a tool of my government. I was paid to destroy the tools of other governments because those governments disagreed about something and they sure as fuck weren't going to be destroyed themselves. But as I ran forward into the night in a painful limping motion and with tracer rounds zipping past me and getting closer, I realized another thing: I was being paid to be shot at. You can't have a war if the enemy hasn't got anyone to shoot at.

'So, that was that.'

'That was that,' Brenda said, throwing her arms out. Some of the coffee sploshed from her mug and I caught a smell of it and realized she'd laced it with vodka. I wondered what kind of night she'd had. I wondered if that was the reason she wanted me to tell her these stories, any stories that kept her from thinking about real life. The stories I was telling her were real, but they weren't real to her. That's what mattered.

'I'd joined the Paras because I couldn't think of anything else to do,' I said. 'When I thought of something else to do, I left. The government called it desertion. I didn't care what they called it. I had to avoid the law for a while and then get a new identity, but that didn't matter.'

I'd been lucky with that bullet, I told her. It had fragmented when it hit the other bloke's helmet, and only a part of it had entered me. It had nicked the bone, chipping it, but that was nothing. It was so long ago now that I hardly thought about it. Whenever I saw the scar, something of the past flickered in my mind, but that was it.

I'd learned two things from my time in the army:

One: I was good with violence. I could take it and not mind. I could handle bad situations and not panic. I could kill.

Two: I wasn't earning enough money.

'That's it,' I said. 'That's all there is.'

'The End,' she said.

'Yeah.'

She put another biscuit in her mouth and chomped on it and pulled her arm across to wipe away the crumbs. She drank some more of her coffee and pulled on her cigarette.

'Tell me about the other ones,' she said finally.

'Which ones?'

'All of them.'

'It would take hours.'

'I've got hours.'

'You've got to sleep. You're tired.'

'Yes. I am tired. But I don't want to go to sleep just yet. Okay?'

'Okay. Which scar do you want to know about?'

'Tell me about those ones on your back. The ones I kiss at night. I know them so well, and yet I don't know a thing about them. I don't understand them. I want to understand. Tell me a story, Joe.'

She used to say that to me sometimes. Tell me a story, like I could tell her something sweet and happy, something to lull her to sleep with.

'After I left the Paras,' I said, 'I ended up in Sheffield, bouncing at a club, doing the odd strong-arm work, repoing, debt collecting, stuff like that. It wasn't bad work. It paid okay, but it wasn't enough. So I started putting out feelers, asking questions, making contacts. Soon, I met a man.'

Michael Sloane had done six years in Strangeways for armed robbery. That should have tipped me off, I suppose.

Still in his twenties with a stretch behind him. Usually, the ones who get sent down are the ones too stupid to avoid it. But I was dumb and fed up with everything.

I was introduced to him by a man called Griggs. Griggs had said, 'Bloke I know needs someone for a job. You interested?' I'd said, 'Yeah.'

And that was that. Easy.

'Easy,' Brenda said, a slight smile in her eyes.

It was a balaclava job, I told her.

'A what?'

'A balaclava job. A post office in Hemsworth.'

'Right. Balaclava. Got it.'

She was starting to slur her words now.

Sloane had said, 'We go in Tuesday morning, before the pensioners've collected their money. It'll be ripe.'

'He seemed to know what he was talking about,' I said.

'Did he?' Brenda said. 'Know what he was talking about, I mean?'

'No.'

At 08.00, we pulled up outside a corner store along a small, grim, grey shopping parade. It wasn't busy, but it wasn't as deserted as Sloane had said it would be. Griggs was driving the car. Sloane got out, pulling down his balaclava. I followed. Sloane was carrying a shotgun. Nobody told me I needed to be tooled up. I'd thought someone would mention it. I'd thought they knew what they were doing. Sloane fished a crowbar out of the car boot and gave it to me, told me to stand there, told me he'd do the business and if anyone gave us grief to smack them with the crowbar.

We walked into the shop and along the aisles of canned

goods and chocolate bars and dusty magazines. We reached the meshed-in cubicle at the back. Some old geezer with a cloth cap and a young pregnant woman with bags of shopping at her feet were waiting for service from a middle-aged Asian woman. The Asian woman looked up and saw Sloane and I saw straightaway that she wasn't going to play ball. Her eyes widened with shock, and then anger kicked in. She waved her arm back and forth. 'No,' she said. 'No. Not again.' Sloane raised the shotgun and told her to give him the money. She started to gather her till and collect the cash into a safety box, all the time waving a finger at Sloane.

Brenda was smiling.

'She had guts, that woman.'

'Yeah. More than Sloane did.'

'What did he do?'

'Threatened her, shouted at her, waved his shotgun about.'

Then the old bloke lifted his stick and started beating Sloane over the head with it. 'Fucking bastard,' he called Sloane. 'Scum, the lot of you.' Sloane covered his head with his arms while the old man pummelled him. Then the lady with the shopping bags started on him.

Brenda laughed.

'I would've liked to have seen that,' she said. 'What did you do?'

'I thought about helping him and decided, fuck him, and fuck Griggs too. The whole thing had been bodged. I was no professional at the game but even I could see that Sloane was an idiot. I turned and started to walk out. I heard Sloane shouting to me to help him, but I carried on walking.'

And that was how I got shot the second time. Sloane let

off both barrels at me. It was a sawn-off and he was being knocked about and I was a good twenty feet away, so the scatter pattern of shot sprayed half the window and shopfront. But some of it hit me in the back and I ended up sprawled over the magazines and by the time I was outside the back of my shirt was soaked in blood. I reached into the car, pulled Griggs out, and drove off.

'God,' Brenda said. 'You were lucky you weren't killed.'

'Damned lucky.'

'What happened to the others? Sloane and Griggs?'

The cigarette burned between her fingers, the mug sat on the table, her hand holding it loosely. She seemed to have forgotten about all that. She seemed to have forgotten everything for a moment, caught up in the sad story of a sad fucking life that I was telling her. I suppose she at least forgot about her own sad story while I was telling her mine. Maybe that's what stories are all about, forgetting. I guess she knew this better than I did.

'I don't know what happened to them,' I said. 'They probably ended up doing long stretches somewhere – they must have done – but they didn't have my real name so they couldn't grass me up. I'd been stupid, but I was clear. Like you say, I was lucky.'

And that was that.

'That was that,' she said.

'Yeah.'

Afterwards, I came back to Tottenham. I didn't know what I was going to do, but I'd learned my lesson.

She mashed her cigarette.

'Promise me you won't get shot again,' she said, flattening

the cigarette, squashing it too much, concentrating all her effort on it.

'I can't do that,' I said.

She finally abandoned the cigarette. After a while, she looked at me.

'I don't want you having any more scars. Please. Promise me.'

'I was stupid before. I worked with idiots. I promise I won't do that again.'

'Promise me you won't get shot.'

'How can I?'

'I don't care if you don't mean it, Joe. I don't care if you lie or pretend. Just tell me, promise me. Promise me that I won't have to see any new scars on you.'

'Okay,' I said. 'I won't get shot. You won't have to see any more scars.'

Well, part of that was true. She wouldn't ever have to see a new scar.

'Tell me a story, Joe,' she'd say.

127

The bullet slammed into my shoulder, spinning me around, throwing me backwards. The walls disappeared and the floor raced up and smashed into my face. I hit it like a sledgehammer pounding into stone. I didn't know what was happening. The floor was where the room should have been and someone was driving a red-hot poker into my flesh, and it was endless, unbearable. The pain pulsed through me, into my marrow. I didn't know where I was, I just felt the pain and the floor pushing into my face. I was in a house, I was in the Falklands, I was in a hospital, I was on the canvas, I stood above a dead man with eyes open and lips pulled back. Everything clouded around me, darkened, and became blurred. An age-old instinct screamed at me to get up. I tried to use my arms to push myself but my left arm collapsed me into a heap. Hot fluid touched my cheek. My left arm felt cold and split by electric pain that ran from my fingers to my neck and down my spine. I tried again to stand, bringing my knees up and using my right arm. It was funny, I felt so useless. I almost laughed. I felt stupid. I was a kid again in the ring. I could see myself from up high, flailing about. Blackness and sickness and a spinning dizziness welled and faded and welled again, and the floor moved from side to side. Something red and shining moved slowly in front of my eyes. I knew it was my own blood. There was a lot of it. I saw a gun on the floor. It was my gun. Someone was dead.

I had to get out of here. There'd been an explosion. A gunshot. Someone had been shot. People had been shot. I'd been shot.

With my good arm, I pushed myself up on to my knees. I stayed like that for a moment while I let the sickness and confusion sink. I remembered where I was, what I was doing there. I remembered a girl's face. I felt a cold sweat break out over me. I was losing blood quickly and it was making me feel faint and weak. I had to get out of here. People would've heard the gunshot. Police would be coming. They responded quickly to reports of gunshots. They came in heavy. I had to get out of here.

I managed to stand. I swayed. I saw my gun on the floor. I saw my blood. I turned.

I saw her then. She was curled up in a ball. She was still in the wardrobe. The gun she'd used was on the floor in front of her. It was a .32 automatic and I'd taken it from less than three feet away. If it had been a 9-mil, I wouldn't have got up.

I picked up my gun and stumbled out. It was hard going; I'd never done anything so hard. Tabbing miles with 140-pound loads over ankle-breaking terrain in bitter cold; fighting the last eight rounds of a twelve-round fight with a broken hand – that shit was easy. This was hard. The blood didn't seep, it poured. The pain pulsed through me, but my left arm was getting cold. It was hanging like meat, swaying at my side. I needed to fix it, but I couldn't stop. I wanted to rest, to lie down and let the swirling fog overtake me. I had to get out.

I should've questioned the girl. She might have seen who killed Beckett. I wasn't thinking clearly. I was on the stairs now and they fell away before my eyes. I leaned against the wall and slid along it, stumbling down, trying not to fall. I should've killed the girl. She'd tie me to the killings. It was too late. I couldn't go back. I could hardly go forwards.

I was fighting hard not to faint, pulling on every flicker of strength I had, trying to hate, trying to push the adrenalin through me. That was my only chance. At the bottom of the stairs, my legs gave out and I hit the floor. I wanted to stay there. I wanted to close my eyes and go to sleep, but something in my mind took over. I went on to auto. I got back up and pushed myself away from the wall. The front door was only yards away. It was miles away. I put one foot before the other. I was learning to walk all over again.

I made it through the door. The fresh air helped; I sucked it in. I gathered all my strength, gritted my teeth. I said, 'Move, you bastard.'

I moved.

My car was across the road. All I had to do was get there. All I had to do was put one foot in front of the other. No fucking problem. I put one foot down. And again. And again.

I opened the car door and threw my gun inside. I held on to the door and fell in.

My heart was thumping now and pumping out blood quickly. It was pouring right out of me. I pulled my belt off and tried to make a tourniquet, but I couldn't get the belt tied off, not with one arm.

I put the key in the ignition and started the engine, but I couldn't change gear. I couldn't move my fucking left arm. With my right hand, I let off the handbrake and put the car into first and let off the clutch. The car lurched forward and smashed into the car in front and stalled. I tried to put it in reverse.

I opened my eyes. It was dark. I didn't know where I was. Then the pain hit and I remembered. I'd fainted, I knew that. There were no police, so I must've been out for a minute only. Something was there, though. Next to me. And then I saw her.

She stood next to the car. She was a foot away, looking at me. Her eyes were wide, her mouth open like she was looking at a magic trick or a dangerous animal in the zoo. I grabbed her and said, 'Who killed Beckett?' She just looked at me. 'Who was it? Did they say anything? Did you see them?'

I shook her. She was so thin. She was skin and bone. She rattled.

Each time I tried to focus, the pain would surge and splinter my body.

It had to be Cole, of course, who'd killed Beckett. He'd found Beckett and sent some men to get his money back. So, if Cole had the money, he must also know that I hadn't taken it, that Beckett had fucked me over. So I was probably clear with Cole. But the police . . .

But it couldn't have been Cole. The door was unbolted, hadn't been smashed.

The police would arrive soon, and in force. And they'd be looking for me.

My mind was clouding over again.

Beckett had let them in. He wouldn't have let Cole in. He knew who he was letting in. He'd trusted them.

I didn't have time to think. I couldn't fuck about with the girl.

I let her go. I thought she'd run away. She didn't. She stood and watched me.

'Go,' I said.

I was supposed to kill her, wasn't I? She'd identify me to the law. Big man, blood leaking out of his arm. Christ, there were probably a hundred things that tied me in to the house. Besides, maybe she could clear me with the law, tell them who'd done the killings.

The police. How long had I been there? My mind was rambling. How long would they take to respond? Not long.

I opened my eyes. I'd passed out again. I saw the girl staring at me. She didn't move.

I opened my eyes again. She was gone. I thought I was hallucinating. I thought I was nearing the end. I didn't seem to mind. You lived. You died. That was how it went.

I got the car started again and crunched the gears, tried to get reverse. The car stalled and jumped and lurched back, smashing into the car behind. I'd had it. I knew it. I was finished. All over.

I fell back in the seat.

I must've passed out again because the next thing I knew she was standing beside the car, shoving my arm. I looked at her for a moment, trying to place her. She was holding something towards me. It was a key. A car key. She pointed along the road to a black Saab. I looked at the car like an idiot. It took me an age to notice the 'Auto' label on the back. I pulled all my strength together in one final effort. I grabbed my bag and coat from the passenger seat, snatched the key from the girl and staggered to the Saab. I flipped the button on the key ring; the alarm blipped off. I opened the door and fell into the driver's seat. I turned the ignition. As the car hummed with life, I heard the passenger door slam shut.

'What are you doing?'

The engine thrummed, filling the silence between us with a kind of tension, a question unasked, unanswered. She looked at me and in her eyes was a look that I couldn't read. It wasn't fear or defiance or suspicion, though it seemed to carry all those things, like they were gathered together inside her, and held there by some kind of need.

But the blood was still seeping from my wound and I could feel the dizzying emptiness getting near again.

'Can't drive,' I said.

'I can drive,' she said.

'Then drive.'

Browne was drunk when he answered the door. He took one look at me and sobered up.

'Christ,' he said. 'In there.'

He pointed to the back of the house. I made it through the hallway and slumped into the seat at the kitchen table. I tried to peel off my jacket. I had no strength. The girl tried to help me, carefully pulling away the blood-soaked cloth. Browne opened a cupboard, grabbed some kind of surgical scissors and sliced through the jacket. Then he cut away my shirt.

'Jesus, man,' he said. 'What have you done?'

I grabbed him, pulled him near.

'Fix me,' I said. 'No medicine. I need to keep – fix me . . .'

When I came to, I was still in the kitchen, still in the seat. Browne, his hands and shirt bloody, was standing back looking at me. He was holding a scalpel. The table was covered in blood-soaked cotton wool, gauze.

'I've done what I can for now,' Browne said, his Scots accent less harsh now that he was more sober. 'I've cleaned it and stitched it. You're suffering from hypovolaemic shock and I suspect the bullet broke your scapula. It went through you, you know. I've given you a penicillin-based antibiotic. I remembered that you weren't allergic to penicillin. That's right, isn't it? I managed to transfuse some blood. In short, you need to get to a hospital.'

'No . . .' I managed to say, 'hospital.'

'I thought not. Well, it's your choice.'

'My blood type –'

'Christ, I know what type you are: O. Same as me.'

I tried to move my arm but the pain cut through me. I was faint still, and weak. I was alive inside a carcass.

'Your arm's going to be useless for a while,' Browne said, wiping his hands on a wet cloth. 'I'll bind it up tightly. Hopefully, you won't die of shock or loss of blood or brain damage. Hopefully, your shoulder isn't splintered too much to heal and there aren't fragments of bullet still inside you. Hopefully.'

'Yeah.'

He flung the cloth into the sink and reached behind him for a glass which he filled with Scotch. He took a couple of swigs. He looked at me for a moment. I was too weak to do anything except sit there. I thought if I tried to move I'd realize I was dead.

'So, you going to tell me what all this is about?' he said.

'Trouble.'

'So I gathered. Who's the girl?'

'Where is she?'

'In the other room. Who is she, Joe?'

'Don't know.'

'Who shot you?'

'She did.'

Browne sighed and puffed his cheeks. 'Okay, Joe. Better I don't know. What's her name?'

I blacked out again. When I managed to open my eyes, I was lying on my back on a mattress. My arm was bandaged and bound to my side. The room was dark, but there was thin daylight behind the curtains, which meant I'd been out for a few hours at least. I could hear a voice speaking quietly in another room. Browne was talking to someone, but I couldn't hear a reply. Was he on the phone? Was he selling me out? I tried to sit up. I didn't make it.

I came to as Browne had just about finished rebandaging my arm. Watery morning light crept around the curtains and paled the living room. Browne fell into the chair opposite my mattress and looked at me through narrowed, red-rimmed eyes.

'Awake, are you? You'll have to stay here for a while. Until you're strong enough to walk. We tried to get you upstairs into bed, but you're too bloody big.'

'What – ?' I said.

My mouth was dry. Browne nodded, held a hand up to silence me, and left the room. He came back with a glass of water, helped me sit up, and lifted the glass to my lips. I drank some of it and fell back again.

'Still getting the headaches?' Browne said.

'Yeah.'

'Have you seen anyone about them?'

'No.'

'I told you a million bloody times, Joe, you've probably got scarring on your brain. You need to see someone.'

'Can they do anything?'

'I'm not a neurologist, I don't know what they can do these days.'

'Can they fix it?'

'You mean can they repair the damage? No.'

'Then what's the point?'

'They can help alleviate the symptoms. The headaches.'

'I can live with headaches. I don't want questions about gunshot wounds.'

He watched me for a moment, then, sitting back in his chair, reached down to the half-bottle of Scotch on the floor beside him and poured a couple of glasses. He offered one to me. I shook my head.

'Take it.'

I reached out with my good arm and took the drink.

'Alcohol is probably the worst thing to give you right now,' he said. 'But I hate drinking alone.'

He poured his drink down his throat. When he saw that I was going to spill mine, he reached over and took it.

'This is the finest cheap Scotch money can buy,' he said. 'Shouldn't waste it.'

I passed out again, thinking that there was something I was going to say.

Images drifted through my mind, nightmarish and clammy and cold, all of them clogging together. It was something I couldn't escape, something I couldn't even see how to escape. I was back in the ring and my brain had been bashed to pulp and I was trying to stand and being choked by confusion, caught in a web.

I'd open my eyes and see Brenda sitting next to me, her hand on mine. I think I touched her face and it felt real. And then I'd remember. My eyes would close, my eyelids weighted down, and I'd go back into the darkness and fear, and I'd be on Mount Longdon, the wet cold making me shake uncontrollably, the boy lying on the ground, grinning at me. And then

I'd look up and see the girl sitting high up on a stool, holding my hand, looking into me. And then I'd go again. It went on like that, for hours – or years, it seemed. And I wouldn't know the difference between waking and sleeping but always I'd see her there, beside me, and I kept wondering if she was real.

FOURTEEN

A bright light woke me. I blinked.

'It's alive,' Browne said.

He swayed as he came into the room, balancing a tray of food. He looked like a circus act. On the tray was a plate of something that looked a bit like fried eggs, beans and bacon. There was a small plate of doughy slices of bread and a mug of tea. I tried to sit up. My head felt light, my thoughts were dull and tied up with themselves. My arm throbbed, but there was little pain, and it was a long way off. I fell back.

'That'll be the morphine,' Browne said. 'It should be wearing off a bit by now.'

'I told you not to give me anything,' I tried to say.

'Yeah. You told me. Now sit up and eat.'

He put the tray aside while he helped me up, padding my back with cushions. He put the tray down on my lap.

'Not hungry.'

'Eat anyway.'

'Where's the girl?'

'Upstairs. Asleep. It's eight-thirty p.m. You came here last night. You'd lost a lot of blood. I thought you might have severed the subclavian artery, but it's all right. I don't think I could've fixed you up if that had been the case. It was the exit wound, mostly. You must've had a high heart rate, pumped out a lot of the red stuff.'

139

'The girl.'

'I told you, she's asleep. She stayed awake, right here by your side, until I gave her a tablet and put her to bed. You've had a blow to the head recently.'

Had I? I remembered the men in my flat, but that was weeks ago, wasn't it? It was years ago.

'Baseball bat,' I said.

'There's swelling there, hell of a lump. I think you were suffering delayed concussion, probably exacerbated by the blood loss. You should've told me.'

There was something I had to say. I was trying to remember what it was. Why was I asking about the girl? I didn't care about the girl. I remembered what it was I needed to say.

'Heard you talking,' I said.

'Imagine that. Me talking. Whatever will I think of next.'

'Who to?'

'Don't trust me, Joe? Suppose I was talking to the police? What're you going to do about it? Now eat.'

I didn't feel like eating. I looked at the food instead.

'Don't tell me what this is about,' Browne said. 'I don't want to know.'

He was right about that. It was better he didn't know. Hadn't we agreed that already?

'She wouldn't tell me anything,' Browne was saying. 'About what happened, I mean.'

He was going the long way around not wanting to know.

'I heard something interesting on the radio, though. Something about a suspected drug deal gone wrong, in Dalston. Three men dead and police searching for a man seen leaving the premises in the early morning. Man was described as big and ugly and very bloody stupid. You, I take it.'

My throat was suddenly dry. I drank some of the tea. It was strong and sweet. It was the best drink I'd ever had. I drank it all and dropped the mug on the floor.

Browne was quiet for a while, biting on his thumbnail, which, I knew, meant he was getting ready to say something significant. He'd done it every time he'd told me that it was time to quit boxing, that I was too old, that I risked permanent brain damage, or whatever.

I waited for him to speak. It was easier to let him take his time, otherwise he'd get crotchety and lose track of what he was trying to say, and then I'd have to wait for him to start all over again. I tried to eat the food, using a fork in my right hand. Browne had given me a knife too. He'd forgotten that I couldn't use both hands.

'Her parents, you know,' he said finally. 'Dead. Well, mother dead. Father ...'

He threw his hands up as if to say 'gone in the wind'.

It took me a few seconds to work out who he was talking about. When I realized, I said, 'So?'

'So? It's a bad thing to lose your parents.'

'Is it?'

'Yes. It is. It is a very sad thing.' He pushed this thought around his head for a second or two, then he said, 'You shouldn't have involved her in this.'

'I didn't.'

'She's so bloody young.'

He wasn't really talking to me. After another moment, he said, 'Are your parents alive?'

I shrugged with one shoulder.

'Don't you know?'

'No.'

'Where'd you think they are now?'

'Dead, or around somewhere.'

'That's sad,' he said softly.

I didn't say anything to that. It didn't seem sad to me. It didn't seem anything to me. Your family were there when you were born. That's all. They fed you until you were old enough to feed yourself, and then you left.

'You're drunk again,' I said.

'Wrong. I'm drunk still. And so what? Who else you going to get to heal your wounds? You want someone sober, go to Harley Street.'

'Where's this going?'

'Huh?

'The girl.'

'Oh, I don't know. Going nowhere, I suppose. Just thought you might like to know about Kid.'

'What?'

'Kid. The girl. That's her name.'

'Her name?'

'Yeah. Kindness. Some name, huh? Kindness. Apparently what they call children out there. In Nigeria. Or was it Ghana? Christian thing. Some name. Beautiful name.'

He left the room, nodding vaguely to himself and trying to walk straight.

He'd aged more than six years in the six years since I'd last seen him. His grey hair had thinned and was now wispy and straggly, clinging to his head in a desperate last stand. His hands had become gnarled. A red strawberry nose and broken blood vessels showed the years of heavy drinking. Mostly, though, what seemed to have aged him was defeat. He'd given up hope and with it he'd lost the spark. The papery skin and drawn face were the look of a man waiting out his time, an advertisement for wasted life. A long way from the success he'd once had.

I ate some food and made an effort to stay conscious. It was hard work. After a couple of hours, I felt reasonable. My arm was beginning to throb, but at least my head was clearer. I was beginning to think.

By the time Browne came in again, I had some idea of what I was going to do. Firstly, I was going to speak to the girl.

'How are you feeling?'

'Okay.'

He stood and watched me for a moment. 'You're welcome,' he said.

'My bag, where is it?'

He went off to get it. When he came back, I said, 'There's money in there. Take some.'

When he looked at me he seemed disappointed or something. He threw the bag to the floor. He was doing his noble act, refusing my money. I let it drop.

'Where's the girl?'

'Her name's Kid. I told you that.'

'Yeah. Where is she?'

Browne shook his head, sighed heavily.

'She's terribly malnourished, you know. I've fed her up a bit, given her some vitamin shots. I need to examine her, but she won't let me. I need to see if she's been abused. She doesn't seem to be injured in any way internally, but . . .' He ran a

143

weary hand over his grey hair. 'Christ, I don't know what I'm doing. She should be in care, in a hospital, not stuck with a drunk and a thug.'

'I need her here.'

He swung round.

'I don't give a damn what you need. It's the girl, man. That's who I'm thinking of.' His fury went as quickly as it had come and he seemed limp, as if he'd spat his strength at me. 'If I thought for one second she'd be better off with the authorities, I'd call them and be damned to you. Aye, and me. But she's gone through enough and I don't want to put her through any more. Not yet, anyway. And, amazingly, she seems to want to be with you.'

I thought he was probably in the middle of a hangover.

'I have to ask her some questions.'

'Can't you let her be?' he said in a tired voice.

'It's important.'

'For a while. Just let her be. She's a bloody child, man. I don't know what she's been through, but I know trauma when I see it. If you push me on this, I'll call the police. I should have done that last night.'

'Why didn't you?'

He slouched over to the sideboard and pulled out a half-bottle of Scotch. He filled a glass and drank it. I decided I could talk to the girl later. I didn't want Browne drunk and angry, he might go and do something stupid.

'Do you know what they did to her?' Browne said.

'Huh?'

Browne smiled. It was what they call a wry smile. I didn't think he was amused at all.

'Do you care about anyone, Joe? Just asking out of curiosity. Call it academic.'

He got like that when he drank. He swallowed the rest of the Scotch.

'Ever had a woman, Joe? Someone you were glad to see? I had someone once. Not my wife. Someone else. Long time ago now. Long time.'

When I thought Browne was finished, I said, 'I need to use your phone.'

But he didn't hear me. He was away in the past, torturing himself a little more with the failure of it all. He stared off into the distance for a moment and then he turned his gaze to me with a look of concentration on his face.

'Yeah. You did, didn't you?'

'What?'

'That woman.'

'What woman?'

'Name 'scapes me. Black woman. Barbara. Lovely lady.'

FIFTEEN

One time, Brenda asked me what I did.

'What do you mean?'

We were at her flat. We were on the sofa, watching a war film on TV. I'd only been seeing her a few days then. I kept thinking she'd tell me it was nice and all but I wasn't really her type.

She'd had a few drinks. I'd had a couple of beers and was feeling tired. My head hurt.

'I mean, what do you really do?'

She was curled up, her head resting on my shoulder.

'You know what I do.'

'Not at the casino. I mean, what else do you do?'

I turned to her now.

'Why do you want to know?'

'Just curious. I mean, I don't care what it is. I just want to know about you.'

I turned back to the film.

'I do a bit of strong-arm stuff.'

'You're muscle, huh? A button man? You work with gangsters? The mob?'

For a moment, I thought that she must be an idiot. People didn't really believe that shit, did they? But when I looked at her, there was a twinkle in her eyes and the corners of her mouth were turned up slightly and I realized she was taking the piss out of me. I didn't seem to mind.

'Because I'm big,' I said, 'some people use me to do some strong-arm stuff, repoing cars, collecting debts, like a bailiff – you heard of a bailiff, right? Well, a lot of that stuff is taking from people who don't want to give it up. You need to have backup so they don't get any funny ideas. That's all I am, backup, insurance.'

It was probably the most I'd ever said to her in one go. I knew, as I was saying it, that I was going out of my way to pretend to be legit. People who talk too much are often lying. I was talking way too much. Besides, she was a pro, why would I care about telling her what I really did? I didn't know why I would, but I suppose I did.

'I bet people always get scared when they see you. I bet they pay up fast.'

'Yeah.'

'Yeah, I'll bet.'

She sat for a moment, thinking.

'I remember when I was a girl – I was ten, I think – and my parents took me on holiday. We went to a place in Devon called Sidmouth. Ever heard of it?'

'No.'

'Well, it's a nice place. There's lots of these winding country lanes with hedges so high you couldn't see more than a hundred yards of road at a time. We rented a cottage for the week. It was so quiet, Joe. Well, you could hear crickets and birds chirping and all that kind of thing, you know, summer sounds. But there was no traffic noise, no shouting, no loud music. No . . . people.'

She was quiet for a long time. She seemed to have forgotten what she was going to say.

'It was nice,' she said again. 'Anyway, I remember this one time, I went out to buy a toffee apple. I'd never had one before and they sold them in this shop and so I went out to get one. I went in and there was this old lady behind the counter and she was looking at me and I smiled at her and started looking around. I thought she looked like a nice old lady, you know. Like you see on TV or something. Like in a book. I mean, she worked in a sweet shop in a small town in Devon. You could've taken it right out one of them old films. I thought she'd smile and tell me I could have the toffee apple for free. And for a moment, I felt happy. And then she came up to me and said, 'Don't try and steal anything.'

I saw her wipe a tear away. She was drunk. But I was listening.

'What I'm trying to say is, I go in a place sometimes and I can see what they're thinking. Only, it used to be something like "there's a little nigger, we'd better keep an eye on her" and now it's "there's a nigger tart, we don't want her here". What I'm trying say is, I know what it's like. To be unwanted. To be looked down on. To be ignored or suspected or whatever. And it hurts, doesn't it? I mean, it always hurts. You can't ever get used to it.'

In the film, British troops were killing Nazis in the name of liberty and country and all the other stuff they tell you is right and just. I said, 'Some of the best people I ever worked with were black.'

Brenda smiled.

'Some of my best friends are black.'

'Huh?'

'Never mind. Go on.'

'Some of the best people I ever worked with and some of the worst people I ever knew were black.'

She thought about this for a moment.

'So, what you're saying is, of all the black people you've known, some have been great criminals and some have been right bastards. Is that it?'

'Yeah.'

'Well, that's nice to know, Joe.'

'It's just how it is. Same with the whites.'

She moved her head over to my chest like she was listening to my heartbeat. Maybe she was checking to see that I was alive.

'I'll sleep with you if you want,' she said. 'For free, I mean.'

I said, 'That's the nicest thing anyone ever said to me.'

I meant it.

Afterwards, lying in bed, she turned over on her side, facing me. 'You were lying,' she said. 'I know you were.'

She must have seen something in my eyes because she sat up, holding her hands up in mock surrender.

'Don't shoot,' she said, trying to smile.

'What do you mean?' I said. 'Lying.'

She lowered her hands. She gave up trying to smile. 'Do you need a gun to repossess cars?' she said.

'Sometimes.'

'Do you need a trunk full of them? Shotguns too?' I clenched my jaw. 'I'm sorry,' she said. 'I weren't spying on you. I just happened to be out back, in the car park one time. That's where I go sometimes – well, that doesn't matter. I saw a fella pull up in a car and you went out to talk to him and he opened up the boot of his car and started showing you these guns.'

I relaxed my jaw. There was a dullness in my head and I felt like I was awake but sleeping. I closed my eyes and the thoughts washed away. I felt like this sometimes, like all the pain was going and my head was floating off somewhere. Sometimes, when it was like that, I had trouble remembering things, I had trouble working things out.

Brenda moved in the bed. When I looked at her, she fidgeted a bit. She looked uncomfortable. A breeze pushed at the curtains and caught some of the cigarette ash in the ashtray on the bedside table and scattered it. The breeze was cool. I looked up at the ceiling. I found myself saying, 'I do armed robberies.'

She didn't say anything right away. I wasn't sure what reaction I'd expected. She might have jumped up and run screaming from the building. But I didn't think so. After a while, she said, 'Banks, you mean?'

'That sort of thing.'

'Who do you work with?'

'Why do you want to know?'

'All I want to know is, do you work for Frank Marriot? Or Kenny Paget?'

'All I want to know is, why do you want to know?'

She shivered and climbed out of bed and shut the window. She got back into the bed, sitting up, her back against the wall. She grabbed a cigarette from the table next to her and lit it. The smoke plumed and spread slowly in a cloud. We both watched it.

'They use children, you know,' she said. 'They have some connections and these kids, these small children, get brought in from somewhere abroad and end up in their hands. They don't make films with them, though. Too easy to get caught that way. They give them to men to use.' She blew some smoke out violently. She brought her knees up to her breasts and hugged them. She wouldn't look at me. 'Tell me you don't work with them. Or with anyone like them.'

'I rob banks.'

'I mean it. You have to tell me honest. Lie to me about anything else, but tell me the truth about this. If you've got any connections with them, tell me. Please.'

'I don't work with Marriot,' I said. 'I never will. And if Paget speaks to me again, I'll probably rip his head off.'

She nodded and smiled a slight smile. I saw tears come down her cheek. She brushed them away quickly. She still wouldn't look at me. What she said next surprised me. What she said was, 'Are you going to kill me?'

I put one hand on her cheek and turned her face towards me.

'Why would I do that?'

'People do, you know. Especially people with guns.'

'I'm not that sort of people.'

'I'm glad,' she said quietly. She pushed herself close to me.

Sometimes, after that, she would hold her hands up and say, 'Please don't kill me.'

She would smile her smile, the one that lit up her face, and her eyes would be bright like they were sparkling, like there was always something she was eager about. She looked so young when she did that, like a small kid. If she'd paid any attention, she might have seen that my eyes were dull and tired. Maybe she never looked properly. Maybe, through her eyes, everything seemed bright, no matter how dull it really was. Sometimes, when she did that, when she held her hands up, I would make a gun of my fingers and point it at her.

SIXTEEN

One time I was in the casino, sitting around, watching the punters spread their dosh about, losing more in a minute than I made in a month. I'd finished for the night and was at the bar, drinking a beer, trying to figure what the fuck I was doing with my life, that sort of thing. I saw my boss, a man called Yates, talking to some short bloke. They were pretty pally, laughing now and then. Yates was a grumpy bastard, spent his time giving his staff grief and complaining about his rotten life. He only ever smiled when he talked with a well-heeled punter. Now he was chatting to this bloke and falling over himself to be friendly. I wouldn't have paid them any attention except that every now and then they'd look my way and that made me itchy. I went to the bar. They came over.

'Joe,' Yates said, 'this is Frank Marriot.'

Marriot held out a hand and I took it, wondering what his game was. I'd been seeing Brenda then for a few weeks and I didn't make a secret about what I thought of Marriot and his pit bull, Paget. I figured he'd come to get me fired. I was about ready to tear his face off.

I'd heard of Marriot before then, of course, and what he did and who he did it to. There were a lot of people who thought he deserved to die and I wasn't about to argue with them. But he was connected way up and brought in a lot of money and spread it around. He was supposed to have some high-placed people in his pocket, one way or another.

I let go of his hand. He smiled. Yates had breezed off somewhere.

'I thought we might have a chat,' Marriot said.

He got on to a bar stool. Matheson came over sharpish.

'What can I get you, Mr Marriot?' Matheson said.

'Rum and Coke. Joe?'

I shook my head. I would've got up and walked out there and then, but I wanted to see what the pitch was. It was something, I knew that much.

Marriot waited until Matheson had put down the rum and Coke.

'Anything else you want, Mr Marriot?' Matheson said, ignoring me.

'That's fine,' Marriot said.

Matheson went back to the other end of the bar where he could ogle one of the busty waitresses who was up that end collecting drinks for an order.

We sat for a while, Marriot and me, admiring the scenery. He was a drab man, like his business. His suit was drab and cheap, his smile was empty, and as drab and cheap as everything else about him. He looked like an accountant. A fucking drab accountant. He wore glasses and had a habit of taking them off and wiping the lenses on his tie. He did that now. He must've thought it made him look smart or businesslike or something.

He took a sip of his drink and placed it on the bar and turned to survey the casino. There were a couple of his girls around, trying to pick up some mugs. When he turned back, he said, 'Kenny told me he bumped into you the other day.'

154

He made it sound like we'd gone for a picnic. Me and Kenny, old pals.

'Uh-huh.'

I was tired of him already. I gulped down the rest of my beer and signalled Matheson to bring me another.

'Your boss seems to think highly of you,' Marriot was saying, 'I hear nobody gets out of hand when you're around. That's good.'

There wasn't much I could say to that. I didn't believe him, anyway. Yates never had a good word to say about anybody.

'Kenny told me you had a reputation as a hard man,' Marriot said. 'Used to be a boxer, didn't you?'

'Some.'

'Paras too, I hear. Falklands, right?'

My skin prickled when he said that. I'd kept quiet about my time in the army. Technically, I was a deserter, even if it had been a long time ago. How the fuck had Marriot found out?

'And now you work for Dave Kendall. Only you're here, earning, what, hundred quid a night? Two hundred? So Kendall can't be doing too much for you.'

'What do you want?'

He spread his hands wide.

'Thought you might like a job. I could always use someone like you. Sometimes we get a spot of bother in our business that needs sorting out. I mean, I run a decent firm, Joe, don't get me wrong. I avoid trouble best I can. None of my girls are into drugs or anything like that; I make sure of it. But, like I say, there's always a use for someone like you.'

'Not interested.'

I turned back to my drink.

'Some of the johns, for example,' he was saying. 'They can get a bit rough; someone like you just needs to have a word with them.'

I watched him in the mirror, back of the bar. He took another sip of his drink and put it down and turned to me and smiled.

'And then there's the girls themselves. They're all right, most of them. Bit stupid, bit flighty, but basically they stay in line. But every now and then they get mixed up with some dumb cunt, get to thinking they might settle down, have kids, all that. Get to thinking they're safe from me if they do. Know what I mean?'

'Uh-huh.'

He took his glasses off and wiped them

'I'm not too keen on my girls having regular blokes. Fact, it's a bit of a rule of mine.'

'Yeah?'

He popped his glasses back on to look at me.

'See, a bloke might get a bit jealous or something. Sort of thing can cause problems.'

'And what if one of the girls wants to leave your employment?'

'It's not a harem. They leave all the time. But while they work for me, they do as I say.' He downed the rest of his rum and Coke and stood up. Even while I sat, he had to look up at me. 'Anyway, give it some thought, all right?'

He slapped me on the shoulder and wandered off.

SEVENTEEN

The cafe was on the Euston Road. It was gone eleven and the place was empty save for an old man in a frayed tweed jacket at one table and a middle-aged woman behind the counter. The strip lighting gave everything a green cast. The old man was asleep. The woman looked bored.

I'd left without seeing Browne and I was thinking now that had been a mistake. My shoulder was splitting again with pain and I felt clammy, hot and cold at the same time. But I had things to do and I needed a clear head.

The man on the other side of the table was called Eddie Lane. He was dressed in a Savile Row pinstripe suit and a Jermyn Street shirt. He was a good-looking bloke, thirty-six, tall and wide at the shoulders but with a torso that tapered to a slim waist, not like my block of granite. He had bright eyes and he always looked like he was amused by something – the rest of us, I suppose. He was one of the best light-heavies I'd ever seen, could've gone far. But he'd given up the ring a few years ago. Now he worked for Vic Dunham. Now he just killed people.

Dunham was the sort of man that people spoke about by connection. 'I once knew a bloke who did a job for Vic Dunham.' He was like that. And Eddie was his shadow. It was a sort of father-son thing, only Dunham was white.

Dunham was organized crime. I didn't like organized crime. For one thing, they weren't that well organized. There were many loose cannons, too many would-be bosses. They were also too hot-headed, too easily insulted or threatened or dishonoured or whatever bollocks it was that got them riled. They often ruled by reputation and that meant they had to maintain face. At least, as they saw it. Mostly, it was macho rubbish. And they kept going to war with each other for one thing or another. That was just stupid; there was plenty of money for everybody. Plus, with organized crime there was the law. They had Serious Crimes and Flying Squad and now even MI5 crawling over them all the time – electronic surveillance, tags, supergrasses and all that. It was too loose. It wasn't professional. No, I didn't like it. But I respected it. I had to, really, just as I respected the law. I was on nodding terms with a few men from some of the local Yardie and East End and Turkish firms, but mostly I left them alone and they left me alone. I had my own thing going on. I wasn't big enough to bother them and, so long as it didn't cross into their turf, there was an understanding.

But Dunham – even I had to admit his organization was solid. And one of the reasons for that was now opposite me.

Eddie was sitting back in his seat, watching me. He had that amused look on his face that made him resemble a forties film star.

'Don't look too good, Joe,' he said.

'I'm okay.'

'Well, you're lots of things, but you're not okay. Not from what I hear.'

'No.'

'It's a mess.'

'Yeah.'

He shifted in his seat. I caught the bulge beneath his jacket. He was a cautious man. I'd been right to come empty-handed; I didn't need grief from Eddie or Dunham to add to my problems. I wasn't in much of a state to use a gun anyway.

'Wanna tell me what's going on?' he said.

'That's what I want you to tell me.'

'You go first. You look like death. I'm eager to know what kind of monster managed to get the drop on you. I remember you in the ring. You were unstoppable. What was it they called you?'

I told him I couldn't remember.

'You're lying, man. What was it?'

He concentrated on it for a few seconds. You would have thought it was important.

'I forget,' he said. 'What the hell was it?'

'What does it matter?'

'Doesn't matter, I guess. Now why don't you tell me what this is all about?'

I told him how the casino job had gone down and what had happened afterwards. I told him about the two men planting money in my flat, and how I'd been set up by Beckett and Kendall to make it look like I'd double-crossed them and taken all the money. I told him about finding Beckett, Walsh and Jenson dead in Dalston, and how the money was gone, taken, I guessed, by whoever had done the killing. I told him how I'd been shot. When I'd finished telling him all that, I waited for him to speak. His eyes smiled. He looked like he was having fun.

'Girl, huh? That's sort of funny, a girl decking you.' I didn't find it funny. 'Was she young?'

'Yeah.'

'Very young? Like, a child?'

'Yeah. So?'

'Beckett's taste. He likes them young. Didn't you know that?'

'No.'

'Yeah. He will not be sorely missed.'

He leaned forward and rested his elbows on the table. He scratched his head. We each had a cup of coffee in front of us. The coffees were cold, untouched.

'Kendall?' he said.

'Dead.'

'Uh-huh. Seems like everywhere you go lately, you're leaving dead people.'

'They're leaving themselves. They keep getting in my way.'

'Don't get me wrong. I don't blame you for killing idiots. It's sort of an unwritten rule with me.'

'Right.'

'I like things unwritten. Know what I mean?'

'Sure,' I said, not knowing what he was talking about, and not caring.

'You're a man of action, Joe. Few words. I don't like words much myself. People lie with words.'

He was talking around the subject. He had a habit of doing that. I never understood it, but he seemed to find amusement in it, so I let him babble. I nodded vaguely. 'Sure.'

'I have a thing about full stops,' he was saying. 'They end words. I got a whole load of full stops on me right now. The nine-millimetre type.'

Now I got it. He was being subtle.

'You mean, if you go out for me on this and I've lied about having the money, you may have to kill me.'

'That's about the size of it.'

'Fine. Now we got all that sorted out, you want to tell me what you know?'

He looked at his coffee for a moment, preparing to say something important. I could tell these things. People often look down when they're going to do that. It's an unconscious thing.

'About five months ago, we were approached by some Albanians. Nice blokes these Albanians, got all the connections. They smuggle anything.'

I'd heard of a couple of Albanian gangs. They were into heroin and slavery, bringing drugs through from the Middle East and Eastern Europe, bringing women and children through from wherever they could, taking away their passports, beating them to make sure they stayed in line, giving them drugs to make them dependent and easily controlled, farming them out to pimps and pornographers.

'This time, they'd brought in a shipment of heroin,' Eddie was saying, 'but their buyer was banged up before they could deliver. Remember Rockley?'

Rockley was doing life for murder and several counts of conspiracy to commit. He was one of the geniuses who turned me off the whole organized-crime thing. Couldn't organize his own fucking family. His brother had grassed him up.

'I remember.'

'So, these Albanians had the stuff but no one to sell it to. They asked us if we were interested. We said no. I heard they went to Cole. I heard he said yes.'

'Why did you turn them down?'

'Lots of reasons. One, we're going legit. Two, they're scum. There are other reasons, but those'll do.'

'How much heroin?'

'How much did you nick from Cole's casino?'

'About a mill.'

'Then, I'd say it was about a mill's worth of smack.'

I was getting it now.

'Cole didn't have the money,' I said, still getting it.

'What I hear, he had a brainwave. Bright man, Cole. He puts two and two together and comes up with a million in cash for the Albanians which he can then claim back from the insurance company. How many people knew the codes and could change a pick-up schedule with the security company?'

'Beckett said only the manager and this Warren bloke.'

'Right. So Cole hands Beckett inside information, but can't implicate the manager because he's too close to Cole. So he uses this man Warren as a decoy for the sake of the police, throw them off the scent that it was an inside job. Plus, he can make sure that the money they take from the casino that night is clean, untraceable. One million cold hard cash for the heroin.'

It was neat, as far as it went.

'A million's not much for someone like Cole.'

'You'd think.'

I stirred my cold coffee.

'Why would Cole buy drugs with money he couldn't afford?' I said.

'You'd have to ask him that, but I hear he's being squeezed by the new firms. It's a tough business these days. If I had to guess, I'd say he was using this deal to try and get back on top.'

'No wonder he's desperate,' I said.

'Yeah. He'll want that money, Joe. Any ideas where it is? Did Kendall grab it and hide it somewhere?'

'No. I think someone took it from Beckett. Kendall was dead before then, so that's him out. I didn't take it. Could Cole have it back?'

'No. He hasn't.'

'How do you know?'

'I know.'

'Right.'

I didn't need to push Eddie on that. I thought that Dunham must have someone inside Cole's mob. Eddie wouldn't tell me if that was the case. The fact that he wasn't telling me told me I was right.

'Then there must be someone else out there,' I said.

'That was my thought.'

'But Cole would still think I've got it.'

'That was another of my thoughts. Great minds think alike, eh?'

A third party. That made things tough.

'Now, Cole looks bad,' Eddie said, 'and he's getting pressure from the Albanians to pay up. They may not be super-smart, these Albanians, but they make up for it by being super-ruthless. They're expanding, and that means they're getting trigger-happy. Cole's getting anxious. Desperate, as you say. You say Paget's after you?'

'Yeah.'

'Hmmm,' Eddie said. 'Not good.'

The woman came over to us. She had a pad in her hand.

'Can I get you something?' she said, making a point of staring at our cups of coffee.

'We're fine, sweetheart,' Eddie said, smiling at her.

She waddled off, muttering something.

'What happened with Paget?' I said. 'Why didn't he get nicked when Marriot went down?'

'He's cunning. Among other things. He jumped ship before Marriot got nicked, offered his services to Cole.'

'And Marriot?'

'Still inside, for all I know. Anyway, I heard he's a wreck now, after – well, after what happened.'

I wondered how much of Paget's desire to get me was for Cole's benefit and how much was personal. It didn't matter. Whatever the reason, he'd try and get me. I said, 'How do I stand with Dunham?'

'I spoke to him. He's willing to take you on, has a high regard for you. That's rare from him. Thing is, what I hear, it won't help.'

'No?'

'No, Joe. Cole's gonna want blood for this. He'll need to recover prestige. Vic's protection isn't going to be worth much – they're not friends, you know.'

'You think Cole will try take me out anyway?'

'I think he'll have to.'

I'd had to take a cab out to meet Eddie. My arm was still useless, the pain surging through me, but I hadn't taken any of the pills Browne gave me. I'd wanted a clear head. Now, riding in the cab, I could feel the cold sweat soaking me and I kept slipping into unconsciousness. The cabbie must've thought I was drunk, but he didn't make a fuss. This was a good fare for him.

The window where I sat was misted up and I leaned my head against it and gazed out. I felt the coldness on my forehead, watched a dark London blur by.

Then I heard Brenda say, 'Poor old Joe, heading for the breaker's yard.'

I opened my eyes. Brenda wasn't there. Someone had said it, I saw the cabbie staring at me in the mirror.

I closed my eyes and heard her voice again, smooth and cool, throaty cool. I was burning up, the sweat soaking me and she put a cool hand to my forehead.

One time, she said, 'I ran away from home when I was sixteen. That was how come I ended up here, doing this. It was this or living on the streets. Me parents split up and I hated me step-dad. Old story.'

Sometimes she asked me about my plans. There was nothing I could tell her. I had no plans. She would tell me that she was going to do a course, become a beautician, whatever that was.

'What do you like doing, Joe?' she said. 'You can't like your job as it is. Being like that all the time, it's just not right.'

We were in a cafe down near Farringdon. I'd gone to see someone and she'd come with me and we'd gone into this place for a tea. The bloke I had to see was thinking of a job and wanted to talk it over with me. Brenda had wanted to come. Maybe that was why she was asking me these questions, telling me about her dreams. It turned out the job wasn't for me and we left the bloke and went for something to eat.

I must have looked pretty dumb, sitting there trying to think of something to say. She smiled and put a hand on my arm. I flinched when she touched me.

'I don't mean anything by it,' she said. 'What I mean is, what do you do when you're not working? You must have something. Everyone's got something.'

'I go to the gym. I read.'

'You read?'

'I can read.'

'I didn't mean that. What I meant was, most people these days don't bother with books.'

'Most people are stupid. And you thought I must be one of them.'

'God, I'm making a mess of this.' She took a deep breath and blew it out and said, 'So tell me, Joe, what do you like to read?'

'History, that sort of thing.'

'You don't like fiction?'

'I'm not interested in it.'

We sat in silence for a while.

'Tell me something else, Joe.'

'Like what?'

'I don't know. Something. About you.'

I couldn't think of anything to say. She said, 'Well, do you . . . do you believe in God?'

'It's a neat scam, I'll give them that.'

'Scam? What do you mean?'

'Scam. Con. Feed people fear and hope, promise them more than they've got and you'll have them eating out of your hand. Politics too. Crime's got nothing on that lot.'

'You admire that? Cons?'

'Sure.'

'Why?'

'It's a good way to get money.'

'So why don't you do it? Cons.'

'People would never trust me enough to believe me.'

'So you went about getting what you wanted another way. You took it.'

'If you like.'

The waitress came to our table and handed us our food. Brenda had a baked potato. She took a long time cutting that thing up and putting the butter and cottage cheese on it. She took way too long.

'That's sad, Joe,' she said. 'All that anger in you. All that hatred.'

I didn't know what she was talking about.

'Anger's got nothing to do with it.'

'No?'

It was all about the money, I told her. That's just the way it was; nothing to do with me. I'd come to learn this. I'd done things the hard way for a while, labouring on the sites, enlisting

167

in the army, trying to find a way of living, trying to find something. And finally I'd found it, I'd reached a way of thinking.

It was something she never understood.

'You take what you need,' I said. 'That's all.'

'That's cynical.'

She was still fiddling with her food, not looking at me.

'Is it?'

She looked up and there was something in the way her eyes were shaped, like she was sad or something.

'Poor old Joe,' she said. 'Heading for the breaker's yard.'

'I've got a way to go yet.'

'You couldn't have been like that all your life. That cynical. There must have been a day once when you wanted to do something else. What did you want to be when you were a boy?'

I told her I'd done woodwork at school. I'd liked making something with my hands. It was the only good thing that school ever taught me.

She'd ask me that kind of thing sometimes, and talk about what she wanted to do and what we could do together.

'You could have been a carpenter, Joe. You still can. You can do a course. They do courses in all sorts of things.'

She'd talk like that, like everything was possible, like we could start again. Sometimes I almost believed her.

One time, I got to thinking about what she'd said. I had the feeling that she wanted me to help her get out from under Frank Marriot. So I went to see him.

He had a large office at the back of a strip club along a narrow side street in Soho. The place was quiet when I went in, only a few staff getting the place ready. A couple of the girls were sitting around, chatting, smoking. I ignored the bloke at the bar who asked me what I wanted. I went into the back.

The office was cluttered with boxes of magazines and photos and videos. There were grey filing cabinets and a computer and desk next to a window which looked out on to a brick wall over the road. In some ways it was like a million other small businesses up and down the country. In some ways.

Paget was in the office when I entered, leaning against the wall by the door. There was no reason for him to be there, as far as I could see. But he stayed where he was, and watched me through slit-like eyes.

Marriot sat behind his desk, scanning one of his magazines, making notes on a pad.

'Hello, Joe,' he said, all bright and breezy. 'Nice surprise. I thought I'd see you again. I told Kenny, didn't I, Ken? I said, Joe'll come round sometime, have a word.'

'You did,' Paget said.

'You been thinking about my offer?' Marriot said.

'I want Brenda off your books.'

He put the magazine down.

'Do you?' he said. 'Well, sure, I can understand that. Young couple like you, in love, whole world ahead of you, full of promise.'

'I want her off.'

Paget made a noise. I turned to look at him. His lips thinned. I think he was laughing.

Marriot sat back. He pulled his glasses off his face, wiped them on his tie.

169

'Any reason?'

'Lots of them.'

'Any reason in particular?'

'Why do you care?'

He slid his glasses back on to his sour-looking face.

'I have to think about Brenda, you see. I'm sort of responsible for her. I have to wonder if you're here off your own bat, perhaps what you want her to do is not in her best interests. I'm just looking out for her. Right, Kenny?'

'That's right.'

'So, give me a reason I can understand.'

'Fuck reasons,' I said. 'I'm not asking your permission. She's out.'

'Well, if it's what she wants.'

'It's what she wants.'

'You sure about that, Joe? Because I don't think she wants to leave. All them blokes. I think she's having too much fun.'

I reached over and grabbed him by the front of his cheap suit and hauled him up out of his seat and pulled him over the desk. It was the first time I saw him lose that smug look.

I pulled my fist back. Then something cold touched the back of my head. I could hear Paget breathing close to my ear.

'I squeeze, your head blows apart,' he whispered. 'I'm good at squeezing.'

I dropped Marriot and walked out.

When I told Brenda what I'd done, she was angry with me. I didn't understand why.

We were at her place. I was washing the plates; she was drying. I'd gone over for a meal and afterwards I'd told her what I'd told Marriot. She stopped drying the saucepan she was holding and slammed it down.

'What did you do that for? Did I ask you to do it?'

'I thought you wanted to quit.'

'I do, it's just . . .'

'Just what?'

'It's not that easy.'

'Why not?'

'Please, Joe. Forget about it, eh?'

'It's a dangerous business. You know that. You know what they're like, the blokes you go with.'

'You don't understand,' she said, like she was talking to a child.

'Tell me, then.'

Marriot was in with some serious people, she said. He didn't like his girls leaving him, she said. She was doing okay, she said.

The more she said all that, the more I thought she was lying, making excuses. I didn't push it. I washed, she wiped. She didn't leave Marriot.

'I've got a date,' she'd say. She always called them that – dates – as if love was involved. Maybe it was easier for her that way. 'Some businessman,' she'd say, 'posh type,' or, 'some copper Marriot's got on the roll,' or, one time, 'some funny little bloke. I seen him around the place.'

It went like that. She talked about them like I talked about jobs I did. Some jewellers, some bank in Stepney, some fucking thing.

If ever we went out, I never took her to places we both knew, places where we might run into Marriot or Paget. I thought I'd do something stupid if I came across them. Brenda never said anything about it, but I got the feeling she understood.

One time, I took her to see a fight. She didn't like it and we left early. On the way out, we bumped into Browne.

'How are the headaches?' he said. 'Are they getting worse?'

I shrugged.

He saw Brenda and introduced himself.

'I'm the one who used to fix him up,' he told her. 'So that he could get back in the ring the next bloody night and get more of his brain pummelled to mulch.' He saw the look on her face. 'Take no notice of me,' he said. 'Joe's all right. To be honest, there's not much up there to damage.'

Outside, Brenda asked me about the headaches. I told her that it was just what happened when you'd fought for a long time like I'd done.

'Do you take anything for them?'

'Codeine sometimes. If they're bad.'

'*Are* they getting worse?'

'Yeah.'

She was quiet for a while. I could see that she wanted to say something, but she didn't seem to have the words.

'All that fighting, Joe,' she said finally.

She hooked her arm in mine and we walked through the night. She didn't say anything, but every now and then she'd tighten her hold on my arm, pull herself closer to me.

She never again mentioned my work or my lifestyle or her work or the pain of life.

Sometimes, when we were sitting watching TV, or in a pub, she would get a faraway look in her eyes. She wouldn't say anything in those moments, but her mouth would frown now and then, and her eyes would seem startled one second, angry the next, like her face was having a conversation with itself. I wondered what she was thinking when she went quiet like that. I should've asked her.

NINETEEN

I opened my eyes and didn't know where I was. It took me a long time to work out that I was in a cab, and that I was alone. I was cold.

My head was fuggy, thoughts far off. The cab rolled through dark empty suburban streets, grey and bleary through the fogged-up window. I watched it all like a man watches his face age.

I was starting to remember. I was going back to Browne's. I'd been to see Eddie. People wanted me dead.

I thought about the meeting with Eddie. Something he'd said twitched inside my mind.

I was wondering what that something was when the cab stopped in front of Browne's. I reached forward and paid the cabbie and everything swam around me. As I fell out of the taxi, I realized that the wet feeling beneath my shirt was more than sweat.

I had a key to Browne's place, but it was more than I could do to get the bloody thing out and put it into the keyhole. I banged on the door. I was surprised when I stumbled into the house. Browne muttered something that I didn't catch. My body weighed half a ton now and I had trouble dragging it to the kitchen. Browne followed me.

'Sit down, for God's sake,' he said. 'What the hell have you done?'

I collapsed on to the seat. I followed Browne's eyes and saw the blood seeping from my arm, dripping on to the floor.

'You've broken the bloody stitches,' he said, pulling off my jacket.

The left side of my shirt was thick with blood. Browne fiddled about with my arm.

'No hospital.'

'No hospital. I know. What the hell were you doing going out? You're lucky to be alive. I don't know how there's a drop of blood left in you.'

He packed tea towels around my arm and went off for bandages.

It was then that I saw the girl standing in the doorway. I'd forgotten about her. What was it Browne had called her? Kid? I was supposed to ask her some questions, wasn't I? I couldn't think what they might be. She stared at the blood with eyes wide with awe and horror, as if she was looking at the terrible slaying of an animal.

'Why are you still here?' I said to her.

Her eyes moved up from the blood.

'I cannot go, sir.'

She pronounced the words exactly, hitting the 't' and 's' with neatness. There was an African accent. I didn't know what country it was from. I could have asked her, but I didn't care enough.

'Don't call me "sir".'

She wanted something, but I didn't know what it was, and I didn't want to know.

'What shall I call you?' she said, looking directly at me,

175

arms straight by her side as if she was talking to a teacher or master or something.

'Don't call me anything,' I said. My face was cold and clammy. 'Just go.'

'I cannot.'

My head was light, floating up to the ceiling. My body was lead. I wondered if Browne had given me something. I was trying to remember if he'd stuck me with a needle. I remembered that something had been on my mind, but I couldn't get a fix on it. I could hardly stay upright in my seat. And the damned girl was there, staring at me, telling me she couldn't go. Couldn't? What the fuck did she want?

'Why?' I asked her.

I didn't hear an answer. I felt myself slump forward in the seat. I saw her hand reach out towards me. She touched my arm as I fell and hit the floor.

I woke with a start. Something was touching my right hand. It was dark and I was still light-headed. I wasn't sure now that it had been anything after all. A dream, maybe.

After a few seconds, or a few hours, I realized I was lying down. I was back on the mattress. I didn't know how I'd got there. The room was black. There was a weight on my chest. I wanted to sit up, but something was pushing me down. My left side was numb.

I lay still for a while, drifting in and out of sleep. Thoughts came to me, tangled with dreams, and were gone before I could make them out. But always, far off, was a feeling of doom, like I was heading for some black hole lying in the black night. It was like it had been all those years ago, walking through the fog, knowing that somewhere ahead of me, maybe only a few yards, soldiers were waiting to cut me in two with their automatic fire.

When I woke again, I knew what the weight was. I could hear her breathing. I tried to lift her off, but I didn't have the strength. She was facing my right side, my good side, curled up, her knees to her chin, her head on my chest. She'd placed herself as far from my damaged arm as she could.

I could feel her heartbeat in my chest. Her hand held mine. She murmured something. I couldn't hear what. She twitched. She was so light I could lift her up inches just by breathing in. She was thin. I could feel her bones digging into me.

I slept again and she became a part of the confusion, part of the knot of thoughts and fears, and even while I wasn't aware of what moved through my mind, I knew she was danger.

When I next woke, it was daylight. I had the feeling I'd been in and out of consciousness for a couple of days. My arm was painful, but the pain had dulled a lot. I tried to flex my fingers. They moved, but not much. They felt swollen and awkward, and I couldn't make a fist. Someone had pumped my hand full of hot water.

I remembered the girl sleeping on my chest. Or I thought I remembered it. I might have dreamed it.

I listened and heard nothing but the odd car rumble past. The house was quiet and had the feeling of emptiness. I stared up at the ceiling and let my head gradually clear.

A few hours later, I heard the front door open and close. Browne looked in on me as he passed the room.

'This time you stay there,' he said.

'How long . . .?'

'It's Sunday. That means you've been out a couple of days, in case you can't work it out.'

He carried on through to the kitchen. It took me a second to see the girl standing in the doorway. She had a strange way of looking at me, always with that amazed and scared stare. And there was something else, something that I didn't understand. She left then and came back a minute later with a mug in her hands. She came over to me, held the mug out.

'Tea,' she said, as if she thought I'd never heard of tea before.

I heaved myself into an upright position and took the mug from her. My throat was dry and my mouth tasted like something dead had gone to live there and died all over again. I gulped the tea. It was sweet, tasted good. When I'd finished, the girl took the mug and held it with both hands, her wide eyes moving from my battered shoulder to my battered face. I thought she'd shrink from the sight of me. I thought she'd move away in fear. Most people did, one way or another. But she just stood there, holding the mug.

'What do you want from me?' I said.

'Nothing.'

'Everybody wants something.'

She looked down at the mug in her hands.

'Why did you help me?' I said.

That question had been sitting at the back of my mind since the night of the shooting. I didn't know why that was. I didn't know why I'd care.

She shook her head a bit. She looked up.

'I'm sorry I shot you,' she said, as if that explained everything. 'I think that you will be okay.'

'What were you doing there?'

She didn't want to answer that. She didn't seem to want to answer anything I asked. Normally, that would have been okay with me, but this was different. The police were after me for multiple murder; Cole was after me for a million hard cash that I didn't have; Beckett and Walsh and Jenson and Simpson were dead; Kendall was dead; I was wanted by everyone and running out of money and, on top of all that, this scrawny child had put a hole in my shoulder that felt as if acid was eating its way through.

'Where'd you get the gun?'

'It was there.'

'Where? In the wardrobe?'

'On the bed.'

'Beckett's?'

'I do not know Beckett.'

'He was the man . . . he was the one called John.'

'John. Yes.'

'Was it his gun?'

'I do not know, sir.'

'Christ, stop calling me "sir". Why did you take it? The gun.'

She wouldn't look at me now. She gripped the mug tightly as if losing it would cost her everything.

'I was scared,' she said so quietly I could hardly hear her. 'I thought . . . I thought you had . . .'

'Had what?'

'Had come to take me.'

When she looked up, I saw that she was crying. She ran from the room.

Browne passed her on his way in. He looked at me.

'I told you to be careful with her.'

Christ.

'I'm going to need a new car,' I said. 'Clothes. A few things.'

'I don't have a car. And I don't think my clothes would fit you.'

'In my bag, there's money in an envelope.'

Browne's eyes narrowed.

'Money? Where'd you get money?'

'Relax. Some of it's mine. Some of it's stuff that they planted on me. That money's all in new notes. Don't take that, it's not clean. Take what you want from the used notes. All right?'

'Not clean?'

'The new money's traceable. Use that and we'll have the law on to us, and Cole. Get an automatic car. An old Ford or something. So long as it runs. I'll give you the name of a couple of places where they'll sort you out and won't ask questions.'

'Fine.'

'And dump the car I've been using. Take it to a railway station, somewhere a long way off. Buy a long-stay ticket. Buy it from a machine, don't leave prints on the coins you use. Watch out for CCTV; wear a hat, something with a wide brim – a baseball cap is good – keep your head low. Wipe the car down.'

'That's not going to help you, Joe. Your blood's all over it.'

'Never mind that. Take care of your prints. My blood's all over everything anyway. And take the girl. Give her some money. Lose her.'

'Okay, Joe.'

There was a noise behind him. She was standing in the doorway. She shook her head.

'No,' she said, 'I want to stay here.'

'It's probably for the best, darling,' Browne said. He reached out and took her by the hand. He bent down. 'I can take you to my sister's. She's a nice lady. She has a cat. Wouldn't you like that?'

'No. Please.'

She drew her hand in.

'Just take her,' I said.

Browne reached for her hand again. She snatched it away from him.

'No,' she shouted.

She ran from the room. Browne stood upright and sighed. I heard the girl run up the stairs and slam the bedroom door.

'Let her stay here for a while,' Browne said.

'It's better she's gone.'

'What do you want me to do? Kidnap her?'

'If you have to.'

He was quiet for a moment.

'She's safer off out of it,' I said.

'She is that,' he said. 'She is that.' He ran his hand over his head. After a moment, he said, 'I'll get you something to eat. Then I'll need to change that dressing. Then, you rest. I'll get those things done.'

After I'd eaten and Browne had gone, I leaned back and wondered why the girl wanted to stay. And I wondered why I wanted her gone. I still needed her to tell me what happened.

The house was quiet. I watched the room get slowly darker. I slept for a few hours. When I woke, it was fully dark. I went out to the kitchen for something to drink. Browne was there, sitting at the table, listening to the radio. He had a near-full bottle of Scotch in front of him. He saw me looking at it.

'Courtesy of you,' he said, lifting a glass in salute. He was drunk again.

'Did you get a car?'

'It's outside. An old Jaguar. How do you feel?'

'Fine.'

'I am, frankly, amazed at what punishment you can take,' he said. He didn't sound amazed. He sounded irritated that I was still alive. 'You know, I once thought you'd been pounded too much in the ring. There was a night, remember, when you fought that Gypsy monster. What was his name? Lawrence?'

'Yeah.'

Lawrence. Christ. The bloke wouldn't go down and he had a right cross like a tank shell. I'd won, but I'd taken punishment.

'I thought, that night, you were finished,' Browne was saying. 'And I mean finished. You were blabbering. Incoherent. You didn't know where you were. I thought, "That's it. His brain is mush." But I was wrong. You could take anything in the ring. Anything.'

I waited. I didn't think he was finished talking. He put the glass to his lips and poured some Scotch down his throat. Then he put the glass on the table and filled it again.

'You've been battered by life, Joe. That's your problem. You've been beaten, clubbed by it so long you've become insensible to it. You're in the twelfth, wandering around on soft legs, not knowing where you are.'

'All done?' I said.

'No. I'm not all bloody done.'

He brushed his hand lazily over his hair from front to back, assuring himself that it was still there.

'Kid,' he said, with his hand on his neck. 'There's something wrong with her. Not everyone is like you, you know. Not everyone is insensible. Some people get hurt by this bloody awful world.'

If he was trying to make a point, he was taking a long time doing it. He sat and stared into space for a few seconds. I waited. It was better to let him get it out of his system.

'It's not physical,' he said. 'I wish it were. But it's not. She's scared and she's been hurt. More than you ever were. She shakes, you know. She wets her bed. She's going to need help.'

He was right. The girl was fucked up.

Browne seemed to remember that his hand was still resting on the back of his neck. He pulled it away and used it to lift the glass of Scotch. Hands were useful for that sort of thing. He drank deeply. He got slushy like this when he got drunk. He usually got self-pitying too. I waited for him to list his failures, his regrets.

'I think she should stay here for now,' he said.

'Why?'

He put the glass down wearily, as if his arm, the glass, everything had become too heavy to bear.

'For some reason, she wants to be with you. Don't ask me to explain it. It's ironic, really. At least, I think it's ironic. In some way. I don't really know any more.'

The girl didn't come near me for a couple of days. She'd be there, sure, looking in through the crack of the door or standing on the landing, her face hardly above the banister, her hands tight on the rail, staring down, watching Browne and me from a safe place, ready to bolt into her bedroom if either one of us tried to go near.

We left her alone. I was itching to speak to her, press her for answers, but I was getting to understand how she'd react. Browne was keeping an eye on me, too, just to make sure I didn't frighten her.

We only really saw her when she came down for meals. Browne's cooking was hopeless, but he tried to do his best.

'I'm sorry it's not very good,' he said to her one lunchtime.

He'd given her macaroni cheese on toast. It was more macaroni than cheese, more toast than macaroni. The girl scraped the stuff off the toast and spooned some of it into her mouth. She chewed it for a while and swallowed and put her spoon down. Browne looked at her helplessly.

'Is there anything you'd prefer?' he said. 'What do you like to eat? What did you eat at home?'

'I like Egusi soup,' she said.

'Egusi soup?' Browne said. 'Egusi soup.'

So that was that. Browne went off to the library and got a book on African cooking. He spent half a day searching out the ingredients, trotting off to somewhere in west London, Notting Hill or Shepherd's Bush or somewhere. He made the soup in the evening and dished it up to us. It was okay. The girl enjoyed it and Browne was happy with that.

After we'd eaten, the girl washed the dishes while Browne dried. She sang quietly and Browne started to hum along with her. He'd had a few by then. He started to jig about. The girl stopped and turned and looked at him. I looked at him. His face was red and shining. He jigged a bit more and slowed down and stopped.

'Highland dancing,' he said. 'I used to be quite good.' He looked at the girl, then at me. His face got redder. 'Well, for God's sake,' he said. 'Haven't you ever danced? Didn't you take that lady friend of yours dancing?'

'No,' I said. 'But I probably should've done.'

Browne spent the rest of the day jotting down recipes.

I had the radio tuned to a London station and listened to the news every hour. There was something about a gunfight in East London, police calling it a fight between rival East European gangs. They obviously didn't know enough, but it sounded like one side could've been Albanian.

There wasn't much on the news about the Dalston killings. The law was sticking to the idea that it was a drugs deal fuck-up. That was good. It helped that Walsh had his habit – they'd found a load of smack under the floorboards.

They'd found Kendall and his wife, too, but they'd put that down to a robbery and they hadn't connected it to the murders in Dalston. Money and jewellery had been nicked from Kendall's house and I guessed that Paget or his men had taken them when they'd gone there. There was nothing at all about the two I'd left in my flat – Dirkin and that boy. I didn't know why that was.

The world turned on. I managed to keep breathing. But that didn't stop Browne eyeing me up all the time, checking my pulse, sticking me with needles, that sort of thing. It kept him busy. One time he got the girl to help change my bandages.

My arm got better. My head got worse. I didn't tell Browne.

We were sitting in the lounge, Browne and me, watching some programme on the box. It was supposed to be a comedy. It didn't matter what it was, it was just something that stopped us having to talk to each other. I was still too fucked up to do anything except sit there and try not to hurt too much. Browne's head bobbed and his eyes closed and opened.

We heard a noise and turned and saw the girl creep in. I glanced at Browne. He glanced at me. It was the first time she'd come into that room when both of us had been there. Browne made an effort and sat up straight.

'Are you all right?' he said.

She watched him for a while, like she didn't know what to make of him. Then she turned to me and it was like everything that had happened to her had gone from her mind. There was a blank look on her face, empty, like she was sleepwalking. Yes, she'd been hurt.

'Talk to her,' Browne said to me.

I couldn't think of anything to say. I tried. I said, 'I knew someone once who had hair like yours. Braided like that. She wanted to be a beautician.'

I waited for her to turn around and walk out or run out and upstairs. But she didn't. She just carried on looking into me, looking for something. I don't know what. I never knew.

After a while, the laughter on the TV got her attention and she turned towards it. She looked at the idiots on the box as they fell about and argued with each other. And then she smiled, and for a moment she was like a child again, with eyes that glowed, lit by something that had managed, for a while, to fill the nothingness that usually spread throughout her.

I had to remind myself that she was a child, not just like a child. She should've been playing games with friends, or learning something in school. Instead, she was on the run from whatever shit she'd had to live through. She wasn't a child, though, except in age. To have a name like Kid, that was the joke.

She came forward and climbed on to the sofa, next to Browne. He didn't say anything, didn't move. He pointed his face in the direction of the TV. Whenever the girl laughed, Browne laughed. I don't think he had any idea what the programme was about. When the girl was quiet, me and Browne were still, as if a movement of the air would destroy her.

So we all sat there. We were a happy family – Browne slumped, trying to focus his eyes on a swimming television, me trying not to bleed too much, the girl forgetting her horrors.

When the doorbell rang, we turned our heads as one.

'I'm not expecting anyone,' Browne said.

We sat there and waited for them to go. Instead, the doorbell rang again and we heard the flap of the letter box open and snap shut.

'The lights are on. They'll know I'm home.'

'Leave it,' I said.

The doorbell rang again. Browne drummed his fingers on his leg.

187

'I'd better go see,' he said. 'Might be a patient.'

'You don't have patients.'

'I've got a few elderly ones, from the old folks' home. I help them out a bit with small things. I need the money, Joe.'

He pulled himself up and padded out to the front door. I heard a woman's voice drift in. The girl was listening carefully.

'I hope I'm not disturbing you,' the voice said. 'I wasn't sure you were home.'

She had one of those posh accents that made her sound like she was ordering her servants about.

'I was out back . . . doing something.'

'It's been such a long time since we saw you last. Weren't you supposed to pop in yesterday?'

'Was I? Oh, I was busy. Tomorrow would be – '

'Anyway, I thought I'd come by, see if you were all right.'

'I'm fine, thanks. I'm a bit busy at the moment.'

'Can't have our doctor getting ill on us.'

The voice got nearer. The front door closed.

'What I wanted to say was that Mrs Clarke's hip is giving her some problems. She won't have it seen to, for some reason. I don't think she likes the idea of an operation. I thought you might have a word with her. I – oh – '

She came into the room then, followed by Browne. He wiped his hand over his head. She saw me and her eyebrows went up. She looked at the girl and her eyebrows went up some more.

'I didn't realize you had company,' she said, turning to Browne. 'Am I interrupting?'

'Well . . .'

She walked further into the room, smiling thinly at me, and

sat herself on the edge of a chair. She wasn't old, probably in her fifties, but she looked old. Her hair was straggly and grey, and her lips were thin, as if she'd spent too much of her time quietly pissed off with the world.

'It's so rare I venture this far,' she said to me.

Her knees were together when she said this, and she leaned forward a bit like she was getting ready to spring up and run out. She held her handbag closer to her. Then she looked at the girl and smiled. The girl watched her blankly.

'Hello. And what's your name?'

'Her name's Ebele,' Browne said.

'Ebele? Is that African?' The girl nodded. 'And how do you know Doctor Browne?'

'I'm looking after her,' Browne said. 'For a neighbour.'

'And this gentleman?' she said, looking at me, smiling nervously. 'Are you looking after him too?'

Browne did his best to laugh. His eyes flicked over my shoulder, trying, I guessed, to see if the bandages could be seen beneath the jumper I was wearing.

'Oh, I've known Joe a long time,' he said, relaxing a bit. 'He popped in to visit.'

'And where do you know Doctor Browne from?'

This she said to me. I shifted in my seat.

'An old patient,' I said.

'Nothing serious, I hope,' the woman said, laughing for some reason.

'This is Sue,' Browne told me. 'Sue runs the old people's home –'

'Nursing home, doctor.'

'Yes. Nursing home.'

'Unusual,' she said. 'For a patient to visit his old doctor, I mean.'

'Is it?' I said.

'One occasionally becomes friends with one's patients,' Browne said, eyeing me. 'All sorts of people.'

'The empathy, I suppose.'

'Empathy. Exactly.'

The chit-chat died out. We all waited for the woman to get the hint. Instead, she looked around at the TV, the carpet, the ceiling. Most of all, she looked at the girl. Her eyes kept going back to her, making the girl edgy. Browne saw it too. The girl's shoulders were hunched, her hands tightening into little fists.

'Where in Africa are you from?' the woman said.

'Would you like some tea?' Browne said to the woman.

'I do not know,' the girl said.

'Don't know?'

'I don't think she understands you,' Browne said. 'English isn't –'

'She seems frightened,' the woman said, looking over at me.

'I do not want to go back,' the girl said.

'Back?'

Browne moved his feet about and wiped his head.

'Tea?' he said.

'She said she doesn't want to go back,' the woman said. 'Back where?'

'To Africa,' Browne said. 'It wasn't nice for her, was it, darling?'

The girl moved her head from side to side. The woman's eyes went from Browne to me then back to the girl.

'Why don't you want to go back?'

'She thinks you've come to take her away,' Browne said.

'Why would I want to do that?'

'Immigration,' Browne said.

'Oh. I see. Don't worry, dear, I won't – '

She reached a hand out to the girl. The girl flinched and backed away.

'Sue, I hope you don't mind, but I really – '

'I am sorry I shot him,' the girl said suddenly.

'Shot him?'

The girl pointed to me and the woman peered at me like I was dying there and then.

'I want to stay here,' the girl said.

'Vivid imagination,' Browne said, 'children.'

'I don't understand.'

'Please,' the girl said.

Browne was sweating. He said, 'It's just her way, Sue. She's a little flighty.'

'She said she shot him.'

'Sue,' Browne said sharply, 'if I might have a word with you?'

The woman stood slowly. Browne led her out of the room. There was some muttering, mostly from Browne. At one point, the woman said, 'I understand completely, doctor.'

I looked at the girl and she looked at me. Then we heard the front door open.

'Whenever you can,' the woman said. 'It would be much appreciated.'

'Certainly.'

The door closed.

Browne came back into the room.

'Bloody woman,' he said.

He collapsed into his chair. The girl scratched her nose and went back to watching the TV.

'Is she a problem?' I said to Browne.

'Problem? She's a bloody nightmare. Nosy old cow. Nobody's safe. I pity those old folks. None of them have any privacy, you know. She knows more of their medical history than I do. Damn it. She'll hound me for months over this.'

'Will she call the police?'

Browne shook his head.

'I told her that Kid had come from a war zone, was still traumatized by it all. Not far off the truth, really.'

'And me?'

He hesitated.

'Did you know I was a prison doctor once?' he said.

'Right. An old patient.'

The girl laughed at something on the box. She was sitting back in the chair, kicking her feet.

'You were a big bloody help, by the way,' Browne said to me. He wiped his head. 'Bloody woman.'

We went back to watching the TV. After a while I heard snoring. Browne was asleep. The girl was asleep next to him, her head on his lap. I watched them for a while. Then I closed my eyes. She hadn't run off to her room this time, and she wasn't having nightmares.

So we carried on like that for a while. I was healing, Browne was staying sober, and we watched the girl get closer to us, like an animal inching its way forward, afraid but starving, edging slowly towards the hand of some stranger, ready to bolt if it was startled.

She started talking, too, but not about that night in Dalston, not about anything that was important. I let it go. Browne had warned me not to push it and I didn't think his loyalty towards a wanted criminal would stretch too far.

She told us something about her family in Africa, but it was always small stuff, never anything personal.

'My father worked in a field,' she would say. 'He used to grow cowpea and sorghum. My brothers helped him and my mother and my sister. I helped him sometimes.'

'Hard work,' Browne said.

'Yes. Hard work.'

Or she would tell us about her teacher and the things she had learned at her school. Browne had the idea of fishing out an old atlas he had and showing it to her, getting her to show him what she knew. The atlas was a couple of decades out of date, still had the Soviet Union, Yugoslavia, that kind of thing. The girl pointed to places and told us what she knew.

'The Mediterranean Sea is here, it looks like a crocodile's head. And Italy looks like a foot. Paris is the capital of Italy where the Pope lives.'

Browne laughed at that, but he smothered it and didn't correct her.

'That's very good,' he would say. 'You know a lot.'

'Yes,' she would say. 'And Scotland is here, I think,' she'd say, pointing to Ireland.

'Near there, honey. Near there.'

We both realized pretty quickly that she couldn't read much English. It didn't seem to stop her. She must've been pointing to the places from memory or sheer guesswork. This is Africa, here is the Nile, like that. Here I was born, here I died.

'What would you like to do when you get older, darling?' Browne asked her one time.

'I would like to be a doctor,' she said.

For some reason, this brought a tear to Browne's eye and he had to excuse himself and go get a drink or three. When he came back, he was carrying an armful of anatomy books and medical equipment. He showed the girl how to use a stethoscope, how to take a pulse. He gave her a book to look at, full of pictures of skeletons, organs, that kind of thing. He pointed things out to her and told them what they were, what they did. She listened, nodded, repeated it back, but we could both see she didn't understand what he was telling her. He carried on, though, for some reason.

I watched all this, waited for her to talk about something useful. She didn't.

Browne tried once or twice to talk to her about her family or about her time here, but she'd clam up. It was plain that she wanted to forget whatever had happened to her here, in London. Browne finally got the message. When he talked to her after that, it was about his sister's cat or his boyhood in Scotland. Since he'd done his dance, she'd become interested in all that.

'I did not know people danced in Scotland,' she said.

Browne brought out his old kilt and told her about the tartan and the sporran and that kind of stuff. He tried to explain about the clans and the history of Scotland. She didn't understand him, but she listened and he was happy with that. He showed her some of the dances, but he couldn't go too long without needing to sit down and refresh himself, as he put it.

194

On the third day, or the fourth, or maybe the fifth, we went shopping, the three of us. Browne wanted to buy some more of that African food and he wanted the girl to show him what to get. Or so he said. He'd been scouring his recipe book and had made a list of stuff. The list was two pages long. He went to the library and used the internet to find a shop in Crouch End, so at least we didn't have to trawl all the way over to west London.

The girl needed clothes, too, and other things. I needed some stuff, but Browne wouldn't get it for me, said it would do me good to get out of the house. So we went shopping. I had to fork out the money for it all because Browne was 'cash-poor', as he called it.

Browne waddled out of the house first, I followed, still a bit weak, and the girl came last, running to catch us up. Christ knows what people thought when they saw us swaying down the road. Browne lurched right, I lurched left, and the girl ran between the two of us, holding our hands, trying to keep us from falling over completely.

We had to use a bus because Browne was about three thousand times over the limit and I still couldn't drive. The girl told us she'd drive, but Browne wouldn't have it. I suppose it would've looked a bit iffy, but I had the feeling that wasn't Browne's reason for not allowing it. I had the feeling he wanted to get the girl out in the fresh air, as if he was introducing an animal to the wild for the first time. I think that was the real reason for the whole shopping trip. Anyway, we went by fucking bus.

Browne got carried away in the African food shop and bought enough to feed us for a month. Every time the girl pointed to something, he bought it. What did he care? I was paying for it. I think he forgot about my arm, forgot I couldn't carry all the shopping. By the time we'd finished getting everything, we had half a dozen bags between us. Browne struggled along with a couple of bags, his face red and shining with effort. The girl tried to help and ended up carrying his Scotch. Browne suddenly decided the buses were too unreliable and we got a cab which dropped us off at the corner of his road.

I saw the car as we neared Browne's. It was opposite his house, too obvious to be law or Cole.

Browne and the girl carried on, not aware of anything, but I slowed my pace and crossed the street and halted by a bus stop, dumping the shopping bags on the seat, using the shelter to conceal myself as much as possible. I turned once and saw that Browne was looking around for me, slowing up. When he saw me, I glanced at the car and he got it. He switched the shopping to one hand, took a hold of the girl's hand and carried on towards his house.

I saw a man get out of the passenger side. He was tall and thin and young, maybe late twenties. Then I saw the driver's door open and I knew what was going on. A woman stepped out. It was that woman, Sue, that fucking nosy posh bint who worked at the old people's home.

'Doctor,' she called out, waving her arm above her head as if he was a mile away.

When the girl saw her, she stopped and tugged on Browne's hand and he leaned down and said something to her. I watched them walk towards the woman, who smiled at the girl and said something to Browne, introducing the man next to her. He smiled at them both, but there was something shifty about him, a tension in his body that his smile couldn't hide. The woman pointed to Browne's house and they all went inside. I picked up the shopping bags and walked off around the block.

By the time I got back, the car was gone. It was cold, but I was sweating with the effort of carrying all that fucking shopping and my right arm was about to drop off. I don't know why I hadn't dumped everything in the nearest bin. It never even occurred to me.

Browne let me in, blowing his cheeks out.

'What did she want?' I said as he closed the door.

'To talk to me about Kid,' he said, walking down the hall towards the kitchen.

I dropped the shopping by the front door and followed him.

'Why?'

'I told you,' he said, as he sat down at the table and broke the seal on the Scotch, 'she's a damned nosy cow, wants to know everyone's business, thinks she can sort everyone out.'

He poured a large Scotch and gulped half of it down. I stood by the table. For a moment it moved away from me, it all moved away, the table, the room, Browne and all.

'What's that got to do with the girl?' I managed to say.

'She said she was concerned for her well-being. Said it wasn't a fit place for a child. I had to agree with her. She intimated that I had a drink problem. Bloody nerve. And she didn't like you either. Told me a child shouldn't be exposed to . . . well – '

'Thugs.'

'More or less. Frankly. She said she'd formed the impression that Kid was becoming unsuitably influenced by such company.'

I heard the words he said, but they didn't connect with any meaning. The room shifted again, I felt clammy.

'Huh?'

'You remember Kid told her she'd shot you.'

'Right.'

My head started to swim around.

'What's wrong?' Browne said.

'Nothing. Who was the bloke?'

'Her nephew. Apparently volunteers at a church in Croydon, Saint something or other.'

'What did he want?'

'Are you sure you're all right? You don't look very good. Is it your head?'

'What did he want? The nephew.'

'I don't think he wanted anything. I think she just dragged him along. He didn't seem happy about it. Poor bugger. Anyway, I told her I'd bring Kid to church next Sunday. I think that's all she wanted to hear, frankly.'

'Did they talk to the girl?'

'Kid, for God's sake. Her name's Kid.'

'Did they talk to her?'

'They tried but she clammed up.'

'Did she say anything? Anything at all?'

'She asked for you.'

'Me?'

'I told her you weren't here. She went up to her room. Now sit down, before you bloody fall.'

I slumped into the seat, sweat clinging to my body. Browne got up and filled a mug with water and slid it along to me.

'Stay put. I'll get us something to eat. You've overdone

it. Don't worry about Sue. I can handle her if I have to.'

With that he downed the rest of his drink and headed upstairs. I heard him wander about, go into the girl's bedroom, come out, call her name, call it again. Then I heard nothing for a while. When I opened my eyes, Browne was in the kitchen again, by the back door. He was closing it.

'Did you open this?' he said. 'This door. It was unlocked. Did you open it?'

It took me a few seconds to realize what he was saying. It took me a few seconds more to understand what he meant.

'Where is she?' I said.

'I don't know. I can't find her. Joe, did you unlock this door?'

'No. Did you see her go upstairs?'

'I . . .'

He ran his hand through his hair, panic in his eyes.

'How was she when the woman was here?' I said.

'She . . . she was scared, kept pulling on my hand, asking me not to let them take her back.'

'Back? Back where?'

'How the bloody hell do I know? Damn it.'

He burst into the garden. I could hear him bashing about with the bins, calling her name. I stood and the room spun. Had the girl come past me when I was out? I didn't think so. The back door was unlocked, but that might have been Browne's fault. He often forgot to lock it. I leaned forward and put my hands on the tabletop to steady myself. I had to think. 'Back,' she'd said. She'd asked Browne not to let them take her back. Back where? She'd been scared like that the first time that woman had called. Why? What was she scared of?

And if she'd run, hidden, where had she gone? Where would she go? I think I knew. I turned and staggered out of the kitchen and up stairs that twisted before me so that I had to stop and fall to my knees and hold on with all my strength.

When I got to her room, I went straight to the cupboard. I swung it open. There she was, curled up tightly, her knees up to her chin, just like she was when I'd found her in Dalston. Her arms were wrapped around her legs, her eyes were squeezed shut.

I put my hand out and touched her on the shoulder and she flinched. Then I heard a noise behind me. I straightened up.

'Is she okay?' Browne said.

My head spun and for a moment I couldn't remember what I was supposed to do. There were dead men downstairs and here was a girl and she had a gun. And then I remembered and I reached out again.

'No,' she said.

'There's something wrong,' Browne said. 'She's shaking.'

'Hey,' I said.

I grabbed her by the shoulder. She threw her hands up and pressed them against her ears.

'No,' she said.

'She was in a cupboard when you found her,' Browne said.

'Hey.'

'Christ, Joe. Leave her alone, man. Can't you see she's reliving it?'

Reliving it, reliving the past, stuck in it. Weren't we all?

'Good.'

'Good? You bloody heartless bastard.'

He tried to push me away, but he couldn't shift me.

200

'If she's reliving it, I can get some answers.'

'Damn your answers.'

'I need to know what scared her.'

'You're bloody scaring her.'

'People are trying to kill me.'

'Aye, and good luck to them. People are trying to kill you and you're trying to kill Kid.'

'I want answers,' I said, knowing there was something wrong with that, with me, with what I was doing.

'You don't want answers. You want to vent your fury, your wrath, like some god who destroys everything, innocent and guilty, anything to serve your will.'

'You don't know what you're talking about,' I said, but his words were catching somewhere.

Now he was trying to shut the cupboard door, his face dripped sweat.

'For God's sake,' he said.

'What is it?' I said to her. 'What can you hear?'

'It goes bang.'

'Bangs? Shots? You heard the shots? Did you see the ones who fired?'

Browne had given up with the door and was pulling at my right arm, trying with all his weight to shift me.

'You've lost control,' he was saying. 'You've been used and you don't like it. Do you, Joe? You don't like being weak and powerless.'

I grabbed her hand and pulled it from her ear.

'Joe,' Browne shouted. 'Joe.'

'Did you see the shooting?' I said to the girl, throwing Browne off.

'It went bang,' she said. She wasn't answering me, she was just talking.

Browne was right, she was reliving it. I don't think she even knew we were there. Something had scared her and she'd gone to a safe place.

'Hey,' I said. 'Hey.'

She screamed and I realized I was shaking her arm, shaking her whole body. My hand gripped the thin black wrist and I knew I could break it with a twist. She was still screaming. Well, her face was screaming, but I couldn't hear the sound of it.

Then something moved inside my head and the room shifted an inch and I looked around and it seemed like I didn't know this place. It was cold and dark and I couldn't understand where I was, and when, and that emptiness opened up inside me. I looked for Browne, but he wasn't there and it was just me and the girl and we were like we'd been before, and I started thinking about the money I was supposed to get, about the money and the bodies downstairs and Cole and Paget after me. Seemed like the more I moved forwards, the more I got sucked back. Always back.

I had to remember that I was at Browne's, but Browne was gone and I swayed for a moment.

Then I saw her, and her eyes snapped open and widened and she held her hand out to me and I thought, Christ, it's happening again.

I felt the splintering pain run through my shoulder, into my arm and I was back in Dalston, and she'd just shot me and Beckett was sitting downstairs with a hole in his head. And I couldn't escape.

Then something stung me and the floor came up and hit me. Again. I was getting to know that floor pretty well. We were old friends.

I opened my eyes a crack and saw smoke everywhere.

'You must be getting old, Joe,' Browne's voice said from a long way off.

I opened my eyes wider. The smoke cleared; the blurring faded; shapes became clearer. Browne sat on a chair and looked down at me. I moved my head a little and saw the girl on the bed, legs dangling, watching me, her hands resting in her lap. I half expected to see a gun pointed at me.

I hauled myself up slowly, resting on my side for a moment.

'Yeah,' I said.

'First you get floored by a small girl, then by an old man.'

I stood, sat on the bed, next to the girl, my weight pushing the mattress down so that she ended up sliding towards me. She didn't move, except to kick her feet a bit. My head felt like it was packed in lead.

'What did you do to me?' I said to Browne.

'Gave you a shot. Knocked you out. Had no choice.'

'My arm.'

'Yes,' he said. 'Sorry about that. I had to do something to get you away from Kid.'

'Right.'

'I'm afraid I opened the wound. But I've restitched it.'

'What did you do?'

He raised his thumb.

'Stuck this in it,' he said. 'Sorry. It must've hurt like a bugger.'

'Yeah.'

'Yes, well, you've only yourself to blame, you know.'

203

The girl said, 'Bugger.'

'Don't say that, darling,' Browne said.

'Yeah,' I said.

'What happened to you? Do you remember? You were acting like a madman. Attacking a small girl, for God's sake.'

'I don't know what happened.'

'Know what I think? I think you had a panic attack.'

'What?'

'I'm serious. You were looking around you as if you didn't know where you were.'

'I didn't.'

'Your head?'

'Yeah. I . . . got confused.'

'You panicked.'

'Maybe.'

Browne sighed, reached down to his bag, opened it and then paused and closed it again.

'Do you know what kind of damage you could have done?'

'I'm all right.'

'Not you, you bloody fool. I mean her. Kid. Know what kind of damage you could have done her?'

I looked at the girl.

'What did you mean, bangs?'

'Leave her,' Browne said.

'You heard the gunshots?'

'Leave her.'

'Bugger,' the girl said.

'Yeah,' I said. 'Right.'

We sat there for a while like that, Browne in the chair, me and the girl on the bed, side by side, her leaning into me, staring vacantly at the wall. I made to get up once, but Browne snapped a stern look at me and I carried on sitting there until the girl fell asleep, then Browne carried her to her bed.

She came down a few hours later, when we were watching an international game on TV. She rubbed her eyes and looked at us, then at the TV. She sat on the floor, cross-legged, and watched England getting hammered and it was like the whole thing a bit earlier had never happened. She didn't mention her fear of being taken away; she didn't mention that bloody woman. She didn't look at me as if I'd attacked her.

Browne told me later that he thought the girl probably hadn't even known we'd been there. He tried to explain it to me, what had happened to her. She'd had a flashback, as he called it.

'I think she's suffering from post-traumatic stress disorder,' he said, 'and she reverted to that moment of fear she'd had in that house in Dalston. Think of it like this: when she was scared back then, what did she do? She hid in a cupboard. And then, when she thought Sue had come to take her away, she got scared again – which is understandable, really, when you think of the kinds of places she must've ended up previously. So, she thought she was being carted off somewhere and panicked and hid in the cupboard. Then, in a kind of mental reversion, she was back in that house in Dalston with those killers downstairs. She'd gone back in time, you see? She was reliving the past. Do you see?'

Reliving the past. Yes, I did see.

'And you,' Browne said, 'you were back there with her, weren't you? For a moment, at least. You reverted as she did. In fact, it was probably her actions that caused your own reactions. That and your battered brain. You know, sad to say, I'm probably the sanest one in this house.' He looked down at his old hands. 'Aye, sad to say.'

So we carried on, like inmates in some kind of suburban refuge, each one of us more fucked up than the rest, each one relying on the others, needing them to get through another damned day without crashing and burning, without self-destructing. And, somehow, it worked. It was like Browne always said about my scars, 'It's the scar tissue that's holding you together, Joe,' he'd say. Well, we were scarred all over the place, and maybe it was that that kept us in one piece. So, we carried on. What else could we do? Life is carrying on. The world turns; we keep breathing. Or not. That's it. There's nothing more.

And we might have continued like that, the three of us. I might have forgotten about Cole and Beckett and the rest of them. We might have been like that forever.

But one morning I woke with a start. It was dark again. It always seemed to be dark lately. Something had clicked in my mind. It had been there for days, worming its way in. It was to do with what I'd said to Browne earlier about the money I had on me. I'd told him to take cash from the envelope because that was my old money, safe to use. The other money was the stuff that had been planted in my flat. I'd told Browne not to touch that because it was traceable.

And that didn't make sense.

I phoned Eddie at Dunham's club and told him I needed to see him.

'I wouldn't come around here, if I were you,' he said. 'Cole's been putting out feelers. He's already approached us.

He knows you and I go back. Might be that I'm being watched.'

'Can you get out without being followed?'

'There are ways. Say, the cafe – same as before.'

'One hour.'

I put the receiver down and looked up and saw Browne standing there watching me. He didn't say anything, just watched me and shook his head slowly. He turned and walked away.

TWENTY-ONE

We sat at the same table as before, each with a cup of coffee. Maybe the same coffee. It was gone midnight. There were more people here this time, a dozen or so, but the tables near us were empty.

This time Eddie was wearing jeans and a white T-shirt and, as far as I could tell, he wasn't armed.

'Well?' he said.

'It was something you told me. You said the money stolen from Cole's place was untraceable.'

'What about it?'

'You know that for sure?'

'No. But it has to be. Why would Cole arrange a robbery of that amount and risk it being traced?'

'He could have laundered it.'

'He could have, but why take the risk? Any other party you involve increases the chances of getting caught. And if he laundered it, he'd have to settle for half the amount he stole.'

'Maybe he only needs half a million.'

'No. Not if the Albanians are offering to Cole what they offered to us. I checked with Vic. It was a straight mill.'

'Maybe Cole had the other half already.'

'Not from what I hear. He's in debt.'

'Right.'

A couple of builders walked in. Eddie turned to look at them. They took a table at the far end of the cafe.

'Why do you want to know?' Eddie said, turning back.

'Those two men in my flat, the ones who tried to plant the money on me.'

Eddie was quiet for a while. A light flickered over our table and made the sound of a fly dying. Then, nodding, Eddie said, 'I see your point. That money in your flat had to be traceable, had to tie you in to the robbery, otherwise why plant it? But if they were using traceable currency, that would mean that the whole million was traceable – which wouldn't make sense.'

Eddie was looking at some sugar on the table. I was looking at Eddie looking at the sugar.

'Dunham owns a casino, right?' I said.

He looked up at me, leaned forward, elbows on the table. 'Yeah.'

'What happens if you have a bad night? If someone wins big?'

'We pay them by cheque, wire transfer maybe.'

'Always?'

'Not always,' Eddie said slowly. 'If they come to the table with cash, they can insist on a cash payment. It's their right. We wouldn't recommend it, of course, but once they're out of our door, we don't have responsibility for what happens to them. Some of our clients come from Middle Eastern embassies, companies, that sort of thing. They're often forbidden to gamble, so if they win, they want it in cash. Some want it in cash for other reasons.'

'So you keep large sums of money on site? Aside from anything you take on the floor?'

'Yeah. We have a contingency amount in the vault.'

'And this comes from a bank?'

'Yeah. Sure.'

'What's the procedure with the serial numbers?'

'We note the first and last numbers in each stack.'

'Why?'

'We have to. Insurance policy insists on it.'

'But after a good night, you'd have lots of cash from the casino floor. Maybe a million or more.'

'More.'

'If someone knocked off your place, what money would they steal?'

He was quiet for a moment, thinking.

'If they knew what they were doing, they wouldn't touch the contingency money. Too hot. They'd take the floor cash.'

'Beckett and Cole would know what they were doing.'

'Yeah. Which means that robbery was a huge cock-up and they stole the wrong money.'

'There's another possibility,' I said. 'They took the floor money and only a part of the traceable money from the contingency pile.'

'Why?'

'The traceable money was taken so they could spread it around my flat and tie me in with the robbery.'

The woman who'd waited on us came over with her pad and a pen.

'Can I get you gents anything to eat?'

Eddie, looking at me intently, shook his head. The woman sighed and wandered off.

'Okay,' Eddie said. 'They nicked the traceable cash only to

set you up. That makes sense. But how does that help? It tells you they've set you up. You knew that already.'

'There's more,' I said. 'The night of the robbery, I heard Beckett outline the plan. They intercepted the money after it had been boxed for the security company. He wouldn't have had the opportunity to fix the currency.'

'So what? Cole fixed it so that Beckett had inside info. Joe, you already know all this. Cole tells Beckett about the timings, the procedure, the security codes. You said yourself that this man Warren was a decoy, that Beckett already had all the information he needed because Cole had given it to him. Then Cole has a man in the casino that night to make sure things go smooth.'

'That's the problem. Cole wouldn't have arranged for Beckett to take traceable cash. Beckett had to do that on his own.'

Eddie sat back and nodded, very slowly.

'I see what you mean.'

'Cole is after me for the money, so he doesn't know that I was set up, so he doesn't know about the traceable cash.'

'I get it,' he said. 'There were two inside men. One there on Cole's part, making sure things are smooth with Beckett. The other working with Beckett, with access to the casino's own cash, framing you for the robbery and stealing from Cole.'

'Yeah.'

'Or maybe it's the same man,' Eddie said. 'Maybe whoever Cole had assigned to assist Beckett was working with Beckett to double-cross Cole and set you up.'

'No, too obvious. Cole would suspect him straightaway. It has to be someone else. Someone Cole doesn't know is involved in the robbery.'

'The third man. The one who took out Beckett in Dalston.'

'Yeah.'

Eddie picked up a spoon and stirred his coffee. He didn't intend to drink it, he just wanted something to do. He dropped the spoon.

'So, the question to ask is – who would be in a position to fix the money, knowing the robbery was about to happen?'

'No. The question to ask is – who could do that and be willing to screw Cole?'

'That's a good question. I can think of a few who'd want to screw Cole. Including me. As for who could arrange the fix, I wouldn't know.'

'Warren is the casino under-manager,' I said. 'Who's the manager?'

'Pat Garner. But John Thurber is Cole's business manager, and he would oversee the operations.'

'And Bill Wilkins is still Cole's number two?'

'Yeah.'

'Anyone else you can think of?'

'Not offhand. But that's a pretty good list.'

We sat quietly for a while, mulling over those few names. I didn't know anything about Garner, and I only knew a bit about Thurber. From what I could remember, he was posh, one of those smart criminals who liked to earn his money from crime then spend his weekends at the golf club, drinking with the chief constable.

Wilkins I remembered from way back.

Eddie said, 'You know what you're gonna do?'

'Find the money, kill whoever took it, give it back to Cole minus my end.'

'That easy, huh?'

'No. What do you know about Garner?'

'Not much. He would've known the routine and where the contingency cash was stored. I haven't heard anything against him, but you never know.'

'Where'd he come from?'

'Huh?'

'Where did Cole hire him from? I don't remember ever hearing his name from before.'

'Far as I know, he was hired by Cole for his experience in running casinos or something. Nothing untoward.'

'He might be bent.'

'He might be. He might be lots of things. He might have been coerced. That being the case, you would need to know who'd coerced him.'

'Yeah. What about Thurber?'

'Capable of it. Shifty and smart. Well educated. But I don't think so.'

'Why?'

'Too discreet. Too smooth, polished. Know what I mean?'

'No.'

Eddie smiled and shook his head.

'Sometimes I think you're pulling all our plonkers, Joe. Know that? You act like you couldn't spell your own name if somebody wrote it down for you. Look, way I see it, whoever's behind this is trying to seriously fuck Cole. That would take someone without fear, or someone ruthless, or greedy, or just plain fucking stupid. Thurber isn't any of those things. He's cautious.'

'And Wilkins? Is he any of those things?'

Eddie frowned and leaned forward and looked down at his coffee.

'He might be,' he said to the coffee. 'He's ambitious, anyway. He started out in north London. Went in with Cole a few years back.'

I'd known a few people who'd done jobs for Wilkins, but that had been a long time ago. For a while, it looked like he was going to be pretty big, but now he was working for Cole. That struck me as odd.

'Why?'

'Something to do with smuggling. Cole was into this and that, beginning to make a name for himself. Wilkins brought connections in with him and became Cole's number two. He has a reputation, though. In short, a bastard.'

He looked up from his coffee.

'You know, I still can't remember what they called you back then.'

TWENTY-TWO

When I got back, Browne was face down on the sofa, dribbling on to a cushion. Half his body dangled over the sofa edge; another inch and he'd be on the floor. I pushed him back on.

The girl was in the kitchen, lit only by the light coming through from the hallway. She was slouched at the table, her head resting on her arms. Her braided hair fell around her like a dark waterfall, lying in twisted silken cords on the tabletop.

She was asleep, her body rising and falling evenly. Her hand twitched and she murmured something. I didn't want to wake her. I watched her, though. Where had she come from? Why was she here? I didn't know a damned thing about her. How old was she, for fuck's sake? Older than she should've been, anyway.

I looked at her hands. How the hell could those hands even hold a gun?

I realized she was watching me, her eyes wide and bright in the dark room. She hadn't moved and, resting there, her face turned to me like that, she looked not like a child at all, but like someone tired of it all. I'd seen that look before.

I tried to think of something to say to her. Nothing came to me. I wondered why I was trying. I gave up and walked over to the fridge and pulled out a bottle of milk. I didn't want the milk, but I drank it.

'Did you see the men who killed Beckett and the others?' I said, my back towards her.

'No, sir.'

I hadn't expected her to answer me. I stayed as I was, with my back to her.

'What did you hear?'

She didn't answer.

'You hear the shots? A struggle?'

'No.' She said it softly, like a whisper.

'What happened?'

'I hid.'

I turned to face her. She was sitting up now, her hands still on the table in front of her.

'Why did you hide?'

'I was scared.'

She didn't see anything; she didn't hear anything. But she was scared enough to hide. That didn't make sense.

She stared at the table. She sat stiffly, as if she was being interrogated. And yet she could have left. That meant she wanted to talk. Did she want to talk about Dalston?

'The men who did the killing,' I said, 'I think they used silencers. You know what silencers are? It means the guns don't make much noise. There was no struggle. They didn't break in. If you didn't see them, how did you know to hide? Was it something else? Did you hear an argument? Did you hear threats made?'

She shook her head, her eyes not moving from the table. She was shrinking into herself, staring out at everything with fear. I'd seen that in the Falklands, on both sides. Young men, boys really, faced death and violence, and realized for the first time that it wasn't like in the films, that it was real and squalid and indifferent, and that morality congealed about it. They would sit there, those boys, their faces white and fixed, their minds turned inwards, a kind of self-defence mechanism. There was a danger the girl was going that way, closing up. If I wanted to get anything from her, I'd have to be careful. I'd have to be subtle.

'Your parents are dead?' I said.

She looked at her hands.

'Who do you live with?' I said. 'Who do you know? Where's your family?'

She still didn't say anything. She still looked at her hands. Whatever it was that had happened to her, it had been bad. She was too small to be hurt that bad. I realized that she was speaking, mumbling really. I grabbed a mug from the side, took the bottle of milk over to the table and poured her some. She drank. I sat down opposite her. I had to know what she knew; now was as good a time as any. When she finished drinking the milk, she put the mug down and wiped her mouth with her hand.

'When I was a child in Nigeria,' she was saying, 'we had a goat.'

You're still a child, I thought. She was quiet again. I waited.

'A kid is a type of small goat,' she told me.

She watched me, waiting for something. I said, 'Mmm.'

Just let her talk. Let her get to things in her own time. She smiled.

'That goat was funny. It would eat everything.'

She stopped there for a moment, maybe remembering the goat. I didn't think so, though, not with the far-off look that had crept into her face, the same kind of look that would cross Brenda's face sometimes.

217

'Goats do that,' I said, just for something to say.

She was a lot like Brenda: the fearfulness, the emptiness. And the same kind of strength, the same will to carry on and not let the lousy fucking world sink into her. Christ, she'd floored me, hadn't she? That was guts.

'When I was born, I was called Ebele. The father at our school told us that it means Kindness.' She said 'father' as 'fadder'. She pronounced each word carefully, like she was addressing the Queen. 'My sister calls me Kid.'

It was the most she'd spoken since I'd known her. I wanted her to continue. I wanted her to tell me what happened at Dalston. I wanted to know who had the money. I wanted to find them and kill them.

But she'd stopped talking. It was as if she were explaining to me something that she thought I wanted to know. There was a silence between us, a strange silence. It had risen from the ground and filled the room, as if the two of us were caught in it and the rest of the world was outside. She wanted something from me, but I didn't know what it could be. I didn't know what I could have to offer.

'How old are you?' she said.

I had to think about that a moment.

'Forty-seven.'

She nodded and her face showed concentration. She was taking it in like it was all vital information.

'Where were you born?'

'Tottenham.'

'Did you have brothers and sisters? I had two brothers and a sister.'

She waited for me to answer.

'I had a brother and sister,' I said. 'Both younger.'

'Do you love them?'

'I don't see them. I don't know where they are.'

There was something going on here and I didn't understand it. She was digging into me, trying to get somewhere, trying to get something from me. I didn't know what it was, or why she'd want to know. I could hear Browne snoring. We both listened to him for a while. She held the mug with both hands.

'We lived in a small village,' she said. 'I liked it. Did you ever see a small village? Did you ever see one when you were young?'

'No.'

'I liked it. Then my father became ill. We moved to Lagos. That is the biggest town of Nigeria. I did not like it.'

She shook her head, as if disagreeing with herself. She carried on for a bit, talking about Lagos and why she didn't like it: the smells, the crowds, the nasty people, as she called them. I tried to remember something from my own childhood, something I could tell her. Nothing came to me. It wasn't that my memory was bad, it was just that there was nothing there for me but empty spaces and concrete.

So I listened to her talking about how her brothers liked football and how her mother was good at cooking and I wondered if she'd have these memories when she was my age.

'Why are you here?' I said to her. 'In England.'

She looked down at her hands. There it was again, the closing up. I was no good at this sort of thing, blundering about. Every time I tried to get some information, she backed away.

'Do you miss it?' I said. 'Nigeria.'

She thought about that and her forehead creased.

'I miss the sky. There is a very big sky and it is blue. In London there is no sky.'

In London, she'd said. Not England, not Britain. I wondered if she'd even been outside of the city.

'I do not like London,' she said. 'But I do not know Tottenham.'

'There's no sky in Tottenham.'

I waited for her to say something else, but she didn't utter a word. She was staring at me now, waiting for something in that way she had, mouth open, eyes wide. Her braided hair was down around her face. Her small hands played with the mug.

My thoughts were muddy and wouldn't clear. The girl was the key, somehow. The things she said, the way she said them, the things she didn't say.

I was limp with fatigue and I felt useless. I was useless. The girl had made me so. I needed answers from her, but I didn't know how to get them. I couldn't use force. How could I? One touch from me and she'd break. I couldn't shout at her. The moment I raised my voice, or darkened my tone, she'd shrink back into herself. I couldn't threaten her. What did I have to threaten her with? And if I'd tried any of those things, Browne wouldn't stand for it; he'd be on the phone to the law in seconds. He was one of those who had ethics. And what could I do to Browne? He'd ignore a threat, and I couldn't kill him. I couldn't kill everyone, could I?

She'd poleaxed me once with a .32 slug and now she was gutting me with her silence. And I, who had never hit the canvas, never; I, who had ripped through banks and security depots and armoured cars; I, who had fought a section of

220

Argentine regulars to a standstill; I, who had ripped and destroyed and smashed anyone who got in my way, was being defeated now by this child. I was being felled by this clump of twigs, this shrub growing at my rotting feet.

I could hear Browne snoring still in the next room. That was how he preferred to go through life, unconscious of it all for as much as possible. It was an easy way out, a cowardly way, but that wasn't his fault – life had made a coward of him. Or so it often seemed. In fact, he still had things that he found worth fighting for. He was a Christian, or had been, or whatever. It was all that Scottish upbringing, rigid Protestant stuff and salt on his porridge. Sometimes he'd get moral and feel a need to do something good. Life had kicked him in the bollocks so many times he'd decided to hide from it in a bottle, but every now and then he'd emerge and go back for another kicking. He still had causes. I was one of them. The girl was another.

Life had hurt her, too, anyone could see that. But she wasn't going under. She had guts. Why? Was there a cause there too? Was she fighting for something? Or was she just fighting for the sake of it?

I had to get inside her mind. I had to root out whatever was hidden there, but how the hell did I do that? I'd never had to communicate with children. I didn't know how to do it.

She was smiling at Browne's snoring.

'I think that he is a good man,' she said.

'Who?'

'Your friend, Doctor James. I think that he is a good man.'

Doctor James. She was talking about Browne. I'd never known his first name.

'He's all right.'

'Why is he sad?'

'Sad? I dunno.'

She looked at me with those wide, starving eyes. I thought that if I didn't feed her something she'd close up on me. She wanted to talk, but not about herself. Maybe she was being subtle. Maybe everything she said was about her and I couldn't see it.

'He's had bad luck,' I said. 'Browne has. James, I mean.'

'Bad juju?'

'Huh?'

'Did he do something bad? Something wrong?'

'Browne? Nah, he just has bad luck is all. He's one of those people.'

'What bad luck?'

'He got fucked over, set up.'

She frowned and her forehead creased and she looked like a toddler trying to work out how to put that square brick into that fucking round hole.

'He got charged with a crime,' I said. 'Nicked. Arrested by the police.'

'A doctor?' she said, amazed that such a thing could happen.

'Yeah, he was a doctor then.'

'Was he a good doctor? I think that he was.'

'He was all right. Did well, small-time but okay.'

'What crime?'

'Rape,' I said. 'You know what that is?'

She nodded her head.

'He didn't do it,' she said.

It wasn't a question. She knew he couldn't have done it, just as I knew it. Some people you wonder about. Some you

222

know. Browne couldn't have hurt anyone if his life depended on it. That was one thing we shared, me and the girl. We both knew Browne. We both knew innocence. Maybe because we both knew the flip side too well.

'No,' I said. 'He didn't do it. Some bird . . . some woman, a patient of his, told the law he'd tried it on.'

'The police?'

'Yeah.'

'But . . . but didn't he tell them the truth?'

'Sure. But the woman had bruises and . . . well, she had some damage to her.'

'Yes,' she said, and I knew she understood what I was talking about. 'But they should believe a doctor.'

'Yeah, well, in this country, a pretty young woman in tears, and evidence of boozing, go a long way.'

'But he should have told them that she was lying.'

'He did. It sounded like desperation. In the end, he was found not guilty anyway.'

'The police said he didn't do it?'

'No. The law thought he did it; they always think people did it – looks bad if they nick innocent people. The jury couldn't reach a majority verdict – they couldn't decide – so he got off. But it was a muddy affair and mud sticks.'

'Mud?'

'Mud, yeah. Bad reputation. Like I've got.'

'What happened to James? After?'

'His practice went belly-up; he boozed. His wife left him and took half his money and both his balls. From then on, pretty much the only work he got was as a medical official at the fights, which is how I know him.'

She leaned forward, her eyebrows raised.

'You believed him, yes?' she said, and I could see that it mattered to her that I did.

'Yeah. Lot of us did. The bird's boyfriend was known to some of us. He was a slimy little cunt.' Her hand went to her mouth. 'Sorry. Anyway, we mostly thought this other bloke had done the raping, or him and the bird had hatched a way of getting money from Browne when they sued him. The boyfriend came to the fights once. He was pissed and maybe he was angry at not getting any dosh after the verdict. One of the other fighters decked him. He was laid out on the floor, a stretcher job. The only man who went to help him was Browne. You understand what I'm telling you?'

'Yes. There are good people.'

'Some, maybe.'

'And bad people.'

'Yeah. Fucking plenty of them.'

'Yes.'

'You sound like you know some,' I said, expecting her to clam up or run away or whatever it was she did to hide from the truth. Instead, she looked up at me and said:

'Why are you sad?'

'What?'

'You look sad.'

I didn't know what that meant. How could I look sad?

'Do I?' I heard myself say.

I was tired. My arm hurt. My head was muzzy. I was thinking that I should go and sleep. I didn't move.

'James said that you were a boxer.'

'Yeah.'

'I think you were a good boxer,' she said.

Her body moved back and forth in small jerks and I realized she was kicking her legs under the table. For some reason it reminded me how young she was.

'You think so, eh? Why? Why would you think anything of me?'

She shrugged.

'Did you have a nickname?' she said. 'Boxers have nicknames.'

I hesitated. I don't know why I did that. Then I lied. I don't know why I did that either. I said, 'No. I didn't have a nickname.'

'What . . . what did you do before you were a boxer?'

'Do? I dunno. Not much. I was in the army.'

'You had friends, yes? I had friends. I had one friend who was called Samuel.'

Then she stopped. She kicked her legs and turned the mug around and looked at the table. I think she was waiting for me to speak, to ask her about this Samuel. I couldn't think of anything to say. What did she want of me anyway? I couldn't get a handle on her, couldn't figure this all out. After a while, I said, 'What did he do, this Samuel?'

She smiled.

'He went to my church. He was a year older than me.'

'Uh-huh. Church, eh?'

'Yes. He was good at singing. Did you have friends when you were young? When you grew up, were you happy?'

She'd stopped kicking now, stopped turning the mug about, stopped everything. She looked at me with those large eyes, her eyebrows raised. She'd stopped everything except that look.

Did I have friends? Was I happy?

I used to listen to others sometimes when they spoke about growing up, when men from my platoon would sit in a crowded, noisy, warm pub and make cracks about the drunken pranks they'd played or the bird next door; or, when lying on my bed in the building site Portakabin, damp and musty-smelling, thick with smoke and cement dust, men from Leeds or Glasgow or Liverpool would talk about football matches they'd been to or scrapes with the law or some film they'd seen at a local fleapit.

I found myself telling the girl all this. I couldn't think of anything to tell her of my own life, of my growing up, so I had to tell her what I'd heard of others' lives. When I finished telling her, she nodded.

'I have heard of Liverpool,' she said. 'They have a football team. My brother had a shirt that said Flower on the back.'

'Fowler,' I said. 'He played for Liverpool.'

'Fowler. Yes. My brother played football. He was very good.'

I said, 'Uh-huh.'

'I do not know Leegs and . . .'

'Leeds and Glasow. They're cities in England and Scotland.'

'Scotland?' she said, a light coming into her face. 'Did they dance, your friends from Scotland?'

'No.'

The light in her face dulled, so I said, 'They might've done. I never saw them.'

'I think that they did,' she said. 'They might know James. They might dance with him.'

Then she was back to kicking her legs, only there was an odd rhythm to the kicks and I realized she was dancing, trying to imitate Browne's Scottish jig.

'Did you have friends when you were a boy?' she said, when she'd danced enough.

'I was never a boy,' I said.

That was a joke. She didn't smile. I think she thought I was telling her the truth, that I'd been made like this, old and battered, stitched together from used parts.

'Did you ever dance?' she said.

'No.'

'Why did you not dance? Did you want to dance? I think that a boxer would be a good dancer. Did you ever play football?'

Brenda used to say this kind of thing to me, ask me the same questions about what I'd done, what I'd wanted to do, to be.

And then I understood. I understood it all and I knew what the girl wanted from me. It was simple, really, and yet, for me, nearly impossible: she wanted me to tell her a story.

All that stuff about the goat, about her father's farm, about her brother playing football, all that was her story. And all the time she was being subtle and I, dull as usual, didn't catch it. The questions she kept asking were cues, and I kept missing them. I was supposed to tell her about my life, about how, as a boy, I'd played football and gone to dances with girls and been happy and normal. She wanted to live it, this normal life, for a moment, even if it was someone else's life she was living.

Yes, she wanted me to tell her a story, something about me, just like Brenda always wanted. They were so much alike, those two. Sometimes, in the night or in the darkness, when I was alone and the shadows closed in and surrounded me,

I'd think of Brenda and Kid, and I'd think of them as one person, and I'd think about how I'd failed Brenda.

'I don't care if you don't mean it, Joe,' Brenda had said. 'I don't care if you lie or pretend. Just tell me, promise me.'

'When I was younger,' I said, 'I liked making things with wood. I could have been a carpenter. I still can. I could do a course. They do courses in all sorts of things.'

'A carpenter,' the girl said to the air. 'They make tables and chairs.'

'You could be a dancer. You could learn Scottish dancing.'

'Would you make me a chair?'

'Sure.'

'Would you take me to dancing?'

'Yeah.'

She got up slowly and walked over and put her arms around me. Her head rested against my shoulder. I sat there stiffly, not knowing what to do with my arms.

'I am sorry for them,' she said.

'What?'

'I am sorry for those men.'

I took her by her shoulder and turned her to face me. 'Why?'

There was that look again, fear and something else. Not sadness, more than that. I'd seen it before in her. It had been there in the car the night she'd shot me. It had been there since, too, only I hadn't been thinking about her, hadn't paid attention to it.

She pulled away and ran from the room. I heard her bedroom door shut. I suppose I could have gone after her.

TWENTY-THREE

Wilkins, Thurber and Garner. Each of them had access to the contingency money in Cole's casino. Each of them could have known what Cole had planned with Beckett. Each of them was in a good position to double-cross Cole and work with Beckett to take the money and set me up. One of them was the man I wanted, I was sure of it. One of them had killed Beckett and Walsh and Jenson, and taken the money for himself.

How was I going to find out which one it was? If I could get to each of them, I knew I could make them talk. Trouble was, I'd never be able to get near any of them, not with things the way they were. They'd all be careful at the moment.

So I couldn't talk to them. But I could talk to someone else.

I found the road straight off and cruised past the house. It looked okay. I circled the block twice before parking my car along the street. It was dark and quiet. I hadn't seen anyone sitting in the cars along the road or standing watching the house. I hadn't seen anything prowling, lurking. I thought I was in the clear.

I was wearing the woollen ski hat and my heavy Crombie-type coat. I walked with my head bowed against the oncoming rain. To onlookers, I wouldn't be easily identifiable. My hands were in the pockets of the coat. My right hand gripped the revolver.

When the door opened, I grabbed the side and pushed with all my weight. The chain had been on but my force and weight ripped it from the door frame. I heard a shocked gasp and a muffled cry and saw a figure stagger backwards. I pushed my way through the door, closed it behind me and pulled out the revolver.

It took a moment for Warren to understand what had happened. He saw the revolver and reached automatically for the telephone. I slapped it out of his hand and pushed him backwards. I stepped on the phone, crushing it.

'Where's your wife?'

'You.'

'Where is she?'

'Up . . . upstairs.'

Mrs Warren called to her husband, asking him who was at the door. I pushed the gun into Warren's ribs.

'We're going upstairs.'

Warren winced, but didn't move.

'She's not well,' he said.

'I don't care.'

'She's pregnant.'

'Move.'

'Please. What do you want?'

'Move.'

'Please don't hurt her.'

For a moment, I didn't move, didn't speak. 'Don't hurt her', he'd said. Not, 'don't hurt me' or 'us'. I put the gun away, grabbed Warren by the shoulder, spun him round and pushed him towards the stairs.

She was sitting on the edge of the bed, tugging out hair

curlers. When she saw her husband walk through the door, she began to say something. She stopped when she saw me. Her face fell, all emotion wiped from it. She stood and lunged forward.

'Sarah.'

Warren reached out, tried to hold her, but she scrambled past him, batting him out of the way and was into me before I knew it. It was an attack like I'd never known. It was desperate and hungry and total. She scraped her nails across my face, both sides, again and again, trying to gouge my eyes out. I lifted my right up and blocked that side, but my left arm was still useless and she was drawing blood. She panted and made a weird moaning sound, and her face was vicious and terrifying. It wasn't human, it was animal. Warren stood in the centre of the room, still and useless, staring at his wife. He could've run. He could've done lots of things, but he just stood and stared. The rush of fury was staggering. With my right hand, I grabbed the woman by her blouse and pulled her forward. She lurched towards me and I shook her hard. She lost her balance enough to stop the frenzy for a moment. I couldn't do much with my left, but I could do enough with my right to make up for it. I should've whacked her, knocked her out. I didn't need a mad woman to deal with. I put my hand around her throat, just beneath her jaw, and squeezed. She went pale, looking into my eyes. She tried to knock my arm away. Warren backed away from us, finding a corner to hide in. I knew I shouldn't fuck about. I knew I shouldn't leave loose ends. I knew I should smack her down and have done with it. I held her tightly. She was fighting for her life now, a strange rasping sound coming from her mouth, her hands clawing at my arm. She was a pregnant woman. If I squeezed too hard, she'd lose consciousness. Fine. Just a small adjustment and I'd hit the pressure points and she'd be out. She might miscarry or something. So what? What was that to me? I'd killed already and was tied into that, if the police ever got me.

All I have to do is squeeze, I told myself. Squeeze. Wasn't that what Paget had said, his gun to my head? 'I'm good at squeezing.' Squeeze and she's out of it and I can get to the bottom of all this shit.

She clawed at me and her eyes bulged and watered, and her mouth made movements. She was trying to talk to me, tell me something.

Do it, my mind said.

I can't, it echoed back.

I let go. She staggered back on weak legs, coughing, gasping for air.

'Don't do that again,' I said.

She collapsed on to the edge of the bed. She sat for a moment and looked at the carpet. Her chest heaved and her face was streaked with tears, but she was oddly calm. She lifted a hand slowly to her hair, touched a curler and took it out. She reached down and picked up a brush. I stared at her. Warren stared at her. She took another curler out of her hair and slowly brushed it down.

I turned to Warren.

'I won't hurt you. I just want some answers. Then I'll go. Understand?'

Warren stared at his wife, stared at me.

'Please . . .'

232

'I'm not going to fucking hurt you,' I said. I was shaking. 'Okay?'

Sweat trickled down my forehead. Blood trickled down my cheeks. Warren was looking at me like I was unrecognizable, like I wasn't human.

'It was a set-up,' I managed to say. 'The robbery. Cole ordered it.'

He wasn't listening. He was watching his wife. She brushed her hair and gazed into a space between here and nowhere.

'It's the baby,' Warren said. He wasn't talking to me. He wasn't talking to anyone.

'Cole ordered the job,' I said. 'You understand?'

'Cole?'

'Your boss.'

'Ordered it?'

'Yeah.'

'I don't . . .'

'I was hired by a man called Beckett. He was hired by Cole.'

'I don't understand.'

She carried on brushing her hair. He kept looking at her, watching a car wreck he was passing.

'It was an inside job,' I said. 'You were a decoy. Cole used you to make it look like a legit robbery.'

My words didn't mean anything to him. He didn't care. I took him by the arm and led him from the bedroom. On the landing, I squared him so that he faced me, and backed him up against the wall.

'Listen to me. I need answers. Give them to me and I'll go. I won't hurt you. I won't hurt your wife.'

'You won't hurt us.'

'No.'

I could see his eyes clear. I eased him towards the stairs and followed him down. I said, 'Do you know a man called Thurber? John Thurber.'

'No.'

'Think.'

'I've never heard of him.'

'Tell me about Pat Garner.'

'Pat? What about him? What's he got to do with it all?'

'He's the manager, isn't he? Was he working the night of the casino job?'

We had reached the downstairs hall. I moved him into the lounge and sat him on the sofa. I pulled a chair up and sat opposite.

'I . . .'

'Was Garner there that night? Think.'

'No. He was off.'

'Why?'

Warren shook his head.

'My wife,' he said.

'Listen to me. Your wife's fine. I won't touch her again. I won't touch either of you. You won't ever see me again once you give me some answers. Someone inside your casino gave the robbers information. Now, why wasn't Garner there?'

'Just a normal night off. That's all. He wouldn't have had anything to do with the robbery.'

'How do you know?'

'He wouldn't.'

'How do you know?'

'He used to make sure nothing untoward happened in the

234

casino. He was honest. He cleaned it up. He wouldn't have been involved in anything illegal.'

'What do you mean, cleaned it up?'

'Look,' he said, 'I'm not saying Mr Cole had anything to do with it. You understand?'

'Fine. Cole's a saint. Tell me about what went on before Garner cleaned it up.'

'Some of the tables were rigged.'

'Who ran it back then? Before Garner.'

'Man called Wilkins.'

'Wilkins? He was the manager?'

'Yeah.'

That didn't make sense. What was Wilkins doing running a casino?

'When?'

'When was he manager? Uh, four years ago. Five, I think.'

'And now he's Cole's second in command, right?'

'I wouldn't know exactly.'

'Was Wilkins there that night?'

Warren thought for a moment.

'Yes,' he said. 'He was. He came in sometimes to hang out. He was there that night.'

'Could he get to the money the security van was supposed to pick up?'

'Yes. He could.'

Was that the reason Wilkins had decided to manage the casino, to set up Cole? That couldn't be it. Wilkins had been manager way back.

'Did Wilkins ever skim?'

'Oh, no. I'm pretty sure about that. I would've known. We

235

knew we were taking too much from the customers, with the rigging, and we were told to keep quiet. Well, I'm not going to make waves, you know, so I turned a blind eye. We all did. When Garner took over, it was a relief. I'm not a dishonest man. Mr Garner knew that if we were caught, we'd lose our licence, and he didn't think it was worth it.'

'So, Wilkins screwed the punters, but not Cole?'

'Yes.'

I thought about that for a moment. A bent casino. That was nothing new. The Sportsman had been bent, and I knew Vic Dunham used his place to clean money, and to take in drugs cash. The smart bastard even paid tax on it.

I had to know why Wilkins would be a casino manager. He had to have had an angle.

'What else did they do there?'

'When Wilkins was boss?'

'Yes.'

'I don't know.'

'Drugs? Laundering?'

'No, no. Nothing like that. Look, I didn't know about any of that, all right? They just ripped off the customers. Bent tables, plants in poker games, deals with some of the women, watered-down champagne. That sort of thing. Nothing very serious, and they never went too far. The public never got suspicious. We used electromagnets on the tables, small things like that. No one at the tables ever knew. We fixed the dealing shoes – cutting back on picture cards – and some of the slots . . .'

Warren rambled on for a while, but I wasn't listening any more. My mind was trying to make connections, stuttering

236

from one thing to another, and there was a mix of thoughts. Something was connecting, though. Something way back.

Warren had stopped talking and was looking at me, and his face was white. He edged back in his seat. He said, 'Jesus.'

It was dark at four in the afternoon, and raining. It was summer, or supposed to be, and I probably thought 'fucking country' or something like that.

There were a handful of customers in the cafe, all at tables, all by themselves. The strip lighting gave everything a washed-out greenish look. Everyone looked sick.

There was the fat woman behind the till and the young waitress in front, leaning back against the counter, staring at her feet. When I walked in, the fat lady saw me and said, 'Coming up.'

I took a seat by the window. The young waitress ambled over with a pot of coffee, her shoulders sagging with the weight of the hour, her feet making sticking sounds on the lino. She half nodded to me and put a mug on to the tabletop and spilled warm coffee into it.

Wind caught the rain a couple of times and lashed it against the plate-glass window. I remember that, the rain. Cars splashed through puddles and their tyres whirred and zipped with the water. People walked with their heads low and their shoulders hunched. Buses and cabs and cars had their lights on. Thunder rumbled, vibrating the window. It died down and the place was quiet again, nobody talking.

The door crashed open and two women burst into the cafe, their heads covered with their jackets. The sounds of the street came in with them, full of water and engine sounds. When the door closed it was quiet again and the sounds were outside and far off.

One of the women had short blond hair, shaved almost, and silverware in her nose. The other had straight black hair and thick black eyeliner. I recognized them. I knew what they did. They didn't work the Sportsman, but they worked nearby, around King's Cross. They shook their wet jackets and sat at a table near me.

The fat woman disappeared out the back. A man in a suit turned the page of a broadsheet. Someone coughed. I remember all this.

The women were talking about something, their voices low. I wasn't interested, but they were near me and the way they huddled close to each other, leaned over the table, gave their words urgency.

'Never catch 'em,' I heard the black-haired one say. 'They never do.'

A man in denims stood and walked over to the till. The fat lady came back with a plate piled with food. The food was steaming. She handed the plate to the waitress and went over to the till. She took a pad from her apron pocket. The man in denims had long, straggly brown hair.

'Fuck,' the blonde said. 'I can't believe it.'

The waitress dropped the plate on to the table in front of me. I was hungry. I cut the steak and watched some blood ooze out.

They started talking again. I tuned out. I cut. I ate. Blood came out. I heard phrases, words. I heard 'police'. I heard 'psycho'. I heard 'her body'.

239

Something was wrong.

I swallowed. I cut another piece of meat and put it in my mouth. The sky flashed and the windows shook from the crack of thunder.

I heard 'some alley'.

I stopped eating.

I heard 'razor or something'.

I heard 'couldn't recognize her'.

I froze, not looking anywhere, not doing anything, just hanging there like one of those drops of water that's about to fall from a leaking tap. It hangs there and hangs there and everything seems to stop. And then it stops some more.

I heard 'Brenda something'.

The meat in my mouth felt different; felt like flesh, not meat; felt like death, not food. It felt bloody and pulpy and disgusting and I wanted to spit it out.

Brenda something.

My insides knotted up. Something cold sucked on my guts. The blood drained from my head.

The waitress was standing next to me. I hadn't seen her come.

Brenda something.

'You want some more?'

Brenda something.

'More coffee?'

Brenda something.

'Are you okay?'

Brenda something.

'Is there something wrong with the steak?'

I can't remember what I did with the half-chewed meat in

my mouth. I swallowed it, I suppose. I can't remember much of anything after those words. I know I grabbed the one nearest me, the blonde. I know I shook her, shouted at her. I wanted her to tell me. I know I hurt her. I didn't care about that. I know people screamed and yelled and tried to pull me off. I know I wound up wet in the street and then I wound up being sick in a pub somewhere off the Pentonville Road. I threw my guts up into a toilet and then I rolled into a ball and felt the stale cold piss and water soak my jacket and my trousers and I didn't care.

They threw me out of the pub and I tried to get back in for more booze. I banged on the door and the barman or someone opened up and started to say something. I grabbed him and hurled him into a parked car and walked back in and ripped a bottle of cheap Scotch from the wall behind the counter, pulling down half the other bottles as well. There were a few others in the pub but nobody stopped me and nobody said anything. I left the pub and walked past the barman, or whoever he was.

I drank the Scotch until I no longer felt the acid burn as it went down. That was what I wanted, to no longer feel. I drank some more and then dropped the bottle to the floor and fell to my knees and held my head in my hands. I felt empty, weak.

I went to the Sportsman. I found Matheson. I grabbed him.

'What happened?'

'I don't know, Joe. Jesus Christ. Please.'

I snatched another bottle of Scotch.

I found another pro outside. I grabbed her.

'What happened?'

'You're hurting me. I don't understand you. What do you want?'

241

I didn't know what to say. I didn't want to say anything. I wanted to keep the moment held like that drip of water, stuck there. I almost cried, then I almost burst out laughing but I caught myself.

'What ha – '

My voice cracked. I took a swallow of the booze and felt the fumes come right back up and into my nose. My head hurt and I realized stupidly that my jaw ached from where I'd been clenching it and grinding my teeth.

'Was it her? Was it Brenda?'

'Please,' she said. 'Please, don't.'

I went back to my flat and wrenched up the floorboard. I took out the rag-wrapped bundle and opened it up. I had a Beretta then. It looked good. It looked sleek. I wanted it in my hand. I picked it up and it felt heavy, solid, like it gave me a purpose or something. I thumbed the safety off and on and let the clip slide out on to my palm. I checked that the clip was fully loaded and rammed it home. I jacked a round into the chamber, let off the hammer and slid the magazine out again. I took a cigarette package from beneath the floorboards and opened it up and tipped another round into the palm of my hand. I pushed this into the magazine and rammed it home. I wanted the thing full. I gripped the Beretta tight in my hand and tried to think what I could destroy.

I didn't want to think about her. A john, they'd said. Some psycho had cut her up. Carved her up and dumped her in an alley.

I tried not to think about it, about her, but the more I tried not to think about it, the more I thought about it. I drank straight from the bottle in gulps and it made me heave. My throat hurt from the throwing up I'd done earlier, but I wanted the pain. I thought the Scotch would help me not to think; I thought that it might blur things. It didn't.

I wanted to kill him. I didn't know who he was. I asked around. Nobody knew. I still wanted to kill someone.

I went to see Frank Marriot. His club was closed. I wasn't armed. I wanted this to be with my hands. I wanted to feel it. They tried to stop me. They didn't.

I found Marriot in his office at the back. He had some Polaroids laid out on his desk. Nice pictures of scared children. He said something. I don't know what it was. He seemed amused. He took his glasses off and wiped them on his tie and started to talk again. He put his glasses back on and pushed them up on to the bridge of his nose. I smashed my fist into the glasses. They shattered; his nose shattered. Everything shattered. I ground the glass into his eye. He'd stopped talking by then.

It took four of them to pull me off. By then, the damage was done. I don't remember much about it. I remember the blood. I was soaked in it. I remember the gore on my hands, the sound of bones cracking, his screams, the smell of his piss.

I heard he was in hospital for weeks. I heard he lost his eye.

It didn't make me feel any better.

I always wonder what it was she'd thought about when she'd been quiet and had that far-off look. Christ, I wish I'd asked her.

TWENTY-FIVE

I left Warren's and drove. I didn't know where I was. I didn't know where I was going, didn't care. I just drove. I didn't know what time it was. It was late, that was all I knew. Too late.

All around me now seemed grey and fogged and coated with soot and grime. The sky was grey. The cars, the road, the buildings were grey and shapeless, blurring into one. My life was grey. I was getting old. It began to turn dusk, or maybe it was the dawn. It didn't matter. The image of the Argentinian kid, dumped on the ground like trash, flickered in my mind. I shook my head to get rid of it. Brenda's face, bloody and screaming for me, came instead. I set my jaw and stared ahead.

I had to think things through, had to make sure I was right. I kept coming back to Dalston – the way the house had looked, the way Beckett and Walsh and Jenson had been killed, the way the locks were off and they'd been relaxing, watching TV, drinking beer. Cole hadn't killed them, I was sure of that. Beckett had done the job for Cole but then double-crossed him. He was in league with someone else, someone close to Cole. Whoever it was, Beckett would have been careful about handing the money over. He would have arranged the time and place. He would've been ready. He wasn't a stupid man. The night he was killed, he wasn't ready. He'd been surprised.

I kept thinking about the girl, too. The way she acted, the way she was scared, the way she looked at me. That look. It bothered me.

There was something else. It was what she'd said. 'I am sorry for those men.' She'd said it so quietly that I hadn't been able to make out the tone she'd used.

I was thinking now that I'd been wrong about a lot of things.

It was the look. Something in the look she'd given me. There was the key. She was the key.

The more I thought about it, the more I knew I was right.

When Browne saw the scratches on my face, he swore at me.

'I don't know why I bother,' he said.

I didn't know either. He went to get some gauze and antiseptic cream, but I told him to leave it.

'Those were done by a woman,' he said.

I agreed.

'Where's the girl?' I said.

He didn't answer me. He was suddenly fearful. He put a hand out towards me. I don't think he knew he'd done it. Above us, at the top of the stairs, a shadow moved. I looked up. The girl clung to the banister, her head no more than a foot above it. She peered down at us. Her eyes were large, but not from fear. She was looking at me with wonder, and for a second she was gone and I saw Brenda's face.

I hesitated.

'Don't,' Browne said.

He seemed to know what I was thinking. Maybe he saw something in my face. Maybe he just feared me with her. I eased him aside and walked heavily up the stairs. The girl watched me climb. I felt a hand on my arm. Browne was holding me with all his strength, trying to pull me back. I lost balance and back-stepped. I could have broken his hold on me easily enough. I could have pushed him aside and taken the girl and shaken it out of her.

'I'm only going to talk to her,' I said.

'She's just a girl.'

'She killed them,' I said.

'What?'

'Beckett, Walsh, Jenson.'

All the time she was watching us. She had the same expression on her face, but now it seemed not a look of wonder, but rather a look of nothing. She looked hollow.

Browne reached up, grabbed weakly at my chest.

'She's just a girl.'

'She killed them. Not with a gun, but she killed them all the same.'

His head waved from side to side.

'You can't know that,' he said. 'You can't know.'

'I know.'

'How can you? How can you be certain?'

'Her hair.'

'What? What are you talking about?'

'It's braided.'

He looked at me for a long time, his eyes holding on to mine, searching them.

'You're insane,' he said finally. He believed it.

I was tired of it all, worn out. Insane, Browne called me. The whole thing was insane. Maybe I was, too. I felt it.

'Someone braided her hair.' I said. 'You can't do it by yourself. I think it was someone close to her. But when she was here, she didn't try to call anyone, she didn't ask us to take her somewhere, she didn't try to go home.'

'They were too far away,' he said.

'No. She'd still try and contact this person. You said it yourself, the girl has suffered. Being stuck with an old drunk and a thug isn't any place for her to be. She'd go to the police, or ask us to take her, or go get a cab, or try to walk home. Or something. But she did nothing.'

I looked up at the girl. Browne looked up. There were tears in her eyes. I knew I was right. His hand dropped away from my chest. He knew it too.

'You're going round in circles,' he said. 'You say she's close to someone, but then you say she doesn't want to go to them. That's a contradiction.'

'No, it isn't. It means the person she's close to is close to someone she doesn't want to be anywhere near.'

'What the bloody hell has all that got to do with those murders?'

'You remember when that woman came over, the second time?'

'You mean Sue? What about her?'

'What did the girl do?'

'She hid. In the cupboard.'

'Right. Just like in Dalston. Remember what you told me? She was reliving it.'

'Post-traumatic stress. Nothing unusual in that. She was scared and she did what she'd done previously.'

'Think about what she said to you, the girl. What did she tell you? Why was she scared?'

'She asked me not to let them take her away,' he said.

247

'No,' I said. 'She asked you not to let them take her *back*. There's a difference. She was only scared of being taken away because she thought she would be taken *back*.'

'Yes. So?'

'Back where?'

Browne looked at the girl. She looked at him.

'I don't know,' he said. 'I don't understand any of it. I don't understand you, Joe.'

'She didn't want to go back to where she'd come from, back to the ones who'd sent her.'

'I don't understand,' he said weakly.

'Christ. She hid in the cupboard at Dalston because she feared the men who were coming would take her back. You understand now? She knew the men who were coming to the house. She knew them. She knew they were coming because they were from the same place she was, the place she didn't want to go back to. Put that together with everything else: she didn't see the gunmen, she didn't hear them, and yet she knew to hide in the cupboard; she knew to have a shooter handy and to use it on whoever opened the cupboard door.'

'You don't know what you're talking about. Are you listening to yourself? One second you say she killed them, the next you say she hid from the gunmen.'

'Beckett, Walsh and Jenson were killed where they sat. They hadn't had time to react because they didn't know the killers were in the house. There was only one way for that to happen – somebody else let the killers in. She was the only other one in the place. She opened the door for the killers, then went upstairs to hide.'

He opened his mouth, then closed it. He put a hand on the

wall to steady himself.

'She's just a girl, man.'

'Beckett had a thing for girls. It was easy to plant her on them.'

'But why? Why would she do it?'

'Because she had no choice. Ever noticed how she talks about her family in the past tense, except for her sister?' I looked up at the girl. 'It's your sister they've got, isn't it?'

Her head moved a bit up, a bit down.

'My sister.'

'And you had to telephone a number, give them an address?'

She shook her head.

'No, sir.'

'No,' I said. 'They would have known the address. They probably sent Beckett there.'

'They gave me a telephone. My sister called me and told me what to do. I had to unlock the door and open it for them. She told me to do that. She told me to hide because the men would want to bring me back with them. I didn't hear anything. I thought everyone had gone. I went downstairs.'

'You saw them, darling?' Browne said. 'The dead men?'

'Yes.'

'Why didn't you run?' I said.

'There was banging on the door. Loud bangs. I was scared. The door was breaking. I ran back upstairs.'

Those bangs had been my bullets.

'That's why you were afraid to say anything?' Browne said to her. 'Because of what they made you do?'

'They said they would hurt her,' she said quietly.

'And I thought it was trauma,' he said.

249

'It is trauma,' I said.

'Christ. Who was it?' Browne said. 'What bloody monster could use a bairn like that?'

'There are people.'

'I'm sorry I hurt you,' she said. 'I was scared.'

'It doesn't matter.'

She whispered something I didn't hear.

'What?'

'You saved me,' she said, wiping her nose with the back of her hand. 'You saved me from them. I was scared. And you came and saved me.'

And then I understood. And Browne, looking at me with a kind of sadness, understood too. It was funny, in a terrible way.

'I didn't save you,' I told the girl. 'I never knew you were there. I went to that place to get some money and to kill some men.'

There I was explaining myself. Fuck the girl. Fuck what she thought.

'Let her believe it, man,' Browne said to me. 'For God's sake, can't you let her believe in something good? Even if it's you.'

He looked older. He looked like his insides had collapsed. He leaned back against the wall, not even trying to stop me now. I didn't move. The girl didn't move. Browne didn't move. We all just hung there, like that fucking drop of water.

'The poor girl,' he said. 'I can't – '

That was when the front door exploded.

They were on us in seconds, bursting in like rats, pouring over each other to get to us. Browne cried out and tried to block them. He lasted a second, less. He was hit and fell and was kicked. I saw him go limp. I heard the back door smash open. I threw one off me and started to climb the stairs. I felt punches on my body as a couple of men threw themselves at me and clung on. I threw out my elbow and heard cartilage crack. I reached round and grabbed hair and yanked it and heard a scream. I smashed a face into the stairs. There were no knives, no guns. They'd been told to take me alive. I couldn't stand and fight: there were too many. I looked up. Kid was frozen, clinging to the banister, her knuckles pale, her mouth open, her eyes wide, her chest heaving. I stumbled up the stairs, kicking out, throwing my arms back in a desperate attempt to get to higher ground. I got closer. I didn't look back. I knew I wouldn't make it. The girl had a chance, though. They were all over the stairs, reaching up for me, grappling for my shirt, my jacket. I leaned forward, touched the stairs with my good arm. I felt them crawl up on to my back. I pushed back with all my strength, roaring with the effort, flinging back my arm, my head. I heard shouts and cries and felt them fall off me. I was free of them for a moment. It wasn't much, but it was enough. I staggered up the rest of the stairs and reached the top. I grabbed Kid and lurched into the bedroom. I threw open the window, lifted her through and dangled her below me. I was leaning as far over as I could so that she was only ten feet or so from the ground. She tried to cling to me but I shook her off and tossed her into the bushes. She cried out as she landed, but she was okay. She got to her feet and stood below the window and looked up at me, lifting her hands as high as she could.

'Run,' I said. 'Go to your sister.'

'Please – '

'Go.'

She didn't budge. They were almost on me.

'I'll come for you,' I said. 'RUN.'

When I turned, they were all over me.

TWENTY-SIX

I was in a warehouse, or some kind of workshop. I had no idea what time it was. There were no windows. The strip lighting was bright and made my eyes hurt. It felt like night. There was a long metal bench along the wall to my right with cardboard boxes beneath. Tools and cans of oil and stuff like that were spattered around. I turned my head as far as I could. The far end was in shadow. I couldn't see the door.

I was in a chair, one of the type used in offices with thick plastic armrests and chrome legs. The chair was small for me, but strong. I pulled against the ropes around my wrists and ankles. They didn't give, not a millimetre.

My head felt light and dull. It was good that it didn't hurt. It was bad that I was woozy. I didn't know what they'd used. Chloroform, probably.

I wanted to close my eyes and sleep. I wanted to close my eyes and not wake up, not have to deal with this shit, with this world. I couldn't afford to feel like that. I fought it, biting my lip and tasting blood. I pulled against the ropes, knowing it was useless but trying to build up the rage, get the adrenalin going.

A door opened somewhere behind. I felt the chill of air on my neck. I was cold with sweat. Men walked in. If I'd been thinking more clearly, I would've feared what was to come. I knew I should've done, and yet I didn't. I seemed away from it all, as if I could stand back and watch myself. I knew I was probably going to die, but the thought didn't mean anything to me; it was just an idea. I tried to make myself think about it, about my death. I should have felt terror or panic or some-thing, but I didn't, and it occurred to me that I didn't care that much anyway. The door closed. I braced myself.

Two men, both in suits, walked to positions in front and to either side of me. I didn't know these men. One was lean and blond and in his forties. He was sinew and tight muscle. The other was shorter and younger with brown hair and a stud earring. The men stood looking down at me. I knew the game. I'd stood where they stood.

I heard another man walk towards me. These two were waiting for him. He came forward and stood between them, facing me. He was short and his stocky build was edging towards fatness, stretching the suit he wore. His square face shone with grease and sweat so that it looked as if, with effort, he was trying to contain himself. He had a nice tan and an expensive haircut, but they couldn't hide his sixty-odd years.

I'd never met him, but I recognized him. His name was Bobby Cole.

'You've caused me a lot of fucking trouble, boy,' he said.

He tapped Blondie.

'Which arm?'

'Left. Around the shoulder.'

Cole looked around the room and wandered off for a moment. The other men didn't move, didn't take their eyes off me. When Cole came back, he had a ball hammer and I started to panic and felt my balls tighten and my stomach sink and the cold sweat break over me because I knew what was coming. He smashed the hammer into my left shoulder. The pain made me gasp; it spread through me and split me apart. I stretched the ropes with the agony. It was good. The anger, the rage, the need to destroy spread with the pain. The three men stood back and waited. I felt faint, but the adrenalin was flowing. I was soaked in sweat. I leaned my head forward and threw up on to the floor in front of me and over the seat. Blood leaked down my arm.

'Where's my fucking money?'

I shook my head. I thought I was going to pass out. I couldn't speak. Cole wasn't stupid. He gave me a minute. He didn't want a corpse. Not yet, anyway.

'Where is it?'

'Haven't got it.'

Cole sighed.

'Hit him.'

The man with the earring stepped forward and planted a quick left-right combination on my face. They were powerful punches, short and sharp. He knew what he was doing, but I'd taken that kind of stuff all my life.

'Where is it?'

'Beckett took it.'

'I know Beckett fucking took it. I hired the cunt to take it.'

'He set me up.'

'Bollocks. Hit him.'

I took some more pounding. It was okay, but it wouldn't be if they kept it up.

'I did the job. He took the money.'

He lurched forward, his hands on my wrists, squeezing them.

'Bollocks, you cunt. I know you and Beckett and Kendall fucked me over. And I know you fucked them over. You think you can kill 'em and you're safe? Huh? You ain't fucking safe from me. I'm going to rip your fucking limbs off if you don't tell me where my money is right fucking now.'

He was in my face now, his eyes bulging and watery, phlegm in the corners of his mouth, and I thought, Christ, he's panicking. He was shitting himself and that was bad. He wasn't thinking clearly. My arm was a nightmare of pain and my head throbbed with dullness. He wasn't going to believe my story. I wouldn't believe it. I had no choice.

'I can prove it,' I said.

'Fuck your proof. Give me my money, or tell me where it is, and maybe I'll let you live.'

That made me laugh. I don't know why. It wasn't funny.

'You'll kill me whatever I say. You'll have to. Now, we can make this hard for both of us, you beating me, me telling you I was set up. Or you could shut the fuck up for a minute and listen.'

He stood back and watched me. He breathed heavily through his mouth. Sweat trickled down his cheek. Blondie and Earring stood by and waited. Finally, Cole let out a long breath. He clenched his jaw. He was calming down, reason finally getting through some of the panic.

'You've got bollocks, boy, I'll say that.'

'Untie me.'

'You must think I'm some daft cunt. Is that what you think, eh? You think I'm a cunt?'

'I don't know you well enough.'

Earring gave me a right to the jaw for that. I could taste

blood. Cole watched while I spat it out. He eyed me curiously, though. I had him thinking.

'Untie me,' I said again.

'So you can clobber me? Forget it.'

'I'm not going to sit here and wait for you to put a bullet in my head. If you want me to talk, untie me.'

'I'll get you talking. Don't worry about that.'

If I could get him to untie me, I had a chance. Not much, but some.

'You're tooled up,' I said. 'I'm not. I can't do anything without getting shot. You can try and make me talk all night and I'll tell you the same thing: I didn't take your money. I'm not getting killed tied to a chair.'

I could see in Cole's face that he was weighing up what I'd said. He was more desperate than I'd thought. They were closing in on him. Sweat beaded his upper lip.

'You don't have all night, do you?' I said. 'You've run out of time.'

Earring and Blondie glanced at each other. They were nervous. Cole's whole firm was just about holding it together, from what I could see. If he had limitless time to make me talk, I had no chance. He'd sit back and let his boys work on me. But if I was right, he didn't have limitless time.

'The longer you keep me tied up, the more I'll stall. I don't know how long I can last. I might go the distance. I've done it before.'

He took a handkerchief from his jacket pocket and wiped the sweat from his face. When he did that, I knew I had him. He couldn't get heavy with me for fear of my passing out. He couldn't knock it out of me quickly because I'd hold on as long as possible and I was used to twelve rounds of punishment. He wiped the phlegm from his mouth.

'Untie him,' he said to Earring. To Blondie, he said, 'Watch him.'

Blondie pulled a semi-auto from a shoulder holster. He took a few steps back and levelled it at me, hip-high, while his mate untied the ropes and moved out of range. I rubbed my ankles and wrists.

I tried to stand, but my legs buckled and I hit the floor hard. I stayed there for a few seconds, on my knees, forehead to the floor, trying to get some blood to my head. The pain throbbed through my shoulder.

'Help him, for Christ's sake.'

Earring stepped forward, but I shook him off and stood. He flinched, taking a step back, ready to spring at me. I looked at Blondie. He seemed calm enough. I didn't want that 9-mil going off in my face. My head had cleared a little. The adrenalin had done that, making my heart beat faster, making the oxygen in my blood flow to my brain. I was thinking better. I stretched my back and looked behind me and saw a large metal roller-door, big enough to let a mid-sized truck through. Next to that was a metal-backed door for people to use. Both were shut and probably locked. I couldn't see another exit. Blondie was out of reach on my right, keeping back, but he was holding the gun in his right hand and if I could make a second for myself and spin left I might be able to hit him in the carotid before he could bring the gun round.

'I'm waiting,' Cole said.

'You hired Beckett to knock off your casino. He hired me, through Kendall.'

'I know that. What of it?'

'Why did Beckett want me? He had his usual crew; he had Simpson for the heavy stuff. They wanted me for a different reason: to fit me up. But that didn't make sense. Why would Beckett bother to stick me with the blame for ripping you off? He would've known you'd still want your money back and when you found out I hadn't got it, you'd go after him.'

'I was after Beckett from the word go. You think I'm stupid enough to think a dumb fuck like you's gonna out-think Beckett?'

'You were stupid enough to hire him,' I said. I expected Cole to explode. He didn't. 'You didn't choose him, did you?'

'You're boring me.'

'It wasn't about the money. Beckett didn't rip you off for a million cash.' The corner of his eye flickered. 'Am I still boring you?'

Slowly, in a voice that sounded like far-off thunder, he said, 'Go on.'

'He didn't care about the money. He had a million quid, untraceable. He could've hightailed it to Ireland, or Scotland or Spain. But he stayed in London.'

'Why?'

'Because he wanted you wasting time. He was waiting. And he thought he didn't have long to wait.'

'Waiting for what?'

He kept his eyes on mine, and they were cold and his eyelids were half closed, as if he was having trouble staying awake, but behind all that there was a kind of murder bubbling slowly and I could understand why people were afraid of him; and

259

I had the feeling that he knew the answer already, had known for a long time.

'He was waiting for you to die,' I said. 'Waiting for the Albanians to finish you off.'

Earring twitched and, from the corner of my eye, I saw Blondie wipe a hand over his mouth. I tensed for an instant, moved on to the balls of my feet. Cole kept his eyes on me. It was a chance, an opening. I might not get another. Drop the left shoulder, spin round left in a curl, right foot out, right arm through the air, hand, palm-up, chopping on Blondie's carotid. He'd drop like that, and I'd have the 9-mil before the others could react.

I watched Cole. He didn't seem to be aware of any of us. Blondie could've handed the gun to me and Cole wouldn't have cared. I knew then I had nothing to fear from him. I let go of the idea of fighting my way out of this.

'Albanians,' he said.

'I heard on the news about a gunfight. That was the Albanians, wasn't it? They're after you.'

'Yeah.'

'It was a hit,' I said. 'On you. A takeover. A coup. The whole thing.'

He nodded, but his face was grim.

'Who?'

'Who suggested Beckett?' I didn't need him to answer that. I needed him to start thinking. 'It was Wilkins, wasn't it?'

'What makes you think that?'

'He was there the night of the job, in the casino. He could've fixed it so the traceable cash was fed to Beckett who gave it to Kendall who used it to set me up.'

'It's not Wilkins,' he said.

'He's taking over your firm.'

'He's not taking over my firm. He's not going to do anything again. We found his body yesterday.'

Christ. If Wilkins was dead . . .

I had to think. The pain in my shoulder was easing up, but my head was getting cloudier. It felt to me like the air was getting thicker, closing in on me. I flexed my arm as best I could. Earring shifted his balance; Blondie brought the gun up and lowered it when he saw I wasn't going to strike. They were uneasy, these two. If the rest of Cole's men were like this, he was in trouble.

'Who killed Wilkins?' I said.

'Fucking Albanians. Who else?'

'Paget.'

'What?'

'It must've been. I thought Wilkins was using Paget. I was wrong. Paget was using him.'

'The fuck you on about?'

'You sent Paget to find me.'

'What of it?'

'Did you send him to kill me?'

'Course I fucking didn't. Why would I do that? I wanted you alive.'

'In Islington, Paget caught up with me, tried to take my head off. Didn't he tell you?'

'No.' Cole's voice was low, barely above a whisper.

My head was still foggy and it took me a moment to understand what was going on. When I understood, I said, 'This isn't news to you, is it? You knew about Wilkins. You knew you were being stitched up. You went to my flat. Yeah, sure you did. You found those men I'd left there. That's why there was nothing on the news about them.'

Cole stood with his shoulders forward and his head lowered some. He glowered at me, his mouth drawn tight. He looked like a bull about to charge. He took a breath and straightened up. We stood there, me waiting for something to happen, Cole glowering and clenching his jaw, Blondie and Earring fidgeting, unsure what was happening but knowing that things were bad. After a while of standing around like a dance formation, I said, 'I want to know what the fuck is going on.'

Cole blinked and looked at me as if he'd forgotten who I was. He glanced over at Blondie.

'Give me the gun,' he said. Blondie handed it to him. 'Get out. Both of you.'

They were reluctant, but they went. When they'd gone, he said, 'Sit down before you fall down.'

I sat. He put the gun into his jacket pocket. He walked up and down a bit with his head lowered and his hands clenching into fists and unclenching. When he'd worked off some of the left-over anger, he stopped in front of me and said, 'Yeah, I was at your flat. I found those two blokes. The boy was all right, except for some breaks. We cleaned it up, got rid of the body, paid off your landlord, what's-'is-name – '

'Akram.'

'Yeah. I asked the boy some questions, dumped him at hospital, told him to keep quiet.'

'Why?'

'Not for your benefit. If the coppers had found them,

they'd've started looking for you and I couldn't have that. I needed to get to you myself.'

'If you questioned the boy, you knew what was going on.'

'I knew some of it. There's more to this than you realize.'

'Maybe you could fill me in.'

He wandered off to a corner of the room and came back with an old chair. He dropped the chair before me and sat down. When he did that, he leaned forward for a moment, put his head in his hands.

'What a fucking mess,' he said.

He sat up straight, took a deep breath.

'I've been having trouble for about a year. The law hit a few of my places; some of my jobs got compromised. Someone was undermining me, I knew that. I thought it was Garner. It had to be him or Wilkins. Whoever it was, they were doing a fucking good job. I was in danger of going under.'

That was what Eddie had told me.

'Then the Albanians came to you,' I said. 'Offered you a load of smack.'

'Right. I don't handle that shit, but I knew I could pass it on at a decent profit. It was a good chance for me to get out from under, a last-ditch thing. I took it, but I didn't have the money up-front and they wouldn't wait long. I was going to fund it with a couple of jobs. One was with Ellis and his mob. Another was the casino job with Beckett. Both got turned over.'

'Ellis?' I said. 'The Brighton job?'

'Yeah. That was my thing. I used Ellis, but it was my job.'

Ellis. What the fuck was happening?

'I was on the job with Ellis before that,' I said.

'Yes,' he said. 'I know.'

'That must've been why they used me for the casino job. Beckett must've realized you'd find me the link between both jobs.'

'After the casino job went arse-up, I looked into it. As you say, you were the only connection between them, aside from me. I asked around about you. I didn't think you were involved, but I had to be sure.'

'Now you know.'

'Sorry about the arm.'

'Forget it.'

'I made a mistake about you. I thought you'd be too stupid to mastermind this shit. You're not stupid, are you?'

I felt stupid. He didn't speak for a minute. When he finally did, it was in a quiet voice, and there was something like regret in there, as if he knew he was at the end.

'I became lazy,' he said. He looked down at his gut. 'I became fat. I'll admit that. It was all too easy. I should've seen what was happening before.'

'They were subtle,' I said, thinking that they'd out-subtled themselves.

'Yeah. Subtle. And I was fat. I was too big to take face-on. I had too many connections, too many men. So they hit me slowly, bit by bit until I was in real fucking trouble. Fucking maggots feeding off me. Are you there yet?'

'The Albanians came to you with this load of heroin,' I said. 'You took the smack, but you couldn't pay up-front so you planned a couple of jobs short-term to pay them off. Paget and Wilkins tried to take advantage of that.'

'Yeah. It was their chance, these maggots. All they had to

do was spoil those jobs and let the Albanians take me out. They sit back and watch it happen, then step in at the end, make a deal with the Albanians by handing over the cash they fucking stole from me.'

I got it then.

'That was their mistake,' I said.

'Mistake?'

'You were still dangerous to them; you could still realize what was happening and get them before the Albanians got you. So, they had to muddy the waters a bit, throw you a few scapegoats, and at the same time take your lifelines from you.'

'They turned over Ellis,' he said. 'And you say that's when they chose to use you?'

It went back further than I'd realized. Back, back. Always back. I was like an animal caught in a trap, and the past was the snare. The more I pulled, the tighter I got caught.

'I only worked with Ellis the one time,' I told Cole. 'The next job Ellis did, they got turned over. Paget and Wilkins must've found out I was in on the previous job. They got Beckett for the casino job, and told him to get me on board so they could set me up. Those two jobs go south and people are going to think I'm dirty. They tell Beckett that I'm the one who'll take the blame. They tell him that you're on your way out and that when you're gone he can come up for air and have a large slice of the money he stole.'

'So what happened? Where did they go wrong?'

'They rushed it. That Albanian deal was an unplanned chance to finish you off, but they had to act quickly. They fucked up. After the casino job, they just had to wait for me to leave my place and then plant the money there. But I didn't

265

leave my place for a couple of days. When I did, they tried to get into the wrong flat – Kendall must've had a copy of my old key. I'd moved, but Kendall didn't know that. They had to get a new key from my landlord and try again. They were running out of time and they rushed it and I caught them.'

The muscles in his jaw flexed. I heard a car pass by outside.

'What was their plan if they'd planted the money on you?'

'I don't know. Maybe the police would've received an anonymous call. Or maybe Paget would have killed me in the flat, with a couple of men loyal to you as witnesses when he found the money. Maybe they would just disappear me and then you could find the money in my flat. You were supposed to think I'd double-crossed Beckett, taken the money and legged it. You were supposed to waste your time looking for me. Instead, I got away and took their evidence with me. Then they started panicking. Paget has been running around trying to tidy it all up. I saw him at Kendall's. He went there to kill him. He tried to kill me. He got to Beckett and Walsh and Jenson.'

'How?'

'Wilkins fixed Beckett up with a safe house, had someone on the inside.'

'Who?'

'It doesn't matter.'

'It matters to me.'

'Beckett went for children,' I said.

'They used a child?'

'They're not Samaritans.'

'What about this Simpson thing? Why'd he get topped?'

'I don't know. I think he lost his bottle when he found out we were robbing you. He seemed nervy during the robbery.

266

Maybe they'd planned to kill him anyway. Jenson and Walsh might not have known what was going on either.'

'And Kendall?'

'He thought he was working with Beckett alone. Beckett thought he was working for Wilkins. Wilkins was probably involved, but if he's dead, it looks like Paget was running it.'

Cole ran a hand through his hair. He was sweating.

'Christ,' he said. 'What a fucking mess. What you say makes sense. But you're wrong about something.'

I didn't think I was wrong. I said, 'Yeah?'

'The Ellis job. You worked with Ellis on the job before the Brighton one? Before it went sour?'

'I told you.'

'Did you know you were supposed to work on that next job too? The Brighton one'

I took a second to work that through. I felt that snare tightening some more. I said, 'What?'

'I made some inquiries; I checked with Ellis. He told me that he used you because his man Caine was fucked up over some woman.' I nodded. I was feeling cold. 'Well, Ellis didn't trust him for the Brighton job either, so he was going to use you for that too. Caine wormed his way back on at the last minute and they dumped you.'

My mind was whirring. I couldn't make the parts fit. I must have looked confused because Cole smiled, if you could call it that.

'You thought you were in this by accident,' he said. 'You thought they picked you for the casino job because you were associated with Ellis, and therefore the Brighton job. You were wrong. Weren't you, boy? It was the other way round. They chose Ellis for the Brighton job – my job – because you were already working with him. They've been fitting you up right from the start.'

My throat was parched. My hands were sweating.

'Who decided to use Ellis?' I said.

'Wilkins. I left – '

The smaller door smashed open. Earring stumbled in, panic all over his sweating face. He hit the floor. Cole jumped up. I jumped up. It was dark outside and headlights flashed past the door and lit up the warehouse like flares, throwing wild shadows everywhere, and I heard vehicles screech on tarmac. Earring was scrambling to his feet, tugging at his pistol.

'They're here,' he said, his voice cracking with fear.

Car doors slammed.

'How many?' Cole said.

'Lots.'

'Close the door,' Cole said.

Earring had his pistol out and was fumbling with it, trying flick the safety off.

'Close the door,' Cole said again, his voice even.

'Don and Jules,' Earring said. 'They're still out there.'

There were single shots from a semi-auto which seemed far away, and then the air crackled with fire from several automatic weapons.

'Close the fucking door.'

Earring dropped his piece and ran for the door. A man I didn't recognize hit the door as Earring got there. He tried weakly to push his way in. His white shirt was sodden red, his face was white. Earring opened the door and the man fell in. Dozens of rounds slammed into the door and sent splinters of wood into Earring's arm. He yelled out. Cole screamed at him, 'Close the fucking door.'

Earring rammed the door, slamming it shut, and threw the bolt. A hail of fire hit the door, but its metal lining held. When I looked back at Cole, he had a mobile phone to his ear. He said, 'I'm at the warehouse. They're on to us. Get everyone and get here. Now.'

'Give me a gun,' I said.

He tossed the phone, pulled some keys out of his pocket, strode over to a corner bench and hauled it out. Underneath this was a plywood board. He threw that aside and I saw a trapdoor laid into the concrete. He unlocked the door and reached in and pulled out some Heckler & Koch MP5s and thirty-round magazines. Earring was backing up slowly, his gun aimed at the door. The other man was crawling towards us, leaving a trail of blood. He wasn't going to make it. I went over to the side and tried to rip out the metal benches but they were fixed firmly into the wall and I couldn't move them. I tossed the cardboard boxes aside, looking for a crowbar. Cole yelled to me and when I turned he threw me a Heckler & Koch. I fired bursts into the wall where the brackets were fixed to the benches. The concrete smashed into dust. There was a huge crash that sounded like a grenade explosion. The roller-door was twisted and bulging. They were trying to ram their way in. The door was holding, but it wouldn't do so for long. I pulled the metal benches away from the wall and threw them on to their sides on the floor to give us some cover. My shoulder was agony and I was leaking blood all over the place now, but I could use my arm and that was all that mattered. Cole slid a magazine into one of the Hecklers and jacked a round into the chamber. He slung another couple of guns over his shoulder and kicked some magazines towards the bench. He was sweating, but his eyes were blazing with the same kind of ecstasy I'd seen in troops under fire. I heard him mutter, 'Cunts.'

They rammed the door again and this time the bolt started to wrench free from the floor housing. Another one and they'd have it. We took up position behind the bench and waited.

'The lights,' Earring said, moving towards the switches. I tugged him back.

'Leave them.'

They could blind us with their headlights if we went dark. There was another boom and screech as they rammed the door again and twisted it and tore it away from its fastening, leaving a gaping slash along the bottom. They reversed the car. There was enough room now for men to squeeze under the door, but I didn't think they would come in until they knew what they were up against. They didn't seem stupid. We waited behind the benches. Earring had set his MP5 to full auto and I reached over and flicked it to the three-shot setting. The way he was panicked, he'd have kept his finger on the trigger and blown his entire magazine in seconds. He stared at me, not knowing what I was doing.

'Keep your eyes front,' I told him. 'Aim steady and breathe slow.'

The first ones came then. Two dark-haired men peered through the twisted crack. I fired a couple of bursts at them and they scarpered. There was calm for a while, probably because they were unsure how many we were. Then something rolled under the smashed door and towards us, and I saw what it was and said, 'Shit.'

I closed my eyes and covered my ears and ducked down behind the bench. I saw Cole start to do the same, but Earring hadn't moved. The flash-bang split the place apart with noise and brilliant white light and I felt the shock wave hit the bench and throw it back and the air seemed to be sucked from my lungs and I fell forwards and gagged and tried to breathe. But I knew I had to do something quickly before they followed up. I had ringing in my ears and couldn't hear a thing and my throat burned from the stench of the magnesium, but I hadn't been blinded. The place was full of white smoke and I couldn't make out if anyone had come under the door. I hit the selector switch on the Heckler to full auto and aimed into the smoke and emptied the magazine to give them something to think about. I reloaded. Noises were distant and muffled because my hearing was fucked, but I heard Cole's gun rattling away on my left. I glanced at Earring and saw that he was on his knees, his eyes shut and his hands over his ears. He'd taken the flash-bang without cover and was probably blinded. He was useless now. We took fire and ducked. Rounds hit the metal benches and the floor around us. Their fire was loose and I thought it might be covering fire. I peered quickly over the bench and saw one of them slide under the door and jump up quickly and run towards us. I fired a short burst and threw him back, dead. They'd decided to take Cole alive, probably because they thought they could get their money from him. Soon, they might decide to be done with it and kill him. We took more covering fire, and then they managed to get the door up a bit and the fire after that was intense and accurate and we had to take cover and I knew we were in trouble, and Earring started screaming something but I couldn't make it

271

out and I didn't think it was language anyway. He started crawling away, trying to get to the small door and the fire was ripping everything apart and sending up clouds of concrete dust, which was choking us. Earring had lost it now and thrown his weapon away and was cowering on the ground and covering his head, deaf, probably, and half-blind. He tried to make a bolt for the small door and ran the wrong way and got wiped out without moving a yard and fell back in a sprawl. I looked at Cole and sweat was pouring down his face and his eyes were blazing and his teeth were gritted and there was madness there and he was going to slaughter every one of the cunts if he could and I had to admire that. I was down to my last thirty-round magazine and I rammed it home and thought, fuck it, and stood and emptied the magazine at them and charged and felt the buzz of a bullet whipping past my head and I slammed into the door and tried to push it down to stop them coming in, but it wouldn't budge and I put everything I had into the effort and still it didn't fucking move and by now I was choking on concrete dust and my eyes were stinging from the flash-bang smoke and bullets were ripping everything apart and I was firing at shadows because I couldn't make out shapes and I thought, I'm dead.

And then I saw Cole standing next to me and he was saying something and tugging at my gun because it was empty and I was still trying to fire it at the gap beneath the door and Cole was smiling madly through a face white with dust and shouting at me and I couldn't hear a fucking word he said.

And then I looked around at the smoke clearing and the concrete walls shot to pieces, lumps of plaster and rubble and dust lying over everything like ash, and the body of Earring on his back as if he'd been crucified on the ground, and the other man in a lump, and three others in pools of blood. And Cole tugged at my arm and I understood. I dropped the gun. The world spun around me and I hit the ground.

I must've been out for a few minutes. When I came to, Cole's men were in the warehouse clearing it up. Cole stood over me and smiled.

'They ain't got me yet,' he said.

My hearing was returning.

He helped me stand, then put a hand in the small of my back and pushed.

'Get out of here,' he said. 'Go.'

I started to leave, then stopped. There was something I needed to know. I turned to Cole.

'How'd you find me?'

'Contacts in the Met. That Dalston thing, when Beckett got killed, they said there was a lot of claret upstairs in one of the bedrooms, but it wasn't the same type as any of the men killed. Once I knew you were injured, it was just a matter of checking doctors, hospitals. Wasn't hard, just took a while. Your Doctor Browne is registered at some nursing home. Woman there remembered you.'

That bloody woman.

There were men outside, standing around, armed and ready. There were cars on a forecourt and the smashed car the Albanians had used on the roller-door. The men watched me as I came out. Cole said something and one of the men handed me some car keys and pointed to a Ford. I got in and drove off.

TWENTY-SEVEN

My shoulder was throbbing, but it was a distant pain. My arm was cold and caked in dried blood. My ears were still ringing and the magnesium and concrete dust had dried my mouth and scorched my throat. I stopped once at a late-night shop and took a bottle of water from the shelf and threw a fiver at the man behind the counter. He looked up and saw me and stumbled backwards over some stacked newspapers. I gulped the water and threw up. I took another bottle and poured it over my head.

If Cole's men had been a minute later, we wouldn't have made it. Or maybe we would've. I don't know. There wasn't much of a fight outside. Cole had been expecting some kind of an attack and he'd made sure his men were close to hand and in force. When they turned up, the Albanians legged it. It wasn't a victory, it was a reprieve.

When I got to Browne's, I was faint. I staggered in and he looked at me and didn't say a word. He didn't look too great himself. He had a cut lip and the start of a black eye. He followed me into the kitchen and gathered some gauze and disinfectant and that sort of thing. After he'd cut away my shirt, he said, 'Is she safe?'

I heard the words, but it took me a moment to understand them. He meant the girl.

'Don't you know?' I said.

'She got away from here, that's all I know.'

'How do you know she got away?'

'I heard them talking. They didn't know who she was.'

'Didn't they ask you?'

He glared at me.

'Of course they did. You think I'd tell them anything?'

He wiped the blood away with alcohol-soaked cotton wool. Then he cut away the old stitches and pulled them out with tweezers. He said something, but I missed it. I thought about the girl. I couldn't remember her name. I said, 'What happened?'

'You know what happened. They came and took you away.'

He did the work on me impatiently, as if he was fixing a kettle that kept breaking. He started stitching, swabbing now and then. There wasn't much pain. I thought that was bad. I should've felt something. I had trouble focusing and I think I passed out, but so briefly as to not be noticed by Browne.

'By the way,' he said, 'are they coming back? It would be nice to know.'

'They won't be back. Did you call anyone? Police?'

'One of them stayed here. He said they said they'd kill you if I called anyone.'

'What happened to him?'

'He got a call and left.'

'You call the police or not?'

He stopped his work and looked at me. He had that look of disappointment he sometimes had.

'I should have done, shouldn't I? I mean, why would I care what happened to you? The girl got away and I thought they still had you and I didn't call anyone and I should have done.'

He dropped the needle and threw the cotton wool down. 'Damn it. What you did was a good thing.'

Everything blurred for a moment, and Browne's voice sounded muffled. I shook my head to clear it.

'What?'

My tongue felt thick.

'You saved the girl, man. I don't know where she is, but I know you saved her from them.'

I didn't know what he was on about. Brenda was dead.

'I didn't save her,' I said.

Browne stared at me. I didn't like the look on his face.

'You're slurring.'

Then I was back in the ring, sitting in my corner with the fight doctor – with Browne – asking me if I was okay. Then I blinked and I was in a kitchen and Browne was there and I didn't know what the hell was going on.

'I'm fine,' I said.

'You're not bloody fine.'

I wondered where Brenda was, and when I thought of her I had this feeling, this sickening gut-twisting feeling that something was badly wrong. I wasn't in the ring, though. I had to remember that.

'Tired.'

'The girl. Don't you remember?'

What was he on about? He was talking about a girl, not Brenda. No, not Brenda. I couldn't separate them in my head. Where was Brenda? Christ, where was she? I had to go to her. I had to save her. Didn't I? I had to do something.

'Joe?' Browne was saying. 'Joe? You understand what I'm saying? Kid. You saved her. Don't you remember?'

I had to think. There was a girl. The girl. Kid, yes. Had I saved her?

The next thing I knew, Browne had my head in his hands. He was peering into my eyes, moving his hands over my head, feeling for bumps. I didn't catch what he said. I brushed him off.

'I'm fine.'

He looked at me a moment longer, then tied off the suture and wrapped my shoulder in bandage.

My head was clouding over again and thoughts clogged and jammed and I watched as Browne dug some food out of the fridge and filled a glass of milk. He seemed to be a long way off and kept looking at me like he used to when I was in the ring and, again, I didn't know where I was or why I was there and I watched Browne move in slow motion and all the while thoughts or memories were moving sluggishly, as if they were sinking in oil, and I was back in a corner of the ring and I could see Brenda there, ringside, watching me and I thought, she's in danger. I must have said it out loud because Browne turned and said, 'Who?'

I had to fight the confusion. I had something still to do.

Browne dropped the food and stuff in front of me. When he'd done that, he slumped into a seat. I ate, or tried to, and he watched me and his face became grim.

'You look worse than ever. I didn't think that was possible. You look . . . Jesus.'

'What?'

'You look dead.'

And I thought, yes, I am.

'Yeah.'

277

'What's wrong with you? Joe? What happened?'

But I couldn't get Brenda's face out of my head, and she became a small girl, a kid, and I heard her saying, 'Poor old Joe, heading for the breaker's yard.'

Sometimes, I thought she might be right.

And Browne was there again and I was saying, 'She's in danger.'

And then she was holding my head and looking into my eyes. Sometimes she would ask me questions to which I didn't have an answer. She would want to know what I was thinking, what I wanted, why I did what I did. That sort of thing. I said, 'I don't know.'

And Browne had my head in his hands and was shouting something to me, but there was a ringing sound and his voice was a long way away.

Sometimes she would ask me if we were going to be okay. I didn't ever understand what she meant. I don't think she did. I don't think she expected an answer.

And then she had a knife and was skewering me and sucking something out and I felt empty, hollow. I'd always felt empty, but this was different; now I felt emptier. I didn't think that was possible. It was more than emptiness. It was pain where emptiness used to be, and I thought, it's better this way.

And then I saw Browne's face close to mine and he had a syringe and was pulling it out of my arm and he was frightened, panic in his eyes, and then he was Warren and I was slapping him stupid, and then Kendall as he tried to make a dash for it, and then he was that kid, the Argentine, dying in front of me, lips pulling back in agony. And I wanted to say, 'It's better this way.'

278

But I couldn't, because there was something I had to do, something I had to finish, and it wasn't time. And I thought, one time I didn't see her for a week.

And then I understood, and I knew what had happened, and my heart hit my chest and I slammed back in the seat. I knew why it had been me at the centre of this whole fucking thing – me from the start, played with, at the mercy of unseen hands, thrown into a bloody pit. I knew everything. I think I'd known for years. And the blood drained from my head and I lurched forward and Browne was saying something to me. I heard him, but I didn't understand, couldn't make out the words. And then he was shaking me and shouting something about hospital. The room was sliding and rolling in front of my eyes, and my head felt weightless. I tried to stand and hit the deck and tried to stand again. I was muttering something, but I don't know what it was, and Browne looked at me in horror. I knew where I had to go. I'd been there before, years ago. I tried to make it to the kitchen door and I hit the table and Browne was grappling and pulling at me and I threw him off and I heard a voice say, 'You won't make it, Joe. You're falling apart.'

I thought that was probably right. I thought it had been right for a long time.

279

It happened in a daze, a kind of waking dream. It was early morning, not quite light, and foul. Rain lashed against the windscreen and made the lights blurred and dazzling. I saw it through someone else's eyes. The steering wheel was loose in my hand and the car slid around a road that moved before me. I think I scraped a parked car and set off the alarm. I think I heard a shout.

'Poor old Joe,' Brenda said.

I turned and saw her in the passenger seat, smiling softly at me.

'You're dead,' I told her.

'We're both dead, Joe,' she told me.

And then it was blazing daylight, hot, heavy, the shirt sticking to my body. We were driving through the Essex countryside, green trees and hedgerows lining the narrow roads, passing fields of wheat, brown and swaying in the breeze, catching the sun so that whole fields would shimmer with light. It must've been late summer. The sky was hazy; high white clouds lay in thin layers across the blue like they'd been sprayed from a can. It must've been a couple of weeks before she was killed. 'In London there is no sky,' the girl had said. Well, I saw the sky that day.

I had to keep my hand on the gearstick because of the roads, changing down to slow around a bend, speeding up on a stretch, changing down again for a steep hill. Her hand rested lightly on mine so that whenever I moved through the gears, her hand moved with it. Every now and then, she'd stroke my hand, just to let me know she was still there, still with me.

We had the windows open and the braids of her hair blew about like tiny ropes. She wore a thin cotton dress, and her skin glistened with sweat, though she looked cool. She always looked cool to me, and I wanted to touch her neck, where her throat was, and run my fingers down to the edge of the cotton, but I had to drive, had somewhere to go, had something to do. Hadn't I?

'Here,' she said, pointing to the side of the road where a lay-by opened on to a huge flat field of glimmering bronze. 'Here.'

I turned the car and the sun bounced off the bonnet and blinded me and I slammed on the brakes and Brenda screamed and I turned to her and she stared at me with blood pouring out of the gashes on her face and horror filled me.

And someone shouted at me and I blinked and it was dark and my car was halfway over the wrong side of the road. A van was in front, stopped a few feet from mine, its headlights blinding me. Someone shouted, swore at me. I reversed, swung the steering wheel round and put my foot on the gas and spun the wheels and clipped the van as I passed it. I had to remember where I was. Brenda was gone. I had to remember that. I'd lost her. Had to remember.

My head dropped a couple of times and I opened the window to let in the cold air and rain. My heart banged in my throat and I was drenched in cold sweat. These things didn't matter. All I had to do was get where I was going. It was all clear to me, in my muddled mind. It all made sense, strings of moments tying together into a knot, tying around my throat.

Bowker was twisting around in my head, one of those pieces of string, terrified of me, squealing me up to Paget as soon as he could, strangling me with his shifty eyes.

'Some funny little bloke,' she'd said. 'I seen him around the place.'

Warren was there too, telling me about the scam with the prostitutes at Cole's place. Cole's casino had a scam with the pros run by Wilkins. Marriot ran the same scam at the Sportsman way back. It fitted that Wilkins and Marriot knew each other, probably worked together.

Then there was Cole telling me that the Ellis job I should've done was another of his. Yes, it was there, it had been there for years and now it was around my neck, killing me, and I was fighting it because that's what I did. I fought. Everything. Always. It was all I could do.

'All that anger in you,' she'd said. 'All that hatred.'

All the anger in me. Yes, the rage. It was all I really had, maybe all I'd ever had.

There were the Albanians, too, with their connections. Marriot would've known the Albanians, must've done, would've used some of the women and children they'd brought in.

And then Paget, not out to capture me and question me, but on a mission to kill me.

And the girl. Yes, the girl. Kid. Yes, it had all been there.

I dumped the car a block away and climbed out and watched the pavement fall away from me. I took a few deep breaths and walked, putting one heavy leg before the other, trying to keep in a straight line. Buildings swayed to the side of me, but the rain soaked me and the wind made me cold and that was good. I was dead, heading to the breaker's yard. That was fine. That was okay. Just one thing to do, just one more thing.

I floated through the door. I remember a man putting an arm out to stop me. I remember snapping it. By the time I was in the club, I had the Makarov in my hand. A few shadows were scattered around the place. One of the shadows turned to me and said, 'Fuck.'

He meant it. Every word.

The shadows moved, slowly at first, and then with cries and shouts they flew around. The rain, or sweat, or something, made me shiver and I felt light, out of myself, and the Makarov felt heavy like it was dying in my hand, like it was wasting away. It needed life. I needed to give it life. I gave it life.

I unleashed the gun and death had come, and chaos, and I watched the shadows fly, some one way, some another. One of them slammed into me and bounced off, and I moved my arm and the gun with it and when I'd stopped moving, the shadow stayed on the ground.

I walked through the club. I heard cracks here and there, but they meant nothing to me because I had something I had to do. I was dead anyway, but I had to finish things. I put a fresh magazine in the gun and carried on.

The office was at the back, along a corridor. I remembered that much. As I went down the corridor, a shape appeared and raised a dark object and rounds sprayed all over. I raised my arm and the figure disappeared.

The door was shut and when I turned the handle small holes appeared and splintered the wood. I thought that was funny and I looked at the holes. I think I laughed. I might've cried. I shot the lock away and fell in.

I saw his face clearly, and I saw the ruined eye and I saw what he held in his hand and I heard words come from his mouth and I took his hand and bent it back until it broke and he screamed and crashed to the ground. And someone said something, and I think it was me and, in a broken voice, he said, 'My hand, my hand.'

And I said something else and he looked at me through a ruined face and said, 'I'll get it for you. Please, Joe. Please, don't do anything.'

He crawled to the corner of the room and opened a cupboard and fiddled with something large that looked like an iron safe. He pulled out a big black shape and then another, throwing them towards me. And he said, 'It's all there.'

And I thanked him and all I could think of was Bowker fixing a date with Brenda, and Paget slicing her to death, and all because she was grassing Marriot up to the law, staying with him, fucking the johns, fucking in his films, living in fear because she couldn't bear to abandon the children he used, and all the time she thought she was safe. And all the time Marriot knew she was in with the law and thought I was in on it too. And all that led to her death in some fucking alley, and to this shit he'd plunged me in, his revenge, a long time coming, setting me up with Cole so that he could use me to take over Cole's firm, get back on top, using me because it completed the circle, strangling me with the past. His past. My past.

He stood slowly.

'It was Paget, Joe. Not me. It was him told me about Brenda

grassing me up. It was him carved her up. I didn't know anything about it. I swear to you.'

'Where is he?'

'I don't know, Joe. Honest. He's run. It was him. Look, Joe –'

I shot him in the stomach. He crumpled to the floor and gripped his gut, writhing in pain. His glasses had fallen off. After a while, he tried to crawl away, like some insect with its legs broken off. He left a bloody trail as he went. I don't know where he was going to. I think he was just crawling. It was the only thing he could do. When I got tired of watching him crawl, I put another round in the back of his head. Then I shot him six times more for no reason that I could think of except that my gun still had six rounds left in it.

I reached down for the bags and the fucking floor hit me in the face. When I came to, things were clearer. The Makarov was still in my hand, the bags in front of me. Marriot's blood crept slowly across the floor and pooled around his body, what was left of it.

I opened the bags and checked them. They were full of money, Cole's money, bundles of used twenty- and fifty-pound notes. I counted off sixteen grand and put it in my pocket.

I must've blacked out again. When I came to, I stood slowly. When I heard the noise, I swung round, and that made me dizzy and I staggered. I managed to get the Makarov up, but I knew it was empty. A voice said, 'Hold it.'

I focused on the figure standing in the doorway, and saw that the figure was Eddie. He had his hands out. They were empty. I lowered the gun and he lowered his hands. He shook his head slowly.

'I don't know how you do it.'

'What are you doing here?'

'Symbiosis.'

He was talking circles again. The whole thing was a circle. I was tired of fucking circles. He walked over and kicked Marriot. He was still dead. Eddie smiled.

'I guess you figured it out, huh?'

'Yeah.'

'He had ambitions. That's the trouble with ambition. Was he in it with the Albanians?'

'No,' I managed to say, my tongue thick, my mouth dry. 'Otherwise they wouldn't have gone after Cole. Marriot played them.'

'He gets out of nick and tries to take over Cole's turf.'

'He was after it before he got nicked.'

'How do you know?'

'Paget.'

Eddie nodded.

'Right. That's why Paget was in with Cole. He and Marriot had already arranged it. Paget works Cole from the inside and they take him down. But Marriot gets nicked and they put it on hold and strike when Marriot gets out. Neat. That the money?'

'Yeah.'

'Come on, I've got a car out back.'

He called back to a couple of his men. They came in and took the money. Eddie reached down to give me a hand. I ignored it.

'You're not going to make it by yourself,' he said.

'I'll make it.'

I stood, wavered, and steadied. He said, 'Right. Let's go.'

'What are you doing here?'

He smiled again. He was finding it all amusing, in his way.

'Like I said, symbiosis.'

My gun came up. He saw the gun and made a small movement.

'Don't,' I said. He froze. He wasn't smiling any more. 'You set me up.'

'Joe, come on, you don't know what you're talking about.'

'I know.'

'We've got to get out of here.'

'You led Cole to me.'

'No, Joe. I didn't. You're not thinking straight. I don't know where you've been staying.'

'But you knew I was at Dalston, that I'd been shot in that house. You were the only one who knew. Cole knew someone was there, but he didn't know it was me. You told him. After that, he was able to find me, through Browne, because he knew I'd been hurt and would need a doctor. How long have you known it was Marriot?'

'What does it matter?'

'It matters.'

'I knew he and Wilkins went back. Long time ago. You narrowed it down to three, remember? Wilkins was one of them. I figured it from there.'

'You let Cole get me.'

'Just business. We let you and Cole have some rope, that's all. We knew you'd get there eventually. Vic likes to keep a low profile.'

'You knew I was coming here.'

287

'Yeah, I did. Had some men outside. But we couldn't get involved yet, didn't want to tip off the Albanians. So, we waited. Vic said you couldn't do it yourself. I disagreed. What else could I do? Would you have let me stop you? Nothing could've stopped you.'

He was right.

'And now?'

'Just making sure you're all right. Vic and Cole have come to an arrangement. These Albanians are getting ambitions, getting a bit too big for their Albanian boots. Pretty soon, they're going to start encroaching on our turf. So, my enemy's enemy and all that. We'll get the money back to Cole, he'll pay them off and then, in a while, Vic and Cole will join up and take them out.'

'And Paget?'

'Cole will find him. He's probably got Cole's smack. Now, let's go.'

I stowed the Makarov.

'I'm not finished,' I said.

I pushed past him. I was in the corridor behind Marriot's club. There were doors. I opened one and another. The third was locked. I kicked it open. She was on the floor, bent over a thin woman, her sister. There were bullet holes in the wall, and the woman. For all I knew, I'd killed her. When Kid looked at me, she had an empty expression like she didn't know who I was, or didn't care. I wanted to hold her. I wanted to give her life and protection. I don't know what I wanted. I wanted her to give me something. I couldn't stand straight. I held out my hand. She looked at it. I was dizzy and I was leaking blood again. I hit the floor hard. I didn't know if I had it in me to get up. Not this time. I could feel what strength I had draining from me. I tried to move, tried to get to her. My body was lead. I think I passed out again.

I felt something cold on my cheek. I opened my eyes and saw something small and thin and dark. I saw a small girl, nothing more than bones and skin and huge eyes. She had the same expression Brenda used to have. I knew what it was, then. I knew what it meant, that look. I knew what Brenda used to feel. Kid put her hand on mine. She was soaked in blood.

Eddie watched us. He shook his head and said, 'Jesus.'

I pushed myself to my feet and led Kid, or she led me, I can't say. Eddie stared at us, at me, his face blank for once. whatever he saw, it no longer amused him.

'Fuck,' he said. 'Now I remember what they called you. The Machine. That was it. The Killing Machine.'

PHILLIP HUNTER
TO
KILL
FOR
She DIED for him.
Now he will KILL for her.
PREVIEW

We burned her on the Thursday. It was one of those dull March days. There was no sky, just wall to wall grey, no colour anywhere, no sun, no wind. It wasn't warm. It wasn't cold. It wasn't anything. It couldn't even be bothered to rain.

It didn't matter.

We crawled along the Eastern Avenue and Blake Hall Road and past the Flats, and I watched people trudge by with their heads down and their hands in their pockets, pushing their children and pulling their shopping and dragging their lives about. The whole world was in mourning. I saw an old Sikh bloke by the side of the road. He watched us go by and bowed his head.

I could have carried the coffin in one arm, it was so small. Instead, four of us walked with it; me and Browne and Eddie and some bloke the funeral house laid on. Browne couldn't walk straight.

The service was a rushed job and I had the feeling the vicar, or whatever he was, wanted to get to a wedding or christening or something, anything that was far away from a lump like me and an old drunk Scot and a black gangster and a small dead girl in a small brown coffin who'd never had a fucking chance. He gave us the usual such-a-tragedy spiel and mumbled a prayer or two. When he told us that she was safe now and in God's arms I wanted to grab him by his clean white collar and drag him down to where she'd held her dead, blood-soaked sister and to where she'd been used as bait for a robber who'd liked kids, and I wanted to ask him where his fucking god was then. Eddie put a hand on my arm. He said, 'Take it easy, Joe.'

Maybe he was thinking the same thing I was. Probably not.

Browne wept through the whole thing. I couldn't blame him for being drunk. He'd liked the girl. He'd thought he could help her. He'd thought he could help me. He couldn't even help himself.

Cole came to the funeral. Some of his men were around, out of the way. They were tooled up and edgy, but Cole seemed okay. He and Eddie nodded to each other. Browne avoided him.

We went to a pub afterwards, me and Browne and Eddie. A couple of East European women came in. They told us they'd worked for Marriot and they were glad he was dead and they were sorry about the girl, even though they'd never known her name. Eddie bought them a drink and they cried a bit. While we were there, other people in the pub quieted their talking and avoided eye contact and dribbled out. A thug, an old drunk Scot, a black criminal and two prostitutes sitting in a bar. It sounded like the start of a joke.

Browne was still pissed but downed a few glasses of Scotch and managed to get pissed all over again and bawled some more, which left Eddie as the one to do the talking, even though he'd hardly known her either. He tried, though, and said things like 'She had you two at least' and 'He paid for it, Joe. Marriot. And Beckett too,' and stuff like that and all the time I sat there knowing I might've been the one who'd fired the round that killed her. It had been a blazing fight and my head wasn't right and I'd let loose my old Makarov semi-auto and shot the place to shit. So, yes, I could have been the one.

Then Eddie bought another round and raised his glass and said, 'Here's to Kid.'

And we all raised our glasses to a tiny dead African girl who was so thin I was scared of crushing her to death when I held her, and who looked at me wide-eyed and open-mouthed, like she was looking at something frightening, and who was named Kindness and who we called Kid.

A letter from the publisher

We hope you enjoyed this book. We are an independent
publisher dedicated to discovering brilliant books,
new authors and great storytelling. Please join us at
www.headofzeus.com and become part of our
community of book-lovers.

We will keep you up to date with our latest books, author
blogs, special previews, tempting offers, chances to win
signed editions and much more.

If you have any questions, feedback or just want to say hi,
please drop us a line on hello@headofzeus.com

 @HoZ_Books

 HeadofZeusBooks

www.headofzeus.com

HEAD of ZEUS

The story starts here